The line between survival and extinction was very thin. One careless mistake sent you across with no possibility of return.

Bart was unaware that he had stumbled again and gone down to his knees. He shook his head now as if to clear it, took another deep breath, tried to rise and failed. All right, he told himself, now we crawl.

He shifted the precious load of wood to one arm, placed the other hand flat in the snow and began to hunch himself forward. How far was it to the cave entrance? Never mind; there were no longer dimensions or distances; there remained only the will to go on.

SNOWBOUND SIX

SIX

Richard Martin Stern

BALLANTINE BOOKS • NEW YORK

All of the characters in this book are fictitious, and any resemblance to actual persons, living or dead, is purely coincidental.

To D.A.S.
With love always,
R.M.S.

Prologue

THERE HAD BEEN A SUCCESSION OF INDIAN SUMMER days in north-central New Mexico, bright, crisp, clear. In the towering mountains behind the old capital city of Santo Cristo, nighttime temperatures fell regularly well below freezing, but in the city itself at an elevation of 7,000 feet, bird baths remained relatively ice-free, and the ground had scarcely begun to harden.

But there were ample signs that winter was at hand. Days were perceptibly shorter, and already flights of ducks and immense wavering skeins of geese had filled the sky, heading south. Juncos, locally called snowbirds, had left their mountain forests and come down to city elevation where ground feeding stations would carry them through until spring. An occasional titmouse or nuthatch could already be found.

Chamisa grew in profusion in and around the city; it had now lost its golden crown, and people had almost forgotten that its pollen had been especially annoying this year. Russian thistles, already dried and broken from their stems, roamed free as tumbleweeds in occasional brisk winds, or piled in windrows against lee fences. What piñon nuts there were in this off year had burst from their cones and lay scattered in the dirt, too few to collect. On the flanks of the mountains below the 11,000-foot timberline the gold of aspens was fading among the evergreens.

And there were other, distant but important factors to bear in mind that week:

On the west coast of the continent from Los Angeles north to Puget Sound, there was rain; in the Georgia

1

Strait gale-force winds; in the high elevations of the Sierra Nevada and the Cascades, snow.

Inland, cold arctic air flowed as water flows downhill from Saskatchewan and Alberta through Montana and Wyoming and into Colorado, threatening the lower states, its progress made easy by the peculiar geography of North America, which interposes no east-west mountain ranges as barriers.

In the Gulf of Mexico warm, moisture-laden air, obeying a building pressure gradient, stirred itself and began to move northward across Texas, into New Mexico.

Meteorologists measured, plotted—and watched.

Prudent folk saw to their firewood, snow tires and anti-freeze.

But on the day before the opening of elk season there was only sunshine in Santo Cristo.

PART
ONE

I.

WARNER HARLOW DROVE. He was a capable driver and apparently indefatigable; by the time the big car and trailer passed through the Santo Cristo plaza and turned toward the mountains, Warner had been at the wheel for something over ten hours, 541 miles from Oklahoma City via Amarillo. They had started well before sunup. Here in New Mexico, it was now mid-afternoon.

It was the wrong turn, Warner's first mistake, but no one noticed.

Sue Ann in the front seat beside Warner looked at the dashboard clock. "I'm sure there are nice places to stay here in Santo Cristo," she said. "We could phone and tell Jake and Ethel we're staying, and then go on tomorrow and be in early." Sue Ann was tired, but there was no urgency in her voice. Warner would decide. You could always count on Warner. Besides, the trip was Warner's, not hers. Sue Ann had no intention of looking for an elk to shoot.

"Only twenty-five, thirty miles more," Warner said. "No sweat." Old Jake would want to start hunting at daybreak, and not for the world would Warner upset any of Jake's plans. Warner had hunted deer, but never elk, the big fellows, and he was certainly not going to do anything now that wasn't strictly by the book.

From the rear seat Patty said automatically, "Aren't you tired, Daddy?" Because I am, she thought. She hated the whole idea of this trip, but she was still, as her mother had pointed out, too young to stay home alone. Patty was seventeen.

"I'm fine," Warner said.

"Well, I'm not," Billy said. Billy was fifteen. He spoke in quick sentences, matching a quick mind. "I've got a pain you-know-where, and I'm hungry." There had to a McDonald's somewhere; or at least a Tastee-Freez. Billy expected no result from his protest, but at least he was on record.

"You're always hungry," Patty said. And he never gained an ounce, either. There were so many things boys had going for them. It wasn't fair.

They passed through the low, sprawling city, left the last houses behind and came again into the kind of rolling country they had seen for a hundred miles—brown dirt dotted here and there with piñon and juniper in near-symbiosis, sparse grass, the weird shapes of cholla cactus like souls in writhing torment, occasional fences, a few cattle widely spread.

"Not like home," Warner said. "It's dry, dry."

The sky was blue, immense, without limit; it seemed to dominate them. The early Spanish had been the first Europeans to notice that; nothing had changed since. The big car moved without effort, windows closed against the sound of wind, air conditioner humming softly.

The road began to climb toward the mountains and for the first time the weight of the trailer took on importance. From the rear seat Billy watched with interest as the speedometer needle dropped slowly. "Santo Cristo," he said at last, "is seven thousand feet. At that altitude an internal-combustion engine loses about twenty-five per cent of its power. I looked it up."

"You would," Patty said. Billy was forever flaunting his knowledge. Everybody said that Billy was very bright, and that was probably a good thing, but Patty could have wished for a brother who kept his precocity a little more to himself. Precocity, *and* those built-in male advantages. Too much. "And I suppose you know why too?"

"Sure. The carburetor can't get enough oxygen for

6

good combustion. That's why they have super-chargers."

Warner listened with a mixture of pride in the boy's erudition and faint annoyance at his brashness. "Well, don't worry about it. We've got plenty of power left." The trouble was, Warner thought, the kid always had his nose in a book. When I was his age, I was more interested in other things. And that was exactly why this trip was so important, even worth missing a week of school. It was a chance to get the kid out into a man's world. With himself, and old Jake.

As they approached the mountains, the rounded ridges and gentle slopes with their green and fading gold covering that had seemed so soft and innocuous from a distance began to take on a sharper, harsher, even vaguely threatening appearance as details became clearer. The piñon and junipers disappeared; almost at once they were into the big evergreens, ponderosa pines for the most part, with here and there blue spruce and firs filling the air with their fresh scent. Narrow-leaf cottonwoods grew along a stream that was barely visible.

The road narrowed and began to climb more steeply in long, swinging curves. In places the trees and the suddenly precipitous mountain flanks interfered with vision and made of each curve a venture into the unknown, no longer a safe, easy drive into friendly country. Here and there outcroppings of bare rock and open talus slopes hung menacingly above the road; and occasional fallen trees, now rotting, their exposed roots torn forcibly from the earth, testified to past rock slides where the basic structure of the mountains had broken loose.

From Santo Cristo the mountains had seemed massive and solid, immutable. Seen close up, the evidence of constant change was obvious: through erosion rock weakened, crumbled and slid down toward the mesas and the plains in an inevitable leveling process, sometimes almost imperceptible, sometimes devastatingly sudden. Looking at bare slopes where once trees had grown and lower vegetation had temporarily secured

7

the soil, you thought of earthquakes, houses and entire villages buried in avalanches, tales of mountain terror throughout the ages.

Warner repeated his observation: "Not much like home, is it?"

No one answered.

They passed a hinged road sign folded double into a triangle. On the exposed surface it read merely: *Courtesy.* Billy pondered it. "What do you suppose it says when they open it up?" Again there was no reply. (Unfolded into a diamond shape at need the sign would read: *Beyond this point, chains or snow tires are required.*) They drove on, past another sign and a road leading off to the right toward the ski basin.

Among the evergreens now trees of a different kind began to appear, deciduous, with pale, almost chartreuse trunks. "Aspens," Billy announced. "I read about them too. And they only start at eight thousand feet, how about that? Eight thousand—and climbing! Right on!"

Sue Ann said, "I didn't know Jake's ranch was this high." She looked at Warner.

Warner hadn't known either. As far as he remembered, the subject hadn't even come up in that phone call. "You've been stagnating down in the flatland too long," Jake had said on the phone. "Haul your ass up here and we'll go out and shoot us an elk. Bring the family. Lots of room. Why, goddamn, we haven't seen each other in how long?"

Too tempting. Warner had thought about it for only two days, and then called back. "How do I get there?"

"Easiest thing in the world. You think we're outside civilization?" Directions from Santo Cristo followed, but no mention of altitude.

Warner said now, "I think elk like the high country. Seems to me I heard that somewhere." He glanced at the odometer. "Anyway, we'll be there directly."

The road continued to climb, no end in sight. From the city, Patty thought, the mountains had not looked this big. Now, among them, they made you feel little, and helpless, and her sense of resentment deepened. "My ears are popping," she said.

"Swallow," Billy told her. "Or blow your nose. Hey, there's a backpacker! Will you look at what he's carrying?"

He was a tall young man, lean at the waist, wide through the shoulders; and he walked up the road in the long, deceptively slow strides of the mountain-wise. He wore a knitted watch cap, flannel shirt, jeans and heavy walking boots. He carried a staff; and a sheath knife in a worn scabbard was on his belt. He was unshaven. Above the main pouch of his frame pack was a roll of heavy plastic; a sleeping bag in its stuff-bag was lashed below. He glanced at the car, and merely nodded without slowing as it passed him.

"We could give him a lift," Billy said.

Patty wrinkled her nose in distaste. "He probably smells the way you do when you've been playing tennis."

Tennis, for God's sake! Warner thought; how about Parcheesi? Aloud he said, "He probably doesn't want a lift." He hoped that it was so. He always felt vaguely guilty when he drove past a hitchhiker, even though he knew what State Police had to say about the dangers of picking up strangers. "Anyway, he looks like he knows what he's doing."

For a few moments around the next curve the trees on the downhill side of the road opened, and the view was breathtaking. They paused to admire it.

The city lay far beneath them now, its buildings nestling into the rolling landscape as if they had grown in place, predominantly adobe, brown as the dirt that surrounded them.

To the south sharp hills rose into jagged mountains which in turn seemed to lose themselves against the mass of a single great, rounded hump, distant but astonishingly clear.

A little farther to the right another isolated mountain mass crouched on the horizon as if painted for a stage set; and as far to the right as they could see

9

through the trees, a third series of mountains grew out of a high plateau and disappeared into infinity.

So steep was the drop-off from the road's edge that they could see no ground, only the tops of tall pine trees somehow clinging to the invisible slope.

Sue Ann shivered faintly and thought of the Hall of the Mountain King music from *Peer Gynt;* but not for the world would she have said so; in the family, hers was the only taste for classical music.

Warner said, "They kind of stood it all on end, didn't they? Like those pictures you see of Switzerland."

Patty, despite herself, said, "Wow!"

Billy was doing mental calculations. "I bet we're looking at twenty thousand square miles. More. How about that?"

They started up, the trees closed in again and the view was gone as they swung into the next curve almost gingerly, Warner quite conscious now of the weight of the trailer behind.

He was unaccustomed to mountain driving, and the sight of those treetops below the road had made him uneasy. He was not a fearful man, but in the immensity of that view, he had felt a sudden sense of isolation and insignificance he had not known before, as if the car, the four persons it carried and the trailer it pulled were all venturing into a vast unknown, familiarity left behind. Responsibility began to take on new weight.

He slowed the car and then stopped it entirely to stare at a new and narrow road which forked to the left, downhill, clinging to the mountainside above a talus slope. A sign read: *Service road. FWD vehicles only.*

Sue Ann looked at Warner. "What does it mean?"

Warner shook his head in silence.

"FWD," Billy said, "four-wheel drive. It's a jeep road."

Sue Ann watched Warner now, and waited.

"I don't know," Warner said. "Jake didn't say anything about a jeep road. But that's the way we're supposed to turn, the first left. I don't get it."

Patty said, "Are we going to try it?"

Sue Ann said, "When people give directions, sometimes they aren't exactly right. Maybe the road we want is farther on."

"Or maybe," Billy said, "we've been on the wrong road all along."

In the off-side extension mirror Warner saw the backpacker come around the last curve at his steady pace. Warner set the parking brake, put the transmission in P and got out. "We'll see what he knows," he said, and walked back to meet the young man.

The young man's name was Ben Parker. He was twenty-seven years old with a Master's degree in English literature, which he now considered an irrelevant waste of time and effort; and an honorable discharge from the U. S. Army with the rank of sergeant, which at least, he considered, belonged to the real, if fouled-up world.

His background was rural upstate New York, and he was, and except for one lapse had always been, a loner, self-sufficient, expecting others to be the same, and both resentful and contemptuous when they were not. The world was filled with sham and inequity, and his anger against both lay always close beneath the surface.

He was not favorably impressed by this character coming toward him now, wearing a Fort Worth Stetson hat, a fancy shirt, tailored frontier pants and cowboy boots and who drove an oversized example of gas-guzzling Detroit iron towing a fancy trailer.

Warner wore his friendly salesman's smile. "Hi," he said. "Maybe you can help us. We're strangers in these parts."

Ben stopped, nodded and said nothing. Gratuitous rudeness was not in his nature.

"That road down to the left," Warner said, and left the sentence hanging, a question.

"As the sign says, a service road for jeeps." Ben

glanced at the car and trailer with concealed contempt. "I wouldn't try it with that rig."

"Maybe," Warner said, "there's another road farther on?"

"No other road."

Warner frowned. "Then where does this road go?"

"Nowhere. In another mile it turns to dirt. In two more miles it stops. There's a lake, and some trails." Ben shrugged. "I suppose you don't have a map?" They never did, he thought, no map, no compass, only blind, city dwellers' faith that there would always be someone to ask, a traffic cop to help or a telephone to use.

"I guess maybe we made a wrong turn," Warner said. He thought about it. Then reluctantly, "I guess now we turn around and head back down. I'm obliged to you."

Ben glanced again at car and trailer on this narrow mountain road, opened his mouth, thought better of it and closed it again in silence. "Have a nice day," he said, and walked on. Passing the car he saw Patty and Billy in the rear seat, and Sue Ann in front. He merely nodded to all of them, and disappeared around the next curve.

How long he walked, he was never afterward quite sure, probably only a quarter, maybe a half mile, five, ten minutes, arguing with himself the whole time. And, he told himself angrily, splitting hairs like a professional moralist.

A bunch of flatlanders, helpless as newborn puppies in what was obviously an alien environment. Maybe the dude in the Fort Worth Stetson could get that rig turned around on this mountain road, and maybe he couldn't. And if he couldn't, then what? Strike the question, he told himself; it's no business of mine.

It was the first snowflake touching his face that gave him pause, its sudden cold dampness underlining what he supposed he had known all along, that this time of year the weather was too good to last. And in these mountains change could come with unbelievable swiftness.

12

He stopped and squinted through the thinning trees. He had been thinking about the flatlanders, he told himself, or he would already have noticed the change. The distant mountains could still be seen, but now only in vague outline; and as he watched, angry, low clouds scudding in from the west wiped away what visibility had remained. Overhead what had been limitless blue sky was now hazy, and the fading sun wore a distinct halo.

Snowflakes fell faster, large and lazy, disappearing immediately as they touched the trees or the ground. But the temperature was falling; he could feel it. It would not be long before the snow would begin to hold. A front moving in, he thought. Well, at this time of year it was only to be expected.

And maybe those damned fool flatlanders had turned around all right, and maybe they hadn't. Okay, if they hadn't, he could give them a hand, and in turn they could give him a lift back into town. How about that?

The alternative was to go on as he had planned, over the high saddle and down into the solitude of that meadow he knew where when the snow stopped there would be trout for the catching in the quick-running stream, with maybe deer to watch or an occasional elk, now and then even a bear or the quick glimpse of a bobcat, a hawk circling lazily against the sky, and above all peace and quiet and none of the hassle of a city.

The snowflakes were beginning to hold on the ground now. They could be the beginning of a big storm. So? In the meadow was that deserted cabin, someone's shattered dream, and with what he carried in his pack he could hole up there almost indefinitely. Seven miles or less, something over two hours if he pushed. If he started right now. The arguments pro and con were balanced.

Make up your mind, he told himself; and in sudden decision turned around and began to walk quickly down the road in the direction of the car and trailer.

He heard nothing as he came around that last

curve above the fork in the road, and there he stopped and stared unbelieving.

Car and trailer were both still there, but lying on their sides now, and dangerously close to the outer edge of the service road above the steep talus slope. The car's engine had not stopped and the exposed drive shaft still rotated, turning the rear wheels in futile, somehow pitiful motion.

As Ben watched, the rear car door lifted slowly, and the young boy clambered up and out, shaken and frightened, but still nimble as a monkey. He fell, rather than jumped, to the ground, and the heavy door slammed shut. Turning, he tried to lift it open again.

"Hold it. I'll give you a hand," Ben said. He put his staff down, undid his hip strap and slipped the pack off. Without its weight he felt light and free.

Billy was still tugging at the door without success. "Easy," Ben said. "Take it easy." He lifted the door with a single jerk and held it open with one hand while with the other he reached down to the frightened girl inside, caught her hand and helped her to climb clear. The door slammed shut again.

"Daddy," the girl said. "And Mom! I think she's hurt!"

Ben got the front door open. Warner's head appeared, and he followed, climbing out slowly, working his way past the steering wheel with effort, a big, heavy man, panting now from the exertion. He had lost his Stetson, and in his usually confident face there was only bewilderment. "I don't know what happened," he said. "I just don't know." He stared at the car and trailer lying at an odd angle to one another as if explanation lay there.

Patty said, "Daddy! Mom—"

Holding the door open, Ben had already reached in and switched off the ignition. The sudden silence was lonely. To Sue Ann he said, "Can you move?"

She was almost on her back in a twisted position, crowded against her door. Her hair covered her face. Slowly she brushed it out of her eyes and took a deep unsteady breath. "I think it's only my foot and ankle. They were—twisted."

Warner said, as if he had just thought of it, "Sue Ann, honey. Let's get you out."

"You hold the door," Ben said. It was his platoon-leader tone, unconsciously used. Bending down into the car, both hands outstretched, "Now. Slow and easy. Up you come." He caught the woman by both upper arms and lifted her gently until she was free of the car. "Can you stand?"

Sue Ann nodded silently. She stood awkwardly on one foot, looking at Warner. "What happened? It was all so fast!"

Ben reached again into the car, brought out the Stetson, that symbol, and held it out to Warner. He tried to keep scorn out of his voice. "It looks like you jack-knifed." he said. "Probably the trailer went over and flipped the car with it." A steep and narrow mountain road, a heavy trailer, a driver who probably never in his life had tried to back a trailer in a confined space—it was a recipe for pure disaster. And now? Ben's mind was already looking ahead, and disliking what it saw.

The snow was thicker, smaller flakes, no longer lazily drifting. And they were holding on the ground and on the sides of the car and trailer. Wind was rising too, and the air was perceptibly colder.

Ben picked up his pack with an angry jerk, automatically slipped into the shoulder harness and buckled the hip strap. They all watched him. He looked at Warner. "Now what?"

"Well," Warner said, "we'd better get some help. I belong to the Triple-A. They can send a truck." Confidence was returning. It was bad, but not catastrophic. Things like this did happen, which was why you belonged to the AAA.

For a few moments no one spoke. Then Ben said, each word distinct, "And just how are you going to get hold of them?" Standing here in the snow, he thought, pointing out the obvious—it was ridiculous. No, he told himself; it isn't obvious at all; I'm trying to talk

15

about color to the blind. They don't even begin to understand. He tried patiently to explain. "The nearest telephone is twelve–fifteen miles back down that road. We're at something over ten thousand feet." Despite himself, scorn crept into his voice. "We're in a snowstorm, and from the looks of it, it's going to be a bad one." Then, watching the big man's heavy breathing, "Even if it weren't snowing, could you walk fifteen miles at this altitude?"

Sue Ann lowered her injured foot to the ground, and promptly lifted it again with a little grimace of pain. "Were you going down?" she said. "Couldn't you send help?"

He had already thought of it, of course, and rejected it. The worsening weather had made that decision. "Fifteen miles. If this turns out to be as bad a storm as it looks, maybe I could make it, and maybe I couldn't, but even if I did, it would take me a good five hours and probably more." And by then, he thought, but did not want to say yet, God only knows what kind of shape you four would be in. *If* he could even make it into town, that was.

What galled him was the helplessness of the situation, and the growing sense of inexorability which he could not ignore. It was, he thought with sudden anger, like one of those Greek tragedies he had never much liked when you didn't know what was going to happen, but with the chorus constantly chanting doom you knew that whatever it was, it was going to be bad.

"Then what are you going to do?" Sue Ann said.

"Seven miles from here, over the saddle," Ben said, "there's a deserted cabin. It has a roof, and the last time I saw it most of its windows were still there. I can make it in a little over two hours if I push." The sense of inexorability hammered at him. I *could have made* it, he thought.

Patty began to cry soundlessly. She could not help herself, and the tears rolled down the sides of her nose to drip unnoticed to the now whitening ground.

Warner said, his voice quieter now, "What do you

think we ought to do? I mean, is there anything around here? Anything at all?"

"Nothing but the trees, and another thousand feet up there aren't even trees." Ben's voice was heavy with scorn he no longer tried to conceal. "These are the Rocky Mountains. You've heard of them?"

"There's no need to talk like that," Warner said. He had a temper of his own.

Ben took a deep breath, held it and slowly let it out. He gestured at the trailer. "Do you have blankets in there? Sleeping bags?"

Warner scowled at the question.

Sue Ann said, "We don't sleep in the trailer. We stay in motels."

"Warm clothes? Boots?"

"Only sweaters, jackets."

"Get them. Put them on. All of them. And grab whatever food you can carry. Put it in a sack."

Warner said slowly, "What are you thinking of? I mean, I don't think we'd better go anywhere. I think we'd better stay right here with the car and the trailer."

There was silence. "It's tempting," Ben said. "Believe me, it is tempting."

"If you mean you can leave us and walk your seven miles to your cabin," Warner said, "why, go right ahead." It was the anger of frustration speaking, and he knew it; but stop it he could not. "We'll stay right here. We'll make out until somebody comes along."

The girl was still crying in her soundless way. Billy stood still, his eyes on Ben's face. Sue Ann on one foot leaned against the underbody of the overturned car, and she too seemed to await a verdict.

"Nobody is coming along," Ben said at last, his voice under tight control. "I told you this road goes nowhere. It's only for hunters, fishermen, backpackers, and none of them in his right mind is going to start out in a snowstorm." Standing here, arguing, with the snow getting heavier by the minute—but what else was there to do? "Stay here," he said, "and you'll freeze to death. You can't build a fire in the trailer even if you knew how; you'd burn it down, and your-selves with it." He took a deep breath, and said what had to be said: "I mean it, goddamn it. Stay here, and you're dead. All of you." There was no reaction. They don't believe me, Ben thought; they simply can't believe that it's so. He could almost hear that off-stage chorus chanting predictions.

Sue Ann looked at Warner and waited.

Through her tears Patty watched Daddy too, and waited for him to put this hateful man in his place. She was frightened and getting cold. And the tears would not stop.

Billy said, "You want us to go to that cabin?" He too was beginning to shiver. "I never walked seven miles."

Warner said, "Is that what you have in mind?"

There was no way out, Ben told himself, none. "No," he said, and tried not to let the anger show. "Up ahead there's a canyon. There are caves, one fair-sized one I know of. It isn't good, but it's shelter, and we can have a fire." *We;* the first-person pronoun seemed to hang, echoing. Decision made. "It's the best I know."

"How long?" Suspicion was plain in Warner's tone.

"Until the snow stops and we can see where we are." That *we* again.

Patty said, "All of us? In a cave?" Her voice was suddenly shrill.

Warner shook his head. "I don't like it."

Ben clung hard to his temper. "I'll say it only one more time," he said, spacing the words for emphasis. "I don't like it either, not worth a good goddamn. If I'd had the brains God gave a chipmunk, I'd be well on my way now, over the saddle and headed for that cabin. But I came back, and here I am, and like it or not, we're all in this together. You might try to help. Get those sweaters and jackets and what food you can carry if you have any and let's get going. Your boy here is already shivering."

Warner hesitated.

Patty said, almost pleading, "Daddy."

Billy said, "I'm going to get my sweater and jacket anyway." He turned away and began to tug at the trailer door.

Sue Ann said, "I don't think I can walk." Her tone was apologetic.

"How about that?" Warner said, defiance flaring briefly.

"I'm going to carry her," Ben said. He was undoing the hip strap again. "And you're going to carry my pack. It's heavy, but there isn't anything in it we aren't going to need." He studied Warner's face in silence. Then, "Well?" He watched Warner hesitate still, doubt and defiance showing in equal measure then, slowly, turn away and walk to the trailer door.

"You, too, honey," Sue Ann said to Patty in a quiet voice. Its calm tone astonished her. "Get whatever you think you'll need. Get my things too." And when the girl had turned away, Sue Ann looked carefully at Ben. "Do you really think you can carry me?"

"Yes."

"Is it far?"

"Far enough." The better part of a mile, uphill on a faint, ancient trail.

"I'm not as heavy as some," Sue Ann said, "but I'm not light, either." There was no reply. He has made up his mind, she thought; a stubborn man. She stood quiet as the increasing pain of foot and ankle and the growing cold amid the snow and the loneliness of this alien environment drove away the last of the doubts. "We have no choice," she said at last.

Warner was the last out of the trailer. He carried a heavy hunting rifle with a mounted scope, and he rested it carefully against the bottom of the trailer while he reached high to lock the trailer door. Then he locked the doors of the car. He faced Ben at last, the rifle again in his hand. Beneath the Stetson his face was set. "I'm still not sure we're doing right." My family, he thought, my responsibility, now suddenly abrogated.

Ben had opened the main pouch of his pack. He paid no attention to Warner as he took out a light nylon parka and pulled it over his head. The snow was falling harder, and the wind had picked up; the flakes came at them on a slant, silent, but no longer soft. The ground was already white. Ben reclosed the pack and straightened in silence.

"I just don't know," Warner said then. "So I guess all I can do is hope you know what's best."

"I don't think you're going to need that rifle."

"I'm not going to leave it here for some thief to pick up."

Ben shrugged. "I'll help you with the pack."

It was heavy. Ben lengthened the hip strap and made it fast, and that helped some, but not much. Warner's face remained determinedly expressionless.

"Okay?" Ben said.

"I'll manage."

Ben handed his staff to Billy, knelt in front of Sue Ann, took her piggyback and got to his feet without apparent effort. "I'll lead," he said. And to Warner, "You take the rear. Keep them closed up. If you have to stop, holler." He started off up the road at that deceptively slow pace.

Patty followed, then Billy, and Warner in his cowboy boots that were not all that comfortable for walking.

And the pack did nothing to help his balance, or his wind. He counted steps, and when he came to fifty, he paused, panting, unbelieving still, and turned to look back. In the driving snow, car and trailer were no longer visible.

2.

ON THE CITIZENS BAND RADIO the truckers' channel, Channel 19, usually devoted to reports of Smoky Bears (patrol cars) and general chatter, was beginning to crackle with different, serious talk.

"Break, one-nine."

"Go, breaker."

"I thank you for the break. That Eye-two-five; north of Albuquerque town she's drifting bad, especially on that big hill. I got me an eighteen-wheeler, good tires and a full load, and I made it—just. Another ten, fifteen minutes she'll be closed down for sure. Ten-four?"

"Ten-four. Much obliged for the information, good buddy. Santo Cristo base station, Sassy Grandma, you got your ears on, you got a copy?"

"Sassy Grandma here. Ten-four. La Bajada hill bad. Much obliged for the info."

"Break, one-nine."

"Go, breaker."

"Thanks for the break. This here's Cowboy. You got a copy, Grandma?"

"Ten-four. Come on, Cowboy."

"Two-eight-five that Parque hill southbound to Santo Cristo town, we got one lane already closed, a pick-um-up and trailer broke down. I'm southbound from Taos town, and what's coming behind me is worse than what we got here. What I mean, she's snowin' an' blowin' till hell won't have it. Ten-four?"

"Ten-four. Appreciate the info, Cowboy. Anybody got word on Eye-two-five north from Santo Cristo?"

21

"This here's Red Dog. Drifting in Apache Canyon. She won't stay open long."

"Ten-four. Appreciate it. We're getting the latest from State Police. Keep your ears up and we'll give it to you when we have it. It's going to be a long night. This is Sassy Grandma. Ten-ten on the side. One-nine clear."

In his small foreign-car garage Bart Wallace kept his CB radio open and also tuned to Channel 19 while he worked on the 30,000-mile servicing of the Mercedes-Benz he would never be able to afford.

He was a huge man, tall, thick and broad without fat, with heavy sloping shoulders and enormous hands that, for all their size and strength, moved with delicate precision as if controlled by some constant monitoring force. He was thirty-nine years old and worked and lived alone.

He had a mechanical engineering degree from Berkeley, where, for a time, he had allowed himself to be persuaded to play football as he had in high school. "You're a damn waste," the coach told him finally. "You're big enough and strong enough and quick enough to play defensive lineman on anybody's team —if you gave a damn."

And Bart had smiled, and, because he did not like to injure anyone's feelings by impoliteness, made his simple explanation: "I don't particularly like knocking people down, that's all it is."

He was social but rather private, comfortable with his own company and his own thoughts. He had worked for some years as a design engineer at Lockheed Aircraft in Burbank, and found the corporate life not for him. His wants were simple, he had his friends here in Santo Cristo and he enjoyed working with well-designed machinery. In season there was fishing, camping, nature photography and skiing nearby. What more could a man ask? And he made his place in the community, a man who believed in paying his way.

While he worked on the car now, he listened

22

thoughtfully as the reports came in. When falling snowflakes were visible through his window, he straightened from the Mercedes, in his deliberate way wiped his hands carefully on a red garage cloth and went to the telephone to call the Federal Aviation Administration people at the airport tower. He did not need to look up the number.

"How does it look?"

"Bad." This was Joe Meems's voice. Joe was the tower controller. "There's another storm coming behind this one. You people had just better hope nobody is damn fool enough to get theirselves lost before it's over."

"We'll hope," Bart said. "Thanks, Joe." He hung up and stood for a few moments watching the snow through the window. It was falling more heavily now, and beginning to hold. Here we go again, he thought; time to take some precautions. He picked up the phone and dialed another number.

The phone rang in the fire barn of the Arroyo Volunteer Fire Department south of town, and also in Bessie Andrews' house a quarter of a mile away. Bessie spent her days in her wheelchair. Her telephone and her CB radio were her main contacts with the world, and she served as willing clearinghouse for the local informal Search and Rescue organization. She answered the phone immediately.

"I don't think a stand-by would be out of order, Bessie," Bart told her.

Search and Rescue in Santo Cristo was not the taut, disciplined organization that existed in some localities. It was, rather, a loose amalgam of mountain-wise unpaid volunteers, some with specialized skills, all with basic training in the fundamentals of map reading, communication, survival and the like, each furnishing his own personal equipment and his time and effort in emergencies.

Like Topsy, it had just growed, and maybe one day there would be uniforms, car insignia, graded commands and all that, with members on constant rotating alert, but not yet. Bart had often thought that when

23

that day arrived he would bow out; in the vast Lock-heed organization he had had enough of orders from on high, and inflexible regulations, to last him indefinitely. In the meantime, in their loose fashion he and the others usually, but not always, managed to do what needed to be done.

"Let's alert only a few," Bart said into the phone. "No need to call out all the troops yet. Say Wilt, CJ, Jaime and Steve. If this weather keeps up, we could be needed."

"Will do," Bessie said. "What's an eight-letter word for a big storm?" Bessie and her eternal crossword puzzles.

"Blizzard," Bart said, "which is just about what's coming." He started to hang up. Bessie's voice stopped him.

"Carl?" Bessie said. "Shall I call him too?"

"I'll call him." Carl was a good man, and a trained para-medic, but he was prickly sometimes. No need to expose Bessie to Carl's moods. Bart hung up and stood for a few more moments staring out at the falling snow before he dialed Carl's number.

Carl was in his plumbing shop. "You've got a hunch?" he said. "Is that it? You don't usually hear voices."

Maybe I am jumpy, Bart thought, because of last time. Maybe—

It was as if Carl were reading his mind. "Forget last time," Carl said. "We brought in a deado, a damn fool hunter who got himself lost no more than half a mile from a trail a blind man couldn't lose." There was scorn in his voice. "Sure, we should have found him, but then he didn't have any business being there in the first place. No compass, no map, not even any matches—some of them never learn that the mountains aren't just an extension of Main Street."

True often enough, Bart thought. So why do we even bother to try to save people like that from themselves? He supposed it was a good question, and he supposed too that psychologists would have long and complicated answers for it, but all it really boiled

24

down to was that when somebody got himself into trouble you felt obligated to drop what you were doing and try to give him a hand. Simple as that. It was not the way city people thought, which was one of the reasons he had put cities behind him.

"Okay," he said in his easy way. "Let's hope they all stay where they're supposed to." He hung up and started back for the Mercedes, but the sight of the falling snow stopped him once more.

It was sunny and clear this morning and on into the afternoon, he thought, just as it had been the day that hunter started out. And unless you knew how quickly mountain weather could change, you assumed that the fair weather would last—as the hunter apparently had because he had worn only a light jacket, no gloves and, as Carl had pointed out, had taken no map, no compass, nothing but his rifle and a pocketful of cartridges, not even a pocketknife. He might, Bart thought with sadness, have been going for no more than a stroll down a well-marked country lane.

They would never know the precise details of the tragedy, but the usual picture was probably close to correct. The hunter had walked farther than he thought away from the trail, maybe following what he took to be signs of deer. Weather had closed in, rain turning to sleet turning to snow as the temperature dropped. The hunter was soaked through his light clothing now, and with wind rising as the center of the storm moved in, his chill would turn to hypothermia as his body lost heat faster than it could replenish it, impairing his muscular coordination, confusing his already frightened thinking.

He survived the storm. His footprints in the snow demonstrated that. They also demonstrated how far gone he was, because the tracks wavered, and strayed, shortened and lengthened, turned and twisted as he lurched on until finally he fell and did not get up.

No one's fault but his own, certainly, but that did not diminish the tragedy. Nor for Bart did it ease the pain of failure. We should have found him in time, he thought as he went back to his work; we didn't, and so he died. No rationalization could change that. Maybe this time, if there is a need, we'll be there when it counts.

In the Santo Cristo airport tower Joe Meems looked at the snow through the outward-slanting windows. Suddenly the runway was no longer visible. "It's like, you know, one of those paperweights," he said, "where you turn it upside down and you have a snowstorm, you know what I mean? I feel like I'm inside the paperweight."

"Something like that," the new controller said. "It moves in in a hurry, doesn't it? An hour ago it was clear."

"This country," Joe Meems said, and shook his head. "It can dehydrate you and kill you of thirst, and it can catch you looking the wrong way in a dry wash and hit you with a flash flood that ends you up dead three miles away, or it can freeze you to death in weather like this, or—"

The loudspeaker crackled. "This is Bonanza one-six-five-zero Bravo calling the Santo Cristo tower. Come in, tower."

Joe Meems said softly, "Jesus!" and reached for the mike with one hand while he wrote down the call letters with the other. Into the mike he said, "This is the Santo Cristo tower. Come in, Bonanza one-six Bravo."

The speaker crackled again. ". . . repeat. This is Bonanza one-six-five-zero Bravo calling the Santo Cristo tower. Come in, tower! Come in, tower!"

Joe Meems's eyes were on the falling snow. "This is the Santo Cristo tower and we read you, Bonanza one-six Bravo. What is your location?"

". . . one-six-five-zero Bravo calling Santo Cristo tower. For God's sake, come in, tower! Repeat, come in, tower!"

It was not much of a climb, Ben Parker told himself, two–three hundred feet of elevation at most. But the difference between a forty-pound pack on his back and a woman weighing something over a hundred pounds was considerable. With his forearms beneath Sue Ann's thighs, he kept his fingers locked against his body, leaned forward into the trail and concentrated on putting one foot in front of the other with no thought of distance or time.

Or of what might have been—himself, free, well able to cope. Damn it, when you made your choice, that was it. It was the one lesson he had learned if no other in this life.

Sue Ann ignored as best she could the pain of her foot and ankle and clung to him until her arms ached, trying desperately to make no movement or shift of balance that would disturb the rhythm of his slow walking. The cold seemed to soak into her bones; and this too she tried to ignore.

They were on a trail of sorts, she thought, although with snow now completely covering the ground, and falling heavily to disturb vision, it was really difficult to tell. She was being carried into the unknown as, strange thought, how many thousands of women throughout the ages had been carried, frequently by force? "Are you all right?" she said. Her lips moved awkwardly from growing numbness.

Ben's head nodded, but he said nothing. Breath was precious. One more step, another and one more after that up this trail how many thousands of feet had trodden, but probably not with a burden like this. He sensed rather than heard the sounds behind him, and he stopped, panting, and slowly turned.

Billy and Patty were panting too, but they were still on their feet, each with the assigned sack over his shoulder, and Billy with Ben's staff. But behind them Warner was on his knees, hands braced in the snow, head hanging, the rifle lying on the ground. He looked up and started to struggle to his feet.

"Hold it," Ben said, and tried to keep impatience out of his voice. "Take off the pack and leave it. You've brought it this far, and that's a help." Now why did he feel that he had to give praise where none was due? Just to keep up the troops' morale? "I'll come back for it." He turned back to the trail and started off again.

Warner got himself erect, still on his knees. He got one foot planted, tried to stand, and could not; and the failure both astonished and infuriated him. Damn it, he thought, I used to be stout enough, didn't I? And I'm not over the hill yet by a long shot. Rest a moment, that's the ticket, then—

"Daddy," Patty's voice. "Daddy, please. Leave the pack like he said. Don't—hurt yourself!" Everything else and now this; it was too much. She was cold and she was frightened and she wanted to cry again, but somehow the tears would not come. "Don't be—foolish, Daddy." She had never spoken to her father like this before. "We need you!"

The stranger with Sue Ann on his back had gone on and not even looked behind to see if they were coming. Arrogant of him, Warner thought, and knew that his own failure was coloring his viewpoint. And Billy had followed. That left only himself and Patty, and Warner wished that she were not here either to witness his shame. Slowly, reluctantly, he unbuckled the hip strap and with effort worked his shoulders free of the padded upper straps. The pack fell to the ground, and it was as if a mountain had been removed. Was this how a packhorse felt when at last the packsaddle was lifted from his back? Warner would never again look at a pack animal in the same way.

He picked up the rifle and stood, not easily, but well enough. There was a deep pain in his chest. He forced himself to look at his daughter, and tried to smile. "Your old man doesn't have it," he said. Words were difficult, and they emerged in a cloud of steam. "Sorry, kitten. Let's go." Nothing else to do, he thought helplessly.

"I don't see," Patty said, "how you got it this far, I really don't." Wasn't this exactly the kind of thing her mother sometimes said that always sounded so—patronizing? Patty turned away and started up the trail.

The tears were closer now, much closer, and her head ached from the cold.

Billy tried to match his stride to the footprints Ben was making, and found that he could not. Nor could he stay with the slow, steady pace. Even with Mom on his back, this guy walked as if nothing could stop him —wow! And after they got to the cave, he was going back down the trail too, to get the pack Pop hadn't been able to carry. Summers at camp, there had been counselors who were pretty neat, good swimmers and canoe handlers, able to make fire with sticks, that kind of thing, but Billy had an idea that this guy could do all the counselors could do, and more besides. Billy's confidence rose, and even his wet feet aching from cold in the red, white and blue jogging shoes he was so proud of didn't seem quite so important as he lurched along panting, his sack over his shoulder, and Ben's staff in his hand.

The trail led into a canyon and climbed along the steep left face. To the right the land, as nearly as Sue Ann could see, fell away. In the swirling snow she caught glimpses of huge pine trees and scattered rocks larger than either the car or the trailer they had left behind. It was frightening country, and again she thought of the Hall of the Mountain King, which, as a girl, she had visualized as enormous, harsh and menacing, something like this.

Snow blurred her vision, but she could not spare a hand to brush her eyes. Each breath emerged in a cloud of vapor. The injured foot and ankle throbbed. Unreal, she thought, unreal.

"Almost there," Ben breathed the words.

Had she then spoken her thought aloud? "I'm— sorry," Sue Ann said.

He nodded, and plodded on. Fifty more paces, he told himself, forty-nine, forty-eight . . .

It was Sue Ann who heard it first, merely a faint thrumming sound distorted and deadened by the silent falling snow. It grew louder. "There's an airplane," she said. "It's somewhere over us."

Ben shook his head. Thirty-six, thirty-five, thirty-

29

four . . . He was gasping now, and each breath burned deep in his lungs. His legs obeyed, as he knew they would even after their aching seemed intolerable; the trick was concentration. Twenty-nine, twenty-eight, twenty-seven . . . I ought to be able to see the cave entrance now, he thought—unless I've taken a wrong trail.

Cut it out, he told himself angrily. You haven't taken a wrong trail; you're on the canyon wall that faces south, which is where they always had their caves, or almost always to catch the sun.

Sixteen, fifteen, fourteen . . . and there it was, the opening, smaller than he remembered it, but essentially the same. He could even smile without amusement, and breathing somehow seemed easier.

But there was a roaring in his ears he had not experienced before even near exhaustion, and maybe—

"It *is* a plane," Sue Ann said. "Can't you hear it?"

Ben stopped then with only half a dozen paces to go, and through the pulse pounding in his head tried to listen. She was right, he told himself in near-disbelief. Somewhere up there, and not far—

The roaring sound ended abruptly. Faintly, almost imperceptibly they heard crashing, crackling sounds. And then quiet with only the faint soughing of wind through the big trees in the silent, falling snow.

Ben took another deep, painful breath, leaned forward and started his legs moving again. There was very little feeling left in his hands, but the fingers stayed locked as if in spasm.

Sue Ann said, "They—they crashed!"

"Poor bastards." Ben's voice was almost inaudible. Somewhere off to the right was where the last sounds had come from. It was the best fix he could get as he lurched on.

He reached the cave entrance, stopped, turned his back to the cliff wall and almost fell to his knees. He saw Billy, plodding up the trail and behind him, Patty; and Warner struggling along still carrying his rifle. "You can get down now," Ben managed over his

30

shoulder to Sue Ann. "We're there." The best we can do, he thought. Let's hope to God it's enough.

In Santo Cristo airport tower there was silence. Joe Meems leaned back in his chair, looked up at the loud-speaker and swore softly beneath his breath. Outside the snow continued to fall, a swirling, shifting, opaque curtain reflecting light back into the tower room.

"Bonanza one-six-five-zero Bravo," Joe Meems said. "We never got through to him, and what the hell good would it have done if we had?"

The new controller said slowly, "Could it be a hoax? I mean somebody flying in this weather, does that make sense?"

"The world is full of damn fools," Joe Meems said, "wall to wall." He sat forward. "Okay. We'll find out who he is, and then *if* he filed a flight plan wherever he started from, and *if* he stuck to it, then *maybe* we can get some idea which way he was heading, and go on from there." His thoughts now were on Bart Wallace and his Search and Rescue people. "Goddamn it," he said suddenly, "do you have any idea how big this goddamn country is? They may never find Bonanza one-six-five-zero Bravo until hell freezes over."

Sue Ann dragged herself through the small cave entrance as into another world where at least the snow no longer fell and there was surcease from the biting wind. But cold remained, a dull ache throughout her body, stronger now.

In the dim light she saw a wall at her right hand. Painfully she crawled to it and heaved herself into a sitting position. Her foot and ankle throbbed with each pulse beat. She tried to ignore them by concentrating on her surroundings.

An antechamber of hell was her first thought, and why could hell not be cold instead of hot? My mind is wandering, she told herself; stop it, stop it! She closed her eyes and counted slowly to ten before she opened them again and looked carefully around.

The roof of the cave was not high; Warner and the

strange young man would have to stoop when they stood. And its color was darker than the cave walls, which were themselves a kind of beige with here and there odd markings that did not seem natural. The floor of the cave was cold, dry, fine sandy material, almost certainly pulverized from the basic rock in which the cave had been formed. She was not a good judge of distances or measurements, but she guessed that the cave in its irregular shape was no larger than their breakfast nook at home.

She made herself sit quiet, trying to relax, shutting out the pain and the cold, trying too to forget the crashing sounds in the trees, concentrating on herself, her family and what had without warning happened to them. We are selfish, she thought, self-centered, and the only world that matters is our own. Was this selfishness an affront to the gods? Strange, sudden thought, bringing with it a cold touch of fear.

And here came Billy scrambling through the entrance, pushing his sack of canned goods ahead of him. His teeth were chattering, but his eyes were bright with young enthusiasm for a new adventure, and he looked around the cave and nodded approvingly as if he had expected no less. "Patty's coming," he said. "And Pop. Ben's gone down for his pack. He told me to gather wood for a fire." He hesitated, and his expression showed sudden concern. "You okay?"

Sue Ann managed a faint nod and even a trace of smile. She watched Billy nod again, crawl back out and disappear.

Patty crawled through the entrance. She looked around, shivering, blinking in the dimness, saw her mother and burst into tears once more.

"Crying isn't going to help, honey," Sue Ann said. It required enormous effort to keep her voice calm and gentle, but there was reproach in her tone. At a time like this, she thought, I can only think in platitudes. "We're just going to have to make the best of it. And we're lucky—" She stopped as Warner's bulk filled the entrance. "Here's Daddy." She closed her eyes in relief.

Warner squeezed through on hands and knees, pushing the rifle ahead of him. Inside, he rose to his feet, straightened too quickly, banged his head on the cave roof, sat down hard and said slowly, audibly and with feeling, "Son of a bitch!" And then, in a quieter voice, "It's a goddamn mess, isn't it?" He squinted at Sue Ann. "You okay?"

Billy's same words, Sue Ann thought; at times, not often enough, the man and the boy even sounded alike. Strange, because in temperament, unfortunately, they were worlds apart. She could only nod.

"Oh, Daddy!" Patty said. "I'm cold!"

"Never mind, honey." Warner's voice was soothing. "It'll pass. That guy, whatever his name is—"

"Ben." Her own voice, Sue Ann thought, seemed to come from a distance. "Billy said so."

"Okay; Ben." Warner's tone changed. "We'll have a fire, and that'll help. And sooner or later they'll find the car. Then they'll start looking. Jake will see to it that they do when we don't show." His confidence began to rise again. "Old Jake won't let us down."

The cold and the pain, Sue Ann thought wildly, maybe they were responsible, or maybe it was just being here in this unreal place surrounded by the sense of menace she had felt from the moment they had entered these mountains, or maybe it was just—everything, and when you reached your limit you saw things with preternatural clarity and could no longer evade facts. "We were on the wrong road, weren't we?" she said in a new clear voice.

"Okay," Warner said, "so I made a wrong turn."

Had it always been this easy to provoke defensive reaction? Sue Ann tried to remember, and could not. Her mind had only one focus. "I'm not blaming you, dear. But—" Why must it be up to me to speak the unpleasant truth?

Warner was frowning. "But what?"

"But we were on the wrong road," Sue Ann heard herself say, "and so they don't know where to look, will they? And it's getting dark, and if the snow keeps up, the car will be buried, and—" Enough.

"Look," Warner said. "They'll find us. Why, hell, we're only sixteen—seventeen miles from the center of Santo Cristo, fifty thousand people. Of course they'll find us."

Patty looked now at her mother.

In the silence, feeling all at once the burden of disclosure, "Of course they will," Sue Ann said, and rolled sideways in a faint.

Ben was back. He pushed the pack through the entrance and crawled in after it. Warner was kneeling over Sue Ann, shaking her gently. "Honey, honey," he was saying in a pleading voice.

Ben said, "What happened?"

"Mom fainted." Patty's voice was unsteady.

"Is she breathing? Let me see." He pushed Warner aside and knelt beside the woman.

Sue Ann's eyelids fluttered, opened. In her eyes was a sudden baffled, uncomprehending look almost of fear. Her breathing was labored.

Ben took her wrist and felt the thready, rapid pulse. "Okay," he said, his voice gentle, "okay. Easy now. A little shock. We'll fix you up. Your foot and ankle. Is the pain bad?"

Sue Ann nodded faintly. Her eyes closed again.

"Let's straighten you out," Ben said. To Patty, "Get my sleeping bag." To Sue Ann again, "We'll get you warm, and I'll give you something for the pain." Then to Patty again, "Help her into the sleeping bag. The floor's cold. And raise her feet a little. Undo her belt and waistband, and her bra."

Patty said, "But I can't just—undress her here!"

Ben had already turned away and was kneeling beside his pack, burrowing into its depth. Over his shoulder his voice was harsh, "And just where in hell are you figuring to take her? To a dressing room somewhere?"

Sue Ann's voice, unsteady and weak, said, "Help me. Do as he says."

Warner said, "Will she be all right? I mean, shock, you said—"

"She'll be fine." Reassurance, the books said, that

34

was the important thing. And once you had been taught, you reacted without even thinking about it, without even asking aloud in pure futility just why in hell you were stupid enough to get yourself into this fix in the first place. Never mind; that could wait. "Here," Ben said, and held out a white pill from his pack, and a drinking cup with a little water. "Demerol. It'll take care of the pain." He helped lift Sue Ann to a sitting position.

Her shirt was open to her waist, her belt undone and trousers unzipped, and her brassiere hung loose. Ben ignored it all. "Can you swallow?" He watched her nod. "Good. You're going to be fine." He held the drinking cup to her lips and then laid her back down gently.

Warner said, "Look—" He stopped. In a different, almost placatory tone, "What I mean is, what can I do?" He saw Sue Ann roll her head and smile faintly up at him. He felt better.

"You can help Billy bring firewood," Ben said. "Up this same trail fifty yards you'll find some scrub growth. Bring whatever you can. Any size." He did not look up as he spoke; and once the implied order was given, his thoughts were off in a different direction. "Let's see if we can get this boot off."

It was a fine, hand-stitched, Tony Lama boot, and Ben's first gentle movement of it brought a murmur of pain. "Sorry," he said. "We'll have to do it another way, but we have to get it off."

Patty said, teeth chattering, "But how?"

Warner on hands and knees was beginning to crawl through the entrance. He could not look back, but he knew what was happening: that sheath knife in the worn scabbard was going to ruin a perfectly good fifty-dollar pair of boots, just like that. Well, the hell with it. The last thing he heard was Sue Ann's weak, "Go ahead." He crawled out into the falling snow.

The mutilated boot had been removed by the time Warner and Billy returned from the final trip of their firewood-gathering mission; and Sue Ann, tucked into

Ben's sleeping bag, was resting quietly, her breathing almost normal again.

"I can't be sure," Ben said, steam from his breath punctuating the words, "but I think there's a fracture. I'm not a doctor; I'm not even a para-medic. I've splinted the leg, probably more than necessary, and that's the best I can do." He sounded angry with himself. He looked at his watch. "Another hour of daylight, no more. Let's get going on that fire."

"Hey," Billy said, "rubbing sticks together, huh?"

"I'm the prosaic type," Ben said. It was the first bit of levity they had heard him attempt. "I use matches. And a starter stick."

He built a small pyramid of twigs and small wood, broke off an inch of a brown stick of what looked to be pressed wood, and lighted that beneath the pyramid. The flame caught and grew. "You're the firetender, Billy," he said. "Now let's see about cutting some of those larger pieces."

From his pack he took a coil of what looked to be braided wire contained between two pieces of cardboard. Unrolled, the wire was about eighteen inches long, with a loop at either end. Ben handled it with extreme care. He took a two-foot stick from the pile of gathered wood, trimmed it smooth with his sheath knife, left a small fork at one end and carved a notch at the other. Then he bent the stick into an arc and fitted the end loops of the wire to fork and notch. Released, the tension of the bent stick held the wire taut.

"It's actually a wire saw," he said, and held it out to Warner. "Feel the wire. Gently. Very gently."

The braided wire contained hundreds of sharp barbs, all pointing in one direction. Warner shook his head in wonder. "Take it easy," Ben said, "and you can cut any of this stuff to whatever length you want." He pointed upward, where a slanting hole in the cave's wall showed light. "That hole will let most of the smoke out. I don't know if it's natural or if somebody drilled it a long time ago. It doesn't matter. We have it, and that's all that matters." He picked up his

36

staff and stooping walked to the entrance. "I'll try to be back by dark," he said.

"Where you going?" Warner's tone was demanding.

"Probably on a fool's errand." Ben left it there, dropped to his knees and crawled out of the cave.

The goddamn trouble was, he told himself, that once you allowed yourself to become involved there was no end to the process of entrapment.

He had seen it in the Army. Once you raised your head and looked even two steps beyond your own feet, they began to pin stripes on your arms, and life wasn't a damn bit easier, just filled with more responsibility. Where they had you was in their knowledge that you couldn't resign from the human race. But you could sure as hell try. You retained that privilege.

The truth of the matter, he told himself as he pulled up the hood of his parka, snugged it around his chin and bent into the wind and driving snow, was that he wouldn't even be starting out on this fool's errand if he hadn't in effect been forced into it. That was the part that galled him.

He liked to believe that he didn't give a damn what other people thought, and yet he knew that he was not immune. Sue Ann had heard the plane crash, and she had made sure that he was aware of it too. So what else was there for him to do but go out and at least go through the motions of trying to find it, and see if there were survivors?

No matter that he didn't have the ghost of a chance in weather like this and in these mountains. Why, hell, he had only the vaguest idea of which direction to take in search. And the chances were less than remote that anyone would be left alive anyway. But because Sue Ann did know that the plane was out there somewhere, and because he, Ben, was able-bodied, and because the system decreed that you were supposed to act as if you cared—then, goddamn it, here he was freezing his ass off for what? For nothing.

Whoever wrote the book had seen to it that you were caught up in the system—forever.

3.

BART WALLACE CLOSED AND LOCKED the foreign-car garage and, head down against cold wind and driving snow, walked down the almost empty street toward the fragrant warmth of La Cantina as toward a familiar hearth and a roaring fire.

There were few persons of either sex with whom he had ever felt totally at ease, and Connie, Consuelo Valdez y Hopkins, Spanish, Anglo and Indian all mixed together, was one. Bart could not have said why; he merely accepted the easy, undemanding relationship.

Connie owned and ran La Cantina—good coffee, breakfast short orders, only beer on a limited license to go with the fine spicy southwestern food she served at lunch and dinner. Like him, Bart often thought, she ran her own enterprise, took pride in its quality and yearned for no greater success, which was maybe not the American dream of grow-big-and-get-rich, but had nonetheless its own quiet satisfactions. This lack of driving ambition was just one of the areas in which they thought alike.

Bart filled the cafe's doorway as he went through and closed the door behind him with gentle care. He took off his cap and parka and scattered the snow that in only these two blocks had gathered on them. He wore his beeper on his belt a little self-consciously, but Connie's smile as she saw it bothered him not at all. The cafe was empty. He sat on one of the counter stools and Connie served him black coffee without asking.

"Even bears hibernate in this kind of weather," Connie said, smiling, "but you and your people—" She shook her head, smiling still. "I always wonder why you do it."

It was the kind of implied question which from someone else would be embarrassing. From Connie it was merely part of their easy give-and-take, and Bart could even allow a rare trace of humor to emerge. "I tried hibernation once," he said. "I got restless."

Connie's smile spread. "I should think you'd have liked it, being all alone."

"Would you?"

The smile was less easy now. "Sometimes I think so. More coffee?"

Behind the counter a small FM radio played program music. The music stopped now, and an announcer's voice said, "We interrupt this program for a special announcement. The storm that has moved into central New Mexico has already deposited up to four inches of snow at the higher elevations, and continuing snow is predicted along with moderate-to-strong winds which will cause drifting. Travelers' advisories have been issued statewide. Temperatures are dropping, and it is predicted that by morning readings of zero degrees, or below, will be registered in the Santo Cristo area and the northern mountains. This bulletin is from State Police headquarters. We now resume our regular program of music in stereo."

Connie replaced the glass coffee maker on its warming coil. "In '71," she said, "I was off at college, but out on the reservation sheep and cattle froze to death —along with some people. When a storm like this starts, I think about that."

I'm thinking about our dead hunter, Bart thought; and was silent.

It was then that the beeper sounded its strident note at Bart's belt. So his hunch had been right. Automatically he silenced the beeper, took a slow, deep breath and in his deliberate way got up from his stool already searching in his pocket for a dime as he walked to the wall phone. Connie watched him as he dialed. He showed no anger or even annoyance. The conversation was brief, and one-sided. "Okay," Bart said at last. "I'm on my way." He hung up and walked back to the counter.

"You still haven't told me why you do it," Connie said.

"Maybe I don't know." He finished his coffee, laid money on the counter and picked up his cap. "There's a plane down somewhere in the mountains." His smile now was without amusement. "If its emergency signal is working, we may be able to find it."

"And if it isn't?"

He shook his head. "Let's hope it is." He was at the door when her voice stopped him.

"Why can't they search by air?"

For answer Bart opened the door and pointed outside. The snow was a dense, moving curtain in the gathering darkness. Bart wore a crooked smile. "In the end," he said, "they usually have to call out the poor stupid foot soldiers. It was the same in the Army."

Billy tended the fire with the earnest attention of a neophyte at a solemn ceremony, each twig and stick carefully placed, watched and at need shifted. The wood was fairly dry and most of the smoke it did generate found its way to the ceiling hole and out, but the heavy pleasant fragrance of buring piñon still filled the cave.

The heat from the fire was not much, Bill thought; it seemed to seep into the rock walls of the cave or dissipate itself in the air without doing much good unless you almost put your hands into the flames. He had never thought much about it before, but he could see now that it was no simple matter to heat even a room this size uniformly, or to heat it at all as far as that went. And if, as the announcer on the transistor radio he had brought from the trailer had said, temperatures were going way down tonight, they were going to be an uncomfortable bunch of people by morning. Only uncomfortable? Or worse? The question lurked in the back of his mind, unanswered.

Billy had never been really cold, but if his wet, aching feet were any indication of what it was like, he wasn't sure how much cold he could stand. In the meantime, he tended the fire as carefully as he could, and tried to put gloomy thoughts from his mind.

Sue Ann lay quietly in the sleeping bag. The Demerol had eased the pain of her foot and ankle, relief coming in waves, each stronger than the one before; and she now felt lightheaded, drowsy and simply tired.

Warner had sawed wood with the wire saw until his arms ached, and there was now a neatly stacked pile which, he calculated, would last the night. He was a big, basically solid man, well-fleshed these days, and cold had never bothered him as much as it did others, but even with the fire the cave was far from comfortable to him, and that was not good, but what was the alternative?

Much as he would have liked to think otherwise in order to place blame upon Ben instead of himself for their predicament, he had to admit that they were probably better off here than back in the trailer, which by now was surely covered with snow and without heat rapidly turning into a deep freeze. And as he thought about it, he could see too that Ben had been right about their not being able to build a fire in the trailer without running the risk of burning it down and themselves with it.

There was the trouble, of course: Ben had been right every step of the way so far, and he had been so goddamned offhand about it, so sure of himself, that instead of being grateful to him, all you felt was resentment. It was fatigue, of course, that was making him irritable, Warner told himself, and the knowledge helped not at all. "How do we know he's even coming back?" The words just popped out.

Patty said, "Oh, Daddy!" In her voice was a mixture of impatience and alarm. "Why wouldn't he?"

"He left his pack," Billy said. "He wouldn't be going far without it." The logical mind at work.

"There was an airplane." Sue Ann's voice was

41

dreamy, but not vague. "Maybe you didn't hear it. It crashed somewhere nearby." It was all quite clear in her mind. "When he had done what he could for us, he went out to see what he could do for them."

Warner snorted. "Clark Kent Superman to the rescue." Verbal sniping was less than generous, and Warner knew it, but at the moment he could not refrain. And the silence in the cave merely added to his irritation. That and the cold. He sat down on the floor of the cave, picked up his rifle and began to rub the dirt from it with his handkerchief.

The snow was deeper now, and still falling heavily. The elements came at you gradually and almost imperceptibly, Ben thought, and then all at once, their preparations complete, just as it had been in Nam, they kicked off the real attack and for the first time showed you the full strength of their forces.

For days, weeks, the ground had been losing its warmth. Wherever snow landed now, it held, and began to build, and where there was wind, to drift; dry snow, soft fluffy snow, powder to skiers, a delight to kids and landscape painters, and, Ben supposed, to poets and lovers and God knew who else. They were welcome to it.

Snow covered sharp rocks and broken branches, hid pitfalls and small irregularities and made stable footing impossible. On a trail or a road it would have been different and he could have proceeded at his normal walking pace. But I am not on a goddamn trail or road, he told himself; I am on a fool's errand, and the temptation was strong to turn around and head back for the relative shelter of the cave. He stifled the temptation with effort. Five more minutes, he told himself; no more than that. Then he would have done what he could.

It was a glimpse of red through the trees and snow, where no red should have been, that guided him, stumbling, hurrying now, but hurrying with caution because a twisted ankle or knee at this point could very well be the ball game. And all he could think as he

42

neared the wreckage of the plane was that somehow, some way, all this had been *arranged;* there was no other explanation.

The red plane had flipped over as it hit, sheared both wings and dropped the twisted fuselage, upside down, in a small ravine. When Ben reached it, the smell of gasoline was strong through the snow, and he wondered just what it would take to produce a spark, maybe by tugging at a jammed door, and blow the whole thing to hell, and himself with it. *They* even booby-trapped it, he thought bitterly.

He squatted to look in through one still intact window. There was a man hanging head down from his seat harness. His face was bloody and his eyes were open with the vacant look Ben had seen before but somehow you never quite got used to. Scratch him.

There was another figure Ben could dimly see on the far side of the cabin, also hanging motionless, upside down in its harness. Without doubt another dead one. So, okay, he had done what he could and—

The other figure moved. Or had it? Had it been a trick of the dim light, or even a stiffening of dead muscles? Ben watched and nothing happened. Still. Oh, hell, he thought; he had to make sure.

He clambered down the side of the ravine and up the other side, catching his knee on a projecting broken branch he had not seen through the snow. He swore with feeling. Painful, but not serious. The hell with it. He squatted to stare through the fuselage window.

The figure inside the plane had long hair, which meant nothing at all. The only way to tell sexes these days, Ben had often thought, was either if they had hair on their faces, or stuck out in front. This one stuck out in front. Okay, female. And her eyes were closed, but what did that mean? Sometimes they died with closed eyes; sometimes not. She wasn't moving, was she?

The odor of gasoline was even stronger, a leak somewhere probably still dripping. And the fuselage door was jammed. He tried it gently and gave it up.

One spark with all those fumes, and there would be three dead ones instead of two.

Through the window he had one more long look at the girl. No movement, no sign of breathing. So okay, there it was. He started to stand, and then caught himself. Had she moved again? Or for the first time?

"Damn it!" He spoke the words aloud. "Make up your mind!" He was not sure whether he spoke to the dead girl or to himself. "I'm not—"

His words stopped. The girl's eyes were suddenly open, and they seemed to be looking straight at him, which was obviously an illusion because her face showed no expression, none. But the eyes, like the eyes of a picture on a wall, seemed to follow him as he lowered himself again to a squatting position.

Oh, hell, he thought again, took a deep breath that tasted strongly of gasoline, grabbed the door handle with both hands, leaned his shoulder against the frame and heaved. The door came open with a shriek of metal—and nothing happened.

Ben let his breath out in a long sigh, reached inside to unbuckle the harness that held the girl, and as gently as he could maneuvered her free. He straightened with her dead weight in his arms.

Standing, holding her more or less erect, he shook her gently, while the eyes watched him without comprehension. "Okay," Ben said. "It's okay. Can you hear me?"

The girl's eyes blinked feebly.

"Can you stand? Damn it, help me. Try. I can't carry you all the way. Try to stand."

The girl's body stirred against him, seemed to gather itself, and some of the weight was removed from his supporting arm. "Okay," Ben said again. "Take your time. But not too much. We've got to get out of here." In the cold and the falling snow and the almost overpowering smell of gasoline he made himself count slowly to ten, to twenty, while the girl's body gathered itself further. So far, so good. "Think you can walk?" Ben said.

44

The girl's lips moved, but it was a moment or two before sound emerged. "Where?"

"Damn it, just answer me."

The girl stood wavering almost free of his arm's support. She brushed her hair from her face and drew a deep breath. Her eyes went to the cabin of the plane again for a long, appraising look. "Joe's dead isn't he?" There was neither wild grief nor panic in the tone. She looked again at Ben. "Isn't he?"

"Right." His knee hurt, the snow was still falling hard, and, damn, but it was cold! "Now can you walk?"

"What about Joe?" Her voice was stronger now.

"You said it: he's dead. And I'm not a burial detail." The odor of gasoline was stronger now. Ben took the girl's arm. "Let's get out of here before she blows." He urged her out into the snow.

The girl stumbled, but she did walk. At first she brushed away Ben's hand, but after a few steps she accepted it again and leaned on it. Her chin was set, and in her face was a look of fierce concentration as she put one foot in front of the other and tried not to limp.

"Maybe a quarter of a mile," Ben said. "Maybe a little farther. If you have to stop, okay."

The girl said nothing. Nor did she look at him. And, leaning on his hand, sometimes stumbling, bent forward into the blowing snow, the look of fierce concentration never relaxing, she walked, or, rather, lurched along step after step, her eyes always on the ground, questioning no more.

They came up the last few yards of the ancient trail, now inches deep in snow. "Here we are," Ben said, and the girl dropped to her knees without comment and dragged herself through the cave entrance. Ben followed.

There was the faint warmth inside, or rather a diminution of the cold, and the flickering light from the fire. Nobody spoke, and after the effort he had gone to, the silence seemed like deliberate affront. Like a bunch of goddamn dummies, Ben thought in sudden, unreasoning anger. They think because they were here first that it's *their* cave, no strangers wanted. "Get over by the fire," he told the girl, who was now shaking uncontrollably, teeth chattering from the cold. And to the Harlows as a group, "We've got company. You might try behaving like it."

4.

AT THE TOP OF THE CORK BULLETIN BOARD in the U. S. Weather Service office Brady Shaw, the chief meteorologist, had thumbtacked a hand-lettered sign. It read: *"If you can keep your head when all about you are losing theirs—you just don't understand the situation."* It was Brady's feeling that the statement had almost universal application.

Brady glared down now at the latest weather satellite photo on the table, and at the transparent outline map of the United States that overlaid it. "Here, here and here," he said, tapping the cloud areas of the photograph with his pencil, "one storm system already on top of us, another moving down from the north, and this—maverick churning around to the south and which way it will go is anybody's guess." His tone was almost angry, as if the vagaries of the weather were a personal insult.

"All indications—" his assistant began.

Brady snorted. "Indications!" He was in his late fifties, and he had known for some time, but never really accepted, that he had gone as far as he was ever going to go in his profession, and so he was in effect merely serving out his time until retirement. Low profile was the trick, make no waves, do the job strictly according to the book and look forward to your pension. So be it. "Okay," he said, in a determinedly resigned voice, "the indications are that the storm system to the south will not bother us."

"That was my point," his assistant said.

But because his assistant did not understand the situation, "On the other hand," Brady said, "when you're dealing with weather moving up from the Gulf, indications sometimes don't mean a damned thing."

Now the old man was harking back to the seat-of-the-pants and the aching-corn days of weather forecasting, the assistant told himself, and tried not to smile. "Yes, sir."

"There are times," Brady said, "when I think we might just as well cut open a sheep and study its entrails, for all we can guess about what's going to happen." His eyes were still on the photograph and the map.

"Yes, sir. What forecast shall we issue?"

"Oh, hell," Brady said. "Go by the book. That system to the north is going to louse us up. That's safe enough to say. And the indications are that the system to the south will veer east and leave us alone."

"Yes, sir. That was my thinking too."

Brady tossed the pencil on the table, started to turn away and then turned back. "But let me tell you one thing, sonny. If that system in the south decides to move north and mix with the other two—and I wouldn't bet a plugged nickel that it won't—then we are going to have the goddamnedest mess in this area you've ever seen or heard tell of. It'll make those storms of '71 here and the blizzard of '88 back east look like mild summer weather."

They had added a room to the Arroyo Volunteer Fire Department barn, and in it under lock and key the Search and Rescue group kept their team equipment: litters, carriers, stretcher, first-aid equipment, oxygen pack, climbing ropes, snow anchors, signal kits, spotlights, lanterns, walkie-talkies, portable stoves, maps . . .

Bart Wallace sat at the table and talked on the

47

phone with the State Police. "The Bonanza pilot filed a flight plan," he said. "Roswell to Tucumcari, so if he's anywhere around here he was either way off course or he changed his mind." More likely the latter, he thought, because light plane pilot-owners, like kids on trail bikes, seemed to go wherever the spirit moved them, and never mind regulations.

State Police Captain Inocencio Lopez said, "His emergency transmitter is functioning?"

"Civil Air Patrol can't get a plane in the air to check," Bart said, "and we haven't picked up any signal from the ground."

"So what do you do now?"

There was a note of impatience in the captain's voice, Bart thought. "There's nothing to do tonight, and unless we get some signal or at least a general location there isn't even any point in trying to find him until tomorrow. There are who knows how many thousand square miles of mountains out there and he could be anywhere. I just wanted to keep you plugged in."

"The pilot's name," the captain said, irony strong, "is Joseph Martin, which probably doesn't mean a thing to you, but down in Roswell where he has a ranch and here in the state legislature it's a name that's known."

"Captain, no matter what his name is, we can't do a thing about him until we have some information on where he might be. If we get some kind of fix, we'll get right on it. In the meantime, all we can do is hope."

There were both reason and logic in what Wallace said, and the captain prided himself on being a reasonable and logical man. On the other hand, where the disappearance of a man of Joe Martin's prominence was concerned, a state senator, all kinds of voices would begin to clamor, exerting pressures which would inevitably descend upon the captain's shoulders. And the worst of it, of course, was that he, the captain, was in a position of no real control because both Civil Air Patrol and Search and Rescue were beyond his jurisdiction. He was reduced to impotent hinting, which he disliked. "Last time—" he began, and left the sentence unfinished.

"Last time we brought in a dead man," Bart said. "I'm quite aware of it. He was there, and we failed to find him in time. We hope it doesn't happen again."

The captain had made his point. It was all he could do. "So do I," he said, and hung up.

In the cave, her name, the girl from the plane said, was Lila. "Last name doesn't much matter, does it?" Crouched near the fire in a light wool shirt and slacks she was no longer shaking convulsively from the cold, but her teeth still chattered, and her voice was difficult to control. She looked around at them all with a faint shrug of apology. "Uninvited guest," she said. "I'm—sorry."

Ben was digging into his pack. He came out with a lightweight, long-sleeved turtleneck which he tossed to the girl. "You'd better put this on."

In silence Lila straightened and looked down at Billy. "You'd better turn your back or close your eyes. I don't want to shock you." She pulled out the tails of her shirt, unbuttoned it, shrugged it off. She was naked to the waist, and her high, firm, taut-nippled breasts scarcely lifted as she slipped her arms into the sleeves of the turtleneck and pulled it down over her head. She put her shirt back on, undid her trousers and tucked both sweater and shirt inside. Her face showed no trace of embarrassment. She began to roll back the too long sleeves of the sweater.

Ben said. "They'll come looking for you? You filed a flight plan? Radio contact?"

Lila crouched again with a faint grimace of pain, and held her hands out to the fire. "Joe filed a flight plan." She smiled ruefully. "To Tucumcari from Roswell. Santo Cristo was a last-minute idea. He did make radio contact, though."

"That's something." Ben nodded. "And if there's an emergency signal transmitting from the plane, and if they can pick it up when the storm's over, they'll come looking. And when they find the plane, and not you, they'll scour this area." He looked at Warner. "We just sit tight, maybe a little uncomfortable, a little crowded, but not for long."

Lila said, "Sorry." Her voice was quiet and expressionless, but it brought silence in the cave. "When they find the plane, and Joe, if they find it, that's the end of the search. Nobody knew about me." She glanced at them all, then spoke directly to Ben. Joe is—was—a pillar of the community. A family man. When he took his little weekend trips, he took them alone, if you see what I mean."

"By God," Warner said, "that kind of thing—"

"Warner." Sue Ann's eyes were open again, and her voice was still dreamy, but distinct. Her role and Warner's, she thought, were suddenly reversed, and she could not have said why. "Warner," she said again, "be quiet."

"Mom!" This was Patty in protest. The Lila woman, no bra, flaunting her nakedness in front of everybody, then saying calm as you please that she and Joe, whoever he was, were, well whatever the word was—

"Sorry," Lila said. She was talking to Ben. "I didn't mean to shock people, but I thought you'd better know that nobody's going to come looking for me."

"Then I blew it," Ben said slowly. He resisted an impulse to swear. "I ought to have left some kind of message at the plane." Watching Lila still shivering, he thought: I ought to have brought whatever clothing you had in the plane, too, but all I was thinking of was that gasoline, goddamn it. "And it's too late now," he said.

Warner said, "Now, wait a minute. Why is it too late?"

"Because it's dark and I'd probably break a leg trying to find the plane. And in the morning, if the snow's too deep—" Ben shrugged.

"You weren't worried about leaving a message at the car. You didn't even think of it. You couldn't wait to get us up here where nobody can find us. Why, damn it—"

50

"Nobody is going to find that car," Ben said, "because nobody is going to be looking for it on that road. It's just one wrong road out of hundreds—private roads, logging roads, Forest Service roads, you name it—in ten thousand square miles of mountains."

"We aren't twenty miles from the middle of Santo Cristo."

"For the moment," Ben said, "we might as well be on the moon."

Warner shook his head stubbornly. "Well, I'm not giving up like that. We've got to do something."

"I agree." Ben's voice was determinedly mild, his temper under tight control. They all watched him, and waited. "We'll have some food," he said. "And then some sleep. In the morning we'll see what it looks like." He watched Warner steadily. "Unless you have a better idea?"

Billy said, "I've got this." He held up the small transistor radio. "You said only food, but I brought it anyway."

Ben nodded, glad of the distraction. "Good for you. See what you can get." He turned away and began to dig into his pack.

The little radio gave off only static at first, and then, suddenly, with a volume that caught at them all, an announcer's voice came through clearly in mid-sentence: " . . . advisories have been issued statewide. Up to ten inches of snow are predicted for the Santo Cristo area, and temperatures tonight are expected to drop well below freezing. That concludes our brief summary of news and weather. We now resume our regular programing."

"Okay, Billy," Ben said over his shoulder. "Turn it off and save the batteries. We'll listen again in the morning." In the silence he turned to face them all. "So now we have some idea of what we're up against," he said. "There's nothing more we can do tonight."

Bart Wallace came back into La Cantina almost, he thought, as if impelled by some kind of tropism. The talk with Captain Lopez troubled him, and he knew that the cause of his unhappiness was precisely the same as the captain's: helplessness. Someone was out there in the mountains at the mercy of this worsening weather, and for tonight there was not a thing that he, the captain or anyone else could do about it.

And at a time like that, he thought, a time of waiting, he simply did not want to be alone with his helpless thoughts. Not after last time. It was as simple as that.

As he sat down heavily on a counter stool, "Nothing to do tonight," he said, answering Connie's unspoken question. "The poor devil will have to make it by himself until morning. If he can."

Connie could almost see into his thoughts, understand them, and approve of the concern that underlay them. He was a good man, as few were, she told herself, a man who could put the welfare of a stranger above his own comfort, who could feel real torment because he was temporarily unable to help; a man who gave far more than he received without complaint; the kind of man you would be lucky to have behind you, or with you, in time of need. "I think," she said slowly, "that you'd better try forgetting last time."

But the dead man could not be forgotten. "The last time I shot a deer," Bart said, "I came up to him and he was still alive. His back was broken. He just looked at me. So did that dead man, or seemed to. I never went hunting again. We should have found him, the dead man. We were close to him, and I'd marked off on the grid as covered the place where we finally did find him." Our fault. No, my fault.

Connie wiped at the counter top with her towel. "Why did you mark it off?"

"They said it had been covered."

"Who's they?"

"I don't even remember. It doesn't matter. I was in charge."

Sometimes, Connie thought, you cried out silently for someone to listen, as who knew better than she? It was no longer his words she listened to, but the overtones and harmonics they produced. In sudden decision she folded the towel carefully and laid it on the counter. "No point in staying open," she said. "Not in this weather."

Bart nodded and stood up. "Okay. I'll leave."

"That wasn't what I meant." Her voice was gentle. "Sometimes it's good to talk. Believe me, I know. And I can listen." She hesitated only briefly. "My house. I'll stuff some food into you. A man your size needs it." The sudden gratitude in his face was a pleasure to see.

It was a small Santo Cristo house, one-story, adobe, with *vigas, latías* and a brick floor polished with age. A fine two gray hills rug hung on one whitewashed wall. "Wood in the basket," Connie said. "You might whip up a fire." She watched him hunker down at the corner fireplace. "Stand the wood on end, gringo," she added. "This isn't an Anglo fireplace." She was smiling as she turned away and walked into the kitchen.

Admit it, she told herself, it is pleasant to have a man around the house at least temporarily. But for a steady diet? She didn't know, and perhaps it was just plain fear that had kept her all this time from finding out.

Basta, enough. That kind of soul-searching led nowhere except into the morass of self-pity. She put lard in the frypan and got tortillas out of the freezing compartment of the refrigerator. When Bart appeared in the kitchen doorway, she was busy at the stove, her movements deft and sure. Fine warm odors filled the room. "Beer in the reefer," she said. "Open me one too, hmmm?"

They ate in front of the fire, spicy, tangy enchiladas and refritos, washed down with good Mexican beer. "Tomorrow?" Connie said. Get him to talk, to cleanse himself and his thoughts, she told herself.

"If the CAP can get a plane in the air, and if they can locate an emergency signal, we'll go to work." It was strange, the ease he felt here in her presence.

"Tell me how." She settled back to listen.

"It all depends. How good the signal location is. What kind of terrain. Choppers, snowmobiles, snowshoes, climbing gear—" Bart spread his hands. "One time or another we've used them all. Sometimes it's a quick operation; sometimes it drags on, and you have to set up a base camp and equip it, organize search teams, coordinate them, try to keep the ghouls and glory-hunters out—" He shrugged. "Each time is a little different."

"People you don't even know," Connie said. "The ones you're looking for, I mean."

"They take on identities." It was true. Long before you found the ones you were searching for, you felt that you knew them, and always they had your sympathy tinged sometimes with sad regret at their carelessness—but always the search continued as long as there was hope, and sometimes beyond, because that was the way it was.

As a matter of cold logic, he had often thought, a search operation rarely made sense. Take this present case. According to the flight plan the pilot had filed, Roswell to Tucumcari, if he was indeed anywhere in the mountains behind Santo Cristo then he was well over a hundred miles off course, which was unlikely. The probability was that he had changed his mind, an act of pure irresponsibility. Now, through his own doing, he was in trouble, and a number of decent men, and women, were going to have to punish themselves in the process of trying to find him and bring him safely out of the mountains.

"It makes no sense at all," Connie said as if he had spoken his thoughts aloud. She was smiling. "But you are going to do it anyway, so stop fretting about it."

Bart nodded, and smiled in his gentle way. "You're right, of course."

A sudden gust of wind rattled the windows, and in immediate response the flames in the fireplace leaped, casting strange flickering shadows on the white walls. The continuing howl of the wind was plain.

Connie watched the man carefully. "You aren't out there in this weather," she said.

"True." He could smile again then as he got to his feet. "I thank you for your hospitality, and I guess the word is understanding." Odd that he felt no discomfort or even reluctance in exposing himself in this way. Usually he tended to shut out the world and keep his inner thoughts to himself. "I guess I wanted someone to listen."

There was another sharp gust beating against the stout walls and small windows, and again the flames reacted.

Connie said gently, "Do you want to go?"

For long moments Bart stared down at the girl in silence. "No," he said at last. "I don't. But—"

"Then stay." At what point this decision had been made, Connie had no idea, nor would she have been able to explain her motive. She had known Bart how long, three years, four? And there had never been anything but pleasant easy talk between them. But tonight quite suddenly everything was changed, a silent chord had been struck, and for the first time they were what probably they had been all along but never fully understood, a man and a woman alike in their loneliness, all pretense finally set aside. Maybe it was the weather that was the catalyst, maybe the situation, maybe—but what difference? We'll just see what happens, she thought; one on one, *mano a mano*. "I don't like loneliness any better than you do," she said.

The governor of New Mexico was young, and a sound sleeper. It took a little time for him to react to the ringing telephone beside the bed, and he picked it up angrily. "Yes?"

"Sorry to bother you, Governor." Frank Silva's voice. Frank was the governor's aide.

By the glow of the night-light, the governor could see his wife in one of those sprawled positions in which she always seemed to sleep. A strap of her nightie had slipped from her shoulder, exposing one of her remarkable breasts, which, despite two children, had lost

55

none of their youthful shape and buoyancy. There was always something warm and intimate about waking from a deep sleep and finding his wife beside him. The governor made himself concentrate on the telephone. "So you're sorry. What's it about?"

"Jake Boone, Governor. He wanted your private number. He said he'd beat my ass off if I didn't give it to him."

"And did you?"

"No, sir. I told him I'd call you instead."

It was Governor Manuel Archuleta's boast that he belonged to no man, but there were certain ones you did treat with caution, and Jake Boone was high on that list. Oil and gas meant money, and money meant power, and, well there was no point in antagonizing a man like that just for the hell of it. "He wants me to call him?"

"Yes, sir. His number is 983-9287."

The governor wrote it down. "What's it about?" His eyes were again on his wife's breast. "Never mind. I'll find out for myself." He hung up, gave his attention to the phone and dialed the number. It was answered on the first ring. "What's up, Jake, that can't wait till morning?"

"We got us a storm, Manny, a big one. Snow already ass-deep in places, and that's just the beginning."

"You didn't wake me up for that."

"And I got me a guest, a college chum, and his family, and they're overdue. They ought to have been here five, six hours ago, and not a word. Warner and I were going elk hunting come morning."

His wife stirred, and the governor's eyes went again to her nakedness. Her eyes were open now, looking up at him. She began to smile. Into the phone the governor said, "What do you want me to do, Jake?"

"I called the State Police. They said they'd keep an eye out. Shit. I want action. Warner's from Oklahoma. This is strange country to him. Goddamn it, Manny, I want him found, him and his family."

The governor's wife, smiling still, looked down at

herself, and then again at her husband. Slowly she lowered the other shoulder strap, baring that breast too.

Into the phone, "I can't—" the governor began, and stopped. Only a hassle lay that way, and suddenly he was interested in other matters. "Okay," he said. "Call Captain Lopez. Tell him I said to. Tell him I'll want to know first thing in the morning just what he's done about your friend. That's the best I can do, Jake."

"I didn't think you'd let me down."

The governor hung up. He too was smiling now, the world once more shut out. He lay down beside his wife and gathered her sleep-warmed softness to him.

State Police Captain Lopez did not like Anglos who demanded rather than asked. "We're getting calls from all over the state, Mr. Boone, and somewhere we've got a downed aircraft as well. And it's going to get worse before it gets better. There's another storm building behind this one." He was just clicking his teeth, and he knew it. Jake Boone was quite used to throwing his weight around all the way to Washington.

"Captain," Jake said, "I'm not interested in your problems. I've got a friend lost. With his family. And I want him found."

The muscles in the captain's cheeks stirred angrily, but he kept his voice under control. He picked up a pencil. "Name? . . . Coming from where? . . . What kind of car?"

"I don't know what kind of car. Buick, Olds, maybe one of those big Fords. I've seen it, but, hell, I'm not a garage mechanic."

The captain stifled an impulse to tell Jake Boone just what in the captain's opinion he was. Instead, "You wouldn't know the license number?"

"Hell, no. The Oklahoma State Police can tell you, can't they?"

The captain put the pencil down. "Maybe with this storm he decided to stop for the night. Had you thought of that?"

"Then he'd have called. I've waited for a call.

57

Nothing." Jake's voice altered. "Look, Captain, I know old Warner. If there's one thing he is, it's dependable. Why, hell, he blocked for me for four years! Got me All-American mention. He was coming here, and he hasn't arrived. Something's happened or he'd have let me know, and that's a fact."

"We'll do our best, Mr. Boone."

"Make damn sure it's good enough."

5.

BEN HAD HIS PACK PROPPED AGAINST THE WALL. He leaned against it, legs outstretched, boots off, hands behind his head, staring at the shadows the fire cast on the far wall of the cave. It was cold, and it was going to be colder. Toward dawn, even for him, it would be close to unbearable. Where I damn well ought to be, he thought, is inside my own sleeping bag, snug and warm. Instead—the hell with it.

Sue Ann was still in the sleeping bag, quiet now, eased by the Demerol dosage. Her breathing was even and almost inaudible. Ben could not tell if she was awake or asleep.

Warner still had his boots on, something he would regret come morning, Ben knew and had not bothered to say; he lay close to, and facing, the fire, his heavy body curled into a near-fetal position for warmth. He slept, snoring and snorting occasionally. The layer of fat that covered him, Ben thought, would serve as insulation, holding in body heat. Warner would be better off than the others.

Take Billy, for example. His lean little body would be scant defense against cold, and it was with that in mind that Ben had paired Billy with his sister, wrapped together in the lightweight, reflective survival blanket also from his own pack. At first they had both resisted the intimacy, but they now were sound asleep in the impossible kind of tangle only the young could achieve. Their combined breaths were visible in the dim light.

Lila, close by, said quietly, "You've got a mess on your hands, haven't you?" Her voice shook with cold.

"You'd better come over here," Ben said. He shifted his body to give her room. Lila moved close against him as she too settled against the pack. Ben put his arm around her. Through the down-filled shirt he now wore, he could feel her body trembling. Slowly the trembling lessened. "You'll warm up," he said.

"A mess," Lila said again. "And I don't help." He is a perpetually angry man, she thought, but despite his anger he does generous things. Why?

"Six is no worse than five."

"By yourself," Lila said slowly, quietly, "you could cope? But could you? I mean, what if this keeps up and there's no way out? Could you handle it? Alone?"

"What do I say to that?"

"Yes," Lila said, "you could, couldn't you? That's your sleeping bag she's in, your blanket the kids have, you could have the fire all to yourself instead of sharing it with him, and me, and you have the right clothing, and you're used to it. You'd do fine." She was silent for a moment. "Not that it does any good, but I'm sorry for what we're doing to you."

"We aren't going to be here long."

"How long is long? How long does it take? What *are* the chances of our being found?"

"It could happen."

"But you wouldn't bet on it, and neither would I. Why am I talking like this anyway? I'm sorry about that, too. I guess I haven't quite—got used to everything yet. I'll be quiet. I am getting warmer. You'll let me stay here?"

"Be my guest." Ben felt her settle a little lower, her head against his shoulder, his arm protectively close around her. She was still. "Sweet dreams," he said.

She is not the one to worry about, Ben thought, nor is Sue Ann. They'll last as long as they can without causing trouble. The others are going to be more of a problem. Automatically, he surveyed the situation.

Warner, now, was probably basically a nice guy, but there were tensions in him, bewilderment, helpless anger, and strains Ben didn't even begin to understand between Warner and Sue Ann, between Warner and Billy. Were there strains like that in any family? I'm no goddamned shrink, Ben told himself angrily; I won't even try to sort it out. But it wouldn't take much, he was sure, to send basically nice guy Warner charging blindly like a wounded buffalo.

And Patty, suddenly cut adrift from all the comfort and privacy, and, yes, the *certainty* that had obviously been her world. How close was she to—flipping? That was just what they needed, a set of full-fledged hysterics.

And Billy, whose enthusiasms and bright ideas could very easily get entirely out of hand, and probably would.

But this kind of character analysis, after all, had only minor importance. It was the cold that was the enemy, and in the end, unless something intervened, it was the cold that would triumph. Lila was right; by himself with what he had carried in his pack, he could survive for days, even two weeks or so. But with his protective clothing, bedding and supplies spread in six directions—no way. Unless help found them, or they, meaning he, could summon help, all that they could do added up to only one thing: eventual death by freezing.

Leaning there, thinking of all this, it was, Ben told himself, almost as if he were back in Nam, pinned down and trying to sort out methods and odds for survival for those he was responsible for, the only difference being that this time he could foretell the final result. Goddamn it, how did I get back into that kind of situation, anyway? Pointless anger, he knew, but it would not go away.

"Why don't you try to sleep too?" Lila said quietly

against his shoulder. And then her voice took on an encouraging note. "You'll think of something."

Sue Ann was not asleep. She made herself lie quiet, enjoying the warmth of the sleeping bag, and trying to ignore, or at least overcome, the constant pain in her ankle. She was aware that Lila and Ben were together; she could hear the faint sibilance of their whispering. And it was not hard, she thought, to guess what it was they talked about.

We are the problem, she thought; not they. Alone, Ben could cope without difficulty. He has showed his strength and his resourcefulness, and in his lonely way he would manage. Even with Lila as a burden, he would be equal to the challenge; nor would he turn his back on it. But the four of us, and I particularly, make his task, and maybe even the survival of us all, close to impossible. It was a devastating concept, and the sense of guilt which had been growing would not go away.

As a girl in her small Oklahoma town she had been taught that religion was a matter of right and wrong, black and white, no shades of gray allowed. But growing into adolescence in a world going from the sickness of the Depression into the continuing dim horror of a world war, the old certainties no longer secure, you grew up and grew away from ideas that had once seemed ineluctable, and only occasionally did twinges of conscience or feelings of guilt rise above the threshold of consciousness to haunt you.

College in the fifties with, everyone said, a brave new world to be built by the young. Warner, with his letter sweater and his picture in the Sunday papers after another Oklahoma victory; Warner and his chum Jake Boone, BMOC, Big Men on Campus, and the horizon without limit, freedom. Fundamentalist concepts seemed a long way off then, and since, but somehow tonight in this cave they were beginning to return. The wrathful God of her childhood was watching now. Had they transgressed?

She and Warner were not wicked people; that was

61

not even a point in question. Selfish, yes, but then, how many were not? Warner had come a long way from college, and she with him, even at the start keeping the books of the small oil well supply firm that eventually grew, not into one of the giants, but big enough, comfortable. Not to be compared with Jake Boone's successes, of course, and maybe that rankled a little, but solid accomplishment nonetheless, and achieved without trampling on the rights or the sensibilities of others, and how many could say the same?

Then why was success tasteless, a Dead Sea fruit? And why the inescapable feeling that what had happened today was not merely a series of accidents, sheer bad luck, but was actually a planned pattern of retribution? For what?

Her fault? Because she had fallen into the comfortable and easy pattern of letting Warner make the decisions, indulge his enthusiasms, live his essentially male life while she, in effect, went her own way?

I have been a good wife and mother, and ours has been a good marriage, is not all of that true? If Warner and I no longer share youthful enthusiasms, and in private never behave as we used to without restraint; and if we tend to take each other, our lives and now even the children almost for granted—isn't that how these things always work out if, indeed, a marriage does endure as ours has and so many we know have not?

We have our flaws. Who does not? I pretend that I don't see Warner's receding hairline and his belly that used to be so flat and ridged with muscle, now sagging; and I will not pretend that I do not look at other, young men, Ben, for example, with pleasure. But is that wicked? She listened and heard no answer.

Billy now. "I don't want to go on this elk hunt, Mom." Lying quiet, staring up into the near-darkness, Sue Ann could hear Billy saying it again. "I know, to Dad it's a big deal, and he'll have the head mounted on the wall and everybody'll say what a big man he is. But I don't want to kill anything. And I don't want to watch, either."

"But you'd like to see the high mountains, wouldn't you?"

"Well, that, sure. I've been reading about them, and—"

"Then let's leave it that way, and maybe your father will change his mind."

"You'll talk to him? Okay. I can't. He thinks there's something wrong with me, that I'm queer or something."

And Patty, part woman, part child, comfortable in neither role, still clinging to father worship and resenting me because I no longer, if I ever did, share her adulation. "You're always putting him down, Mom. Maybe he does forget things, but he has lots on his mind."

"Of course he does, honey."

"There you go. It's the way you say things, like you don't really mean them. I can't talk to you any more. I guess maybe I never could."

And what did that mean? "Honey, these things pass."

"Do you really believe that, Mom? Because I don't."

In little ways like that, or maybe they are not little at all, have I been living a lie? Has Warner, willfully blind? And have Patty and Billy seen it and understood the weakness and the inertia that caused it— and remained silent merely enduring?

Sue Ann closed her eyes. Her eyelids stung. She heard Warner give another snort in his sleep. It was the only sound in the cave. "Dear God." Her lips moved, no sound came out, but the words reverberated in her mind. "Please. Please! If this is our fault, don't take it out on the children. Help us. Please!"

Once during the night Bart Wallace stirred in his sleep and said audibly, with unusual vehemence and rare profanity, "He was there all along, you son of a bitch." And then, as if the words had exorcised the ghost that haunted him, he relaxed and his breathing became quiet once more.

Connie lay on her back beside him, hands behind her head, staring up into the darkness. She felt relaxed, comfortably spent, pleased both with herself and with the man beside her. Still, she was making no judgments.

No promises were involved, no commitment of any kind. He and she were, in the current phrase, consenting adults, and that was it. If in the future more than conversation, companionship and sex were to come from their relationship, why, so be it; but she would not press. There was an almost fatalistic streak strong within her, and whether that was Anglo, Spanish or Indian legacy, she had no idea, and didn't much care.

When she was growing up, child to adolescent to woman, she had dwelt sometimes almost desperately on the questions of who was she and why was she impelled this way or that in her behavior. But the answers were never clear, and finally even the questions themselves lost meaning. She was what she was, and that would have to do.

Bart, now, was an enigma because he was not at all the prototypical dropout angrily turning his back on the rat race. There were enough of those in Santo Cristo, heaven knew, and Connie was well acquainted with their looks and behavior. Bart was different.

For one thing, there was no anger in him, only gentleness. For another, in looks, in dress and in behavior he was far closer to the Anglos who were the lawyers, the doctors, the bankers or big-time operators of the town. And yet he chose to be a garage mechanic.

"It isn't much," he had told her—was it only last night?—"but I like to do it, and I do it well. I guess they left conventional ambition out of me."

Well, as far as that went, they had left the ambition out of her, too, hadn't they? And so they were two alike. Warm thought.

And where Bart did differ in another way from some of the Anglos Connie knew was in his lack of arrogance and, well, general abrasiveness. Take Jake

64

Boone, for example, whose face Connie had slapped one day in La Cantina and then made her position clear in front of witnesses: "Take your obscene leer and your foul mouth and your redneck proclivities out of here and don't bring them back."

"Big words," Jake had said. "Did you learn them on the reservation?"

Connie picked up a butcher knife. "I learned how to slaughter a pig, and I'll be happy to show you."

No, Bart didn't fit into that mold either. Like herself, Connie thought, Bart really didn't fit, period. She was smiling as she closed her eyes and slept.

It was the sound of the beeper that awakened them both. Bart rolled out of bed to silence it, looked down at his nakedness and smiled sheepishly. "Not very romantic, I'm afraid. There ought to be a slow awakening and quiet talk."

"The phone is in the living room." Connie too got out of bed naked, put on a robe and, barefoot, padded out to the kitchen to make coffee. There was the fragrance of bacon frying as well when Bart, dressed, came in. "Juice in the reefer," Connie said. "How do you like your eggs?"

"Easy over." He watched her quick, deft movements. "I'll have to eat and run. Two airliners flying high during the night on different courses picked up an emergency signal. We have a fix—of sorts, and we're going to have to work fast."

Connie flipped the eggs over. She watched Bart quietly.

"Another cold front moving down," Bart said. "Readings below zero in Colorado last night. We'll catch it sometime today, and somebody out there and not prepared won't have much chance."

"Then get your juice and sit down and start eating."

Still in her robe she went with him to the door. She held out her hand. "Luck."

"Look," Bart said in his gentle, almost apologetic way, "last night—"

"Last night was last night."

"Something to forget?"

65

"Something to think about." Connie rose on tiptoe and her lips brushed his cheek. *"Ve tu con Dios.* Go thee with God."

Brady Shaw was down in the Weather Service office early driven by he knew not what compulsion to study the night reports that had come in on the teletype machines, and the charts that had been made from them. It was still snowing hard, which was to be expected. By the time his assistant arrived exactly on the hour, stamping his feet and scattering snow from his parka, Brady was already into his third cup of coffee.

"A little colder than we expected," the assistant said, "but otherwise it's behaving just as we predicted." There was satisfaction in his voice.

"I want the satellite pictures," Brady said. "And if you call forty below in Colorado and northern New Mexico a *little* colder—" He shook his head. "Forty below!"

"Still in the ball park." The assistant's voice was easy, unconcerned. "And all the satellite pictures will show is what we already know, won't they, that that northern system is moving down on us?"

"I want to know about the one moving in from the Gulf, too."

"Oh," the assistant said. "That one."

"Yes, goddamn it, *that* one!" There were times when Brady was sure that he was just not cut out to be a meteorologist; he lacked dispassion. "They're just lines on a chart and figures on paper to you," he said. "To me they're poor damned truckers trying to get over the Divide. or hunters who'd damn well better head for shelter, or airports that may have to close down, or power lines that could break, leaving whole towns without light, heat—" He made himself stop.

His assistant had heard it all before, and was not impressed. He was silent.

"Along about noon," Brady said in a new, quieter voice, "it's going to be cold enough right here in Santo Cristo to freeze the balls off a brass monkey, and when the telephone starts to ring, I want to be able to say whether it's going to ease up, which I doubt like hell, or get a lot worse before it gets any better."

"The northern system will pass through—" the assistant began.

"Unless that son of a bitch up from the Gulf moves in and fouls up everything," Brady said, "and don't tell me it can't do it because the book says it can't. I've been around here long enough to know better. That's why I want those satellite pictures. I've got a feeling in my bones that we're just seeing the start of the trouble."

The sun was not yet over the eastern mountains, and already State Police Captain Inocencio Lopez had been on duty for twenty-four hours. Now, another cigarette in the endless chain burning in the overflowing ashtray, and a cup of tepid coffee in front of him, he spoke on the telephone with the governor, who was always an early riser. "We have the license number and the make of the Harlow car and trailer," the captain said. "Oklahoma has cooperated fully, and their check shows that the Harlows didn't register at any motels as far as the state line. On our side, we can't find any trace either. And they aren't on the road to Mr. Boone's ranch." God only knew how many man-hours that information represented. All because Jake Boone could and did throw his weight around.

"So," the governor said, "what does that add up to?"

"Either they're snowbound on the Interstate and a highway crew will find them eventually—"

"Or?"

"Or they took a wrong road and could be anywhere. When Civil Air Patrol can get off the ground, if they can, they'll be flying searches looking for a downed aircraft." The captain paused for effect. "Joe Martin from Roswell," he said, and waited for reaction.

The governor whistled softly. "Joe Martin? Jesus! You're sure? Nobody told me."

"We had to check it out. It was his plane. And he

67

left Roswell in it yesterday afternoon, headed for Tucumcari—"

"Then what's he doing here? Never mind. Silly question. You have a location?" The governor listened while the captain explained about the two commercial airliners picking up emergency signals during the night. "Go on," the governor said.

"Wallace and his S&R people are moving out to look," the captain said, "I've asked CAP *if* they can get in the air to look for car and trailer as well. And Wallace too. The best we can do, Governor."

The governor was silent for a few moments. Then, "Joe Martin, Inny, is the senate minority leader. You know that. And just between us, he's a pain in the ass too. But if we don't find him quick—oh, hell, you see what I mean. There are people who wouldn't put anything past me, anything, even leaving Joe Martin out there to freeze to death." The governor was thinking while he talked, weighing political factors, appearances, probably public reaction. "You see what I mean?"

"Yes, sir."

"What's the weather forecast?"

"Bad, and getting worse. Temperatures well below zero, more snow, drifting conditions. Roads will be closed all across the state."

The governor was silent, thoughtful. He said slowly, "And this Oklahoma friend of Jake Boone's, with his whole goddamned family. That makes it a real ballbreaker. It was bad enough last time, that dead deer hunter from wherever he was—Arkansas? People will start thinking this state is a death trap." And tourism was one of the state's major industries. There was no need to say it. "I don't want any mistakes this time."

"No, sir."

"Tell you what," the governor said with sudden inspiration. "Put one of your men on it to coordinate the whole operation, and keep me informed what's happening."

Oh, Jesus, the captain thought, there's nothing one of my men can do except get in the way. Wallace and his people know their business. Aloud, "I don't think, Governor, that that would be—helpful."

"Well, I do, goddamn it. I want Joe Martin and the Harlow family found, and I want a man of yours right on it to see that they are. Is that clear?"

It was, the captain thought, just the kind of snap decision men in authority tended to make heedless of consequences, as if by virtue of their office they had only to wave a hand or issue an order and everything would be all right—instead of frequently much worse. Still, he was in no position to argue.

The captain sighed. The taste of stale tobacco and tepid coffee was strong in his throat, and suddenly sour as his thoughts. He lifted his shoulders and let them fall wearily. "Yes, sir," he said.

Bart Wallace had a 7.5 minute 1:24000 United States Geological Survey topographic map of the mountain area directly behind Santo Cristo spread on the table in the equipment room of the firehouse. He made himself concentrate, all memories of last night put aside. "The bearings intersect here," he said, and touched the map lightly with his pencil. "I wish we had three bearings, but two is all we have." The five people around him stared thoughtfully at the map.

"The only good thing you can say for it," Carl said, "is that it's fairly close. But those contour lines are practically on top of each other." By trade Carl was a plumber, by temperament a volatile skeptic with definite ideas; a solid, middle-sized man, dwarfed as he stood beside Bart, but unfazed in any company. He said now in his positive way, "If the plane's down in that canyon he hasn't a chance."

"I know that canyon," Jaime said. His voice held a faint lilt of Spanish. He was a wood-carver and cabinetmaker, by avocation a mountain climber and skier. "We've done some rock work in there." He showed white teeth in a quick smile. "She is a bitch in more ways than one." He turned the smile fondly on the big girl who stood beside him. "No offense, *guapa*."

Steve merely shook her head, her eyes still on the

map. She was not the only female in the Search and Rescue group, but she and Jaime were the climbing experts and were usually called out for rough terrain. She looked now at Bart. "What he's saying," she said, "is that that whole area is unsafe and ought to have been blocked off a long time ago."

"Unsafe how?"

They all looked at Jaime.

Jaime spread his hands and shrugged. "The rock is unstable. In the canyon there are caves, very old caves—" He shook his head and showed the white teeth again. He touched the map. "But they built a road here up toward the lake, and also a service road here down the side of the mountain, and when they built, they blasted, and while I am no geologist, I think they weakened the entire structure. Every winter since there have been rock slides—" He made a quick, sharp gesture. "On the other hand, if that is where the plane went down, then that is where we have to look, no? You agree, *guapa?*"

Steve nodded absently. She was looking again at Bart. "How good a fix would you guess it is?"

Wilt and CJ, the remaining pair, stood quiet waiting for Bart's judgment. Wilt was almost Bart's height but nowhere near his bulk, a lean, quiet and resilient man. During the summer season Wilt guided pack trains into the mountains; from late October to April he was his own man, skiing, hiking and working sporadically on a monumental history of the Spanish land grants in the northern New Mexico area. Of them all, Wilt knew the mountains best.

CJ was an artist, a painter of landscapes, in times of monetary need also broiler chef at whichever of the city's hotels would hire him. He was a short man, stocky, usually taciturn, but given to occasional temper outbursts. He and Wilt had long worked together on rescue operations.

Bart took his time over Steve's question. "How good a fix?" He shook his head. "Two commercial aircraft flying at night at thirty, thirty-five thousand feet and five hundred miles an hour—" He shrugged.

"And with those canyon walls and the peaks in the area there could have been echoes, the signals bouncing. The fix is questionable at best. But it's all we have until CAP can get a plane in the air." Through the windows the snow was a visible swirling pattern in the still faint light. "The snow is *supposed* to let up in a few hours. They'll try to fly then."

Carl said, "Then I say we wait."

"We can't." From the time when, naked, he talked on the phone in the living room of Connie's little house, he had thought it through in his careful way, considering possibilities, weighing odds, knowing that whatever course he chose *could* be the wrong one, but knowing too that a decision had to be made.

It was the weather forecast that settled it. "How long the snow will stop, *if* it stops, is anybody's guess," he said. "And what's coming next is worse than what we have now." He paused for emphasis. "Forty-below temperatures and more snow. I'm betting that a quick search, just the six of us, three teams on snowshoes, is our only chance. We'll take two jeeps." With his forefinger he traced on the map the road Warner had driven yesterday. "I think we can get up to just about here. Jaime, you and Steve take this sector." He drew a circle with his pencil. "Line in your UTM grids and check it out as best you can—fast. CJ, you and Wilt cover this sector." Another circle. "Carl and I will take this one. One walkie-talkie for each team." He looked around at them all. "Okay?"

Steve said slowly, "No base?"

There were variables, too many variables, but what it all boiled down to was that how long the search *could* continue, even with a base which would take precious time to establish, depended entirely on the weather. At the predicted forty below zero, or even close to it, no search in the open would be possible. "I don't think so," Bart said. "We'll use the jeeps as base, and take what we may think we'll need in them, ropes, a litter, first-aid gear, that kind of thing, and we go in as fast as we can and get them out fast or—" The memory of that dead hunter was strong. "Or we

71

don't get them out at all until after this second storm has passed. And the weather people aren't saying when that will be."

"Them?" This was Jaime. "I thought the pilot was alone, amigo."

"There's a car and trailer," Bart said, "with a family from Oklahoma, and nobody has any idea where they are. We're supposed to keep an eye out for them too. That's all I know." Except that Captain Lopez had said there was pressure from above, strong pressure. Which doesn't affect us, Bart thought, and then changed his mind as the door opened and a State cop walked in, closed the door and nodded to them all.

"Carter, lieutenant, State Police," he said. "Governor's orders. I'm assigned to your group—"

"I don't think red lights or sirens will do us any good," Bart said mildly.

"—to coordinate your operation," Carter finished.

There was silence. Jaime said, "To coordinate with who, whom?"

"I think," Bart said, "that the lieutenant is using a figure of speech." His voice had altered subtly. "You mean, you're in charge, is that it, Lieutenant?"

In silence Carter nodded slowly. He did not smile.

They all looked at Bart. "Let's gather our gear and move out," Bart said. "It's light enough now to see what we're doing."

Warner awakened, shivering with cold, stiff, and with an urgent need to urinate. He got up slowly, painfully, almost fell down again and then sat on the cave floor and tried to rub feeling into both feet. The process itself was painful, and what he knew to be a senseless train of impotent anger began in his mind. The goddamned handmade boots were no good for walking in snow up a mountain trail, as he had discovered yesterday, and they were sure as hell not good to sleep in, so unless you had a horse or a fancy dress ball, what the hell good were they?

His bladder claimed preeminence, and he got painfully to his feet again, crossed the small cave on careful steps and crawled out through the entrance straight into a snowbank.

When he returned, shaking badly with cold now and covered with snow, Ben was feeding the fire, and Lila, kneeling, was talking quietly to Sue Ann; her breath was visible. Patty and Billy still slept.

Warner went over to kneel near the fire, hands out to its warmth. "It's still snowing." He tried to keep his teeth from chattering.

Ben nodded as he sat down to pull on and lace his boots. "We're going to need more wood. We'll see about that after some food."

"Just how long do we have to stay here?" And then, quickly, "Okay. That's a silly question, isn't it?"

A little of the basic good guy was finally showing, Ben thought. "Whether it is or not," he said, "I can't answer it. One step at a time." He rose, crouching. "How deep is the snow?"

"Deep enough," Warner said. He watched Ben crawl out through the entrance and after a time return, as snow-covered and obviously as chilled as he had been. The sight lifted Warner's spirits.

He was normally a good-natured, gregarious man, and it annoyed him now to find himself almost sullen and openly suspicious, too quick to take offense, unable to give generous credit where credit was due. Oh, he was cold, and stiff, but physical punishment had never broken him down before.

On the face of it, God knew they owed this Ben character a bunch, and under almost any other circumstances Warner would have been quick to admit it.

The trouble was that here he had been thrust into such an ignominious role that any kind of praise or even open appreciation would only sound like brownnosing. Beside, goddamn it, he simply could not help resenting Ben's leadership and ability, and that in itself was for him a new reaction.

He had been in subordinate positions before without resentment. Why, hell, all during college he had joyfully cleared the way, and usually ended with his nose in the turf, for old Jake to carry the ball to glory;

73

and never felt a jealous twinge because he knew that what he was doing was vital, that he was doing it well and—perhaps most important—that those who understood these things recognized his importance in the football scheme of things.

Here it was different. Here he was useless, merely a burden, of less importance to their safety or even survival than, say, fifteen-year-old Billy, whose mind kept bouncing around with fresh ideas and knowledge, gleaned God only knew where, and who had already moved into a position second only to Ben in the local pecking order. Less than Sue Ann, who was seeing matters with new clarity; less than that Lila female, who had already shaken off an airplane crash and now, without flinching, faced right up to facts most people would have tried to sidestep.

He was, Warner thought grimly, just about on a par in the scheme of things with Patty, girl-woman, frightened and bewildered. It was humiliating.

Ben primed and lighted his small gasoline stove, and set a pan of snow to melt. When it was liquefied, but not heated, he removed it from the stove and stirred in six spoonsful of powdered orange juice mix, filled his drinking cup and passed it around, Sue Ann first.

Patty and Billy were awake and untangled, yawning, stretching and looking uncomfortable. Warner said, "Outside."

Billy nodded and disappeared through the cave entrance. He was back shortly, teeth chattering as he beat his hands together. "Still snowing, and it's cold! Hey, how about that? Orange juice!" He began to burrow into the sack he had carried from the trailer.

Patty swallowed. She looked at her mother. "In the snow," Sue Ann said. "There is no other way." She watched Patty disappear reluctantly.

Warner said, "Sue Ann, honey—"

Lila said, "We'll manage."

A voice said suddenly, ". . . for a downed aircraft registered to State Senator Joseph Martin of Roswell and believed to be in the mountains behind Santo

Cristo. A Search and Rescue team with the cooperation of the State Police is combing the area. When
weather conditions permit, Civil Air Patrol aircraft
will assist in the search."

Billy turned down the volume of the radio. He
said apologetically, "You said today we'd listen
again."

He thought of bringing it, Warner told himself; it
didn't even occur to me.

"Right," Ben said. "Turn it up again."

". . . weather report. The storm which has dropped
up to nine inches of snow in the Santo Cristo area is
expected to move out of the area by midmorning, but
further heavy snow and severe cold warnings have already been issued for the storm which is moving in
behind it. Temperatures as low as forty degrees below
zero were recorded last night in southern Colorado
and the northern New Mexico towns and villages, and
temperatures in the Santo Cristo area are expected to
fall well below zero late this afternoon and tonight.
Tomorrow the forecast is for further snow, and continued extreme cold. More travelers' advisories have
been issued—"

"Turn it off, Billy," Ben said. And in the sudden
silence, "Have any of you ever tasted dried eggs?
And we have some bacon too. Most, if not all, the
comforts of home." He watched Patty crawl into the
cave. She was shivering, covered with snow and crying. "You'll feel better," Ben said, "after we get some
food in you." He hoped. He was near the end of his
patience with Patty. He opened his pack and began
to take out carefully wrapped bundles.

Billy huddled close and tended the fire, while Ben
cooked on his small stove. The odor of food mixed
with piñon smoke filled the cave. Lila knelt beside
Ben. "Want me to take over?" Her unsteady voice was
pitched low, for his ears only. "I'm not too bad, and
as long as you're shooting the works instead of ration-
ing it—"

"You heard the forecast." After last night's brief
talk, she was one person he could confide in. He kept

his voice scarcely audible. "We're thirty-five hundred feet above Santo Cristo. Figure three and a half degrees colder for every thousand feet you go up. That's something over twelve degrees. If they're going to be well below zero down there—" His voice stopped.

Lila said quietly, "Even here in the cave you think we can't handle it? It was bad last night, but—"

"Damn it," Ben said, "I'm the only one with warm clothing. And last night was mild compared to what's coming. We'll get what wood we can—if we can, and we'll do our damnedest."

"But," Lila said quietly, "you think we aren't going to be here—alive, long enough to worry about stretching your food supply, is that it?"

"There's enough food to last one man for two weeks," Ben said, keeping his voice down too. Damn it, she asked for it, he thought. "It'll last all of us for— as long as we're going to need it. As long as we can keep that fire going and the temperature in here above the point where we freeze to death or even get frostbitten fingers and toes, we're going to be damned uncomfortable, but all right. After that—" He shook his head with an angry jerk. "Don't burn the bacon." He rose then, and, crouching, walked over to Sue Ann. "How's the pain?" I'm a goddamned Florence Nightingale, he told himself angrily.

Sue Ann smiled faintly.

"Okay," Ben said, "we've got more Demerol. We'll give you another fix." He turned away. To Patty he said, "Instead of sitting there feeling sorry for yourself, you might see if there's anything you can do for your mother."

Patty wiped her eyes with the back of her hand. "You can't talk to me like that."

"I just did. Shall I repeat it?"

"That," Billy said from the fire, "is telling it like it is."

Warner thought to interfere, and changed his mind. "What about that weather report?"

Ben turned to face him. "What about it?"

"Are you going to get us out of here?"

76

Ben was conscious that Lila watched him carefully. He said, "We'll eat breakfast. We'll see about gathering wood—just in case. And when the snow lets up, I'll see what I can do about—getting help."

"You carried Sue Ann up here. Can't you carry her out?" Warner was conscious that he sounded querulous, and he could not help it. Goddamn.

"Not through three-foot drifts, and more."

"Eggs and bacon ready," Lila said. She did not look at Ben. "Come and get it before the grease sets."

6.

THEY HAD DRIVEN THE TWO JEEPS, in four-wheel drive and low transmissions, slipping and sliding through the falling snow as far as they could up the road Warner had blundered onto yesterday. Now, prudently, they backed and filled and maneuvered until the cars were turned around and pointing back downhill before they switched off the engines and got out. It was still snowing hard, it was cold, and not yet full daylight.

One by one Jaime pulled two pairs of snowshoes out, his and Steve's, from beneath a Stokes litter, a frame first-aid pack, an oxygen pack and a coil of climbing rope. He bent to secure his snowshoe harness; in long johns, two pairs of socks, heavy trousers, a turtleneck sweater and a goose-down parka, his movements were clumsy. He straightened at last. "One day," he said in his Spanish-lilted English, showing the white teeth, "we are going to be called out in bright, warm sunshine, and our search will be what the British call a piece of cake, no?"

Wilt straightened on his long legs and stamped his

snowshoes experimentally. "That will be the day. I hope I'm not nursemaiding a pack train of dudes back in the wilderness. I'd like to see Steve in a bikini."

Bart listened and said nothing. Banter was good; it meant that despite Lieutenant Carter's presence they were loose. If only the man would have the sense to keep his mouth shut—

Carter did not. "I've been thinking," he said. "All six of you had better head for that spot you have marked on the map. Then—"

Carl, the plumber, kneeling, said something inaudible.

Carter said, "What did you say?"

Carl looked up. Slowly, distinctly, "I said, 'Shit!'" He bent to his snowshoes again.

Bart too was kneeling. The lieutenant stared thoughtfully at his broad back. "You understand, do you not," he said, "that on orders of the governor I am in charge?" It was not precisely what Captain Lopez had told him, but the lieutenant was making his own interpretation.

Bart finished binding his snowshoe harness and stood up. "That's the way we understand it." His voice was quiet, almost expressionless, and he stood without movement, towering over the lieutenant. "You just sit right here and stay in charge," he said gently, "and keep the radios open on both frequencies. You're our base." He looked around at the others. "All set? Then let's move out. Steven, you and Jaime on up the road. CJ, you and Wilt over that way. Stay in touch. Carl—"

Lieutenant Carter said sharply, "Just a minute! I don't want you splitting up until—"

There was a sudden sound like a distant rifle shot muffled by the falling snow. It was followed quickly by another. And then came the faint continuous drone of a jet engine at high speed.

"Sonic boom," Carl said. "Some military jet jockey—"

It was Steve who said, "Wait! Listen!"

A new sound began, gently at first, a distant rumbling, growing in volume, like summer thunder high in the mountains. It seemed to come from everywhere, and they were silent until it died away.

Lieutenant Carter said, "Thunder? In this weather?" His voice was incredulous.

Carl said bitterly, "Guess again."

"That," Bart said, "was a snow avalanche." And maybe rock slide, as Jaime predicted, he thought. A bad omen. He looked around at them all. "All right, let's move out. Take care, and keep in touch." He looked at his compass and started off into the trees. Carl followed.

Inside the cave, they heard the sonic booms too, and they felt the power of the avalanche the booms had triggered in the sudden vibrations of the rock beneath their feet. They all looked at Ben, who was hunkered down beside his pack. "Snow slides," he said, and even produced a faint false smile of reassurance. "Early and late in the season they happen." Damned fool pilot, he thought angrily, with no idea what trouble he could cause.

"The snow's unstable," Billy said. "I read about them, avalanches. Anything can set them off, isn't that so, Ben? I mean, in ski areas they set them off on purpose so they won't start at the wrong time and bury somebody."

A very bright kid, Ben thought, with apparently the curiosity of Kipling's mongoose to run and find out when he did not know something.

"They say," Billy was saying, "that even somebody yelling or whistling can set them off sometimes. How about that?"

Lila shivered. She was thinking again of that airplane, upside down in the ravine, and Joe, now only a frozen dead body hanging from his harness, while she was in here at least for the present alive, if almost numb from cold. But, dear God! in these mountains in winter how narrow was that line between survival and extinction. She never thought of it before; it was as if the sudden deep rumbling and the shaking of the

79

ground beneath her feet had jerked aside a curtain to expose her own mortality. "Nice country they've got here," she said in a voice that was not quite steady. "They pile it up and they shake it loose, is that it?"

A small piece of rock rattled suddenly down the uneven inside wall to land on the floor of the cave beside Sue Ann.

"By God," Warner said, "will you look at that! I mean, what if the whole thing decides to go? Then where are we?"

Panic could be near, Ben thought. He stood to dominate the scene. "This cave's been here a long time without collapsing. Those markings on the walls are petroglyphs, and they weren't done yesterday. Cool it."

Billy put another stick on the fire. He said almost inaudibly, "They didn't have sonic booms back then, though."

True enough, Ben thought, but the kid doesn't have to say it aloud. Things are bad enough without hunting for further calamity.

"I don't think it's safe," Warner said. "I mean—"

"Goddamn it, just what do you mean?" Ben said sharply. "That we ought to move to another motel?" In the sudden silence he pulled his parka over his head, pulled up the hood, snugged it beneath his chin and put on the gloves he had taken from his pack. "I'm going to gather what wood I can find. I'll bring it to the entrance. You can take it from there." He crawled outside and was gone. The cave seemed suddenly cold and empty.

An angry man, Lila thought again; but doing nonetheless everything that he can.

"I think he's hateful," Patty said. "Nobody has to be like that!"

Sue Ann said in her dreamy voice, "Honey, he has five of us on his back. He—"

"And you always take his side! Even against Daddy!"

Warner said, "Kitten—"

But it was Sue Ann's voice that dominated. "Yes,

80

honey, I do." The memory of those night thoughts was strong and the sense of guilt still vivid. We are here, she thought, and Ben is our only hope; it is as simple, as devastating as that. "I rode up here on his back," she said. "We are all of us here in this cave, at least alive, because of him. We can put up with a little of his temper, because without him——"

"That isn't so!" Patty said. "Daddy would have thought of something, wouldn't you, Daddy?"

The poor guy, Lila thought; put right under the gun by his own daughter. He still doesn't have a clue about what to do, and how can he admit that? She said, "Sure you would, if you'd had the time."

Warner straightened his shoulders. "I doubt if I'd have been able to think of anything," he said. "I doubt it very much. I thought we should have stayed with the car. And maybe we should have, at that." He was silent for a few moments, looking around at them all in sudden, unaccustomed contrition. "I'm—sorry."

"Nobody's blaming you, dear," Sue Ann said. "It's just—one of those things."

"But you are blaming him!" This was Patty again. "We—all are! That's what makes it—worst of all!"

Jaime and Steve had the easiest going, up the road, no trees or brush to contend with; but under the best of conditions, uphill at ten thousand feet in deep snow snowshoeing is not easy work. Jaime led at a slow, steady pace, bent forward against the slope and the driving snow. Steve followed, not too close, lest a sudden slip or stop entangle them. Breath was precious, and they did not speak.

She was a tall girl, this Stephanie Jordan, large-boned, strong, calm, a farm girl from California's Central Valley with light coloring and blue eyes that spoke of a distant Nordic ancestor lured to the new land by tales of adventure and gold. She lived alone in Santo Cristo making a precarious living by her pottery. In the winter she worked as a ski instructor at the Santo Cristo Basin. She was almost, but not quite, as good on rock as Jaime was. Few were.

They passed the place on the road where the trees were open and yesterday the view had been limitless. Today the view extended only a matter of yards out into the still falling snow. Jaime pointed upward. "I think it's beginning to clear." The words were an effort.

Steve nodded and said nothing. They moved on.

They came around the next bend, where the service road took off to the left, steeply downhill, and there they stopped short. Both the main road and upper part of the service road had been swept clean of snow. Uprooted trees and large rocks filled the area. It was a scene of devastation.

"Jesus!" Jaime said, giving the name the Spanish pronunciation. "Hay-soos! That avalanche—" He left it there, the sentence unfinished. He and Steve stared in awe.

It was Steve who pointed upward to the top of the mountain mass, marked now by a dark gash where the slide had begun. "It's still—unstable," she said. "That snow overhang could start another one. We'd better get past it while we can." She bent to take off her snowshoes. Jaime's voice made her straighten quickly.

"Jesus Christ!" Jaime said, this time in clear English. "Look down there!"

Below the service road where the talus slope ended and the trees began, debris from the avalanche had slowed, stopped and piled into a mass. There were uprotted trees, brush, rocks too large for a man to lift —and the gleam of metal, the half-buried shape of a car, and a trailer smashed almost beyond recognition.

In stunned silence Steve took the walkie-talkie from her parka pocket and raised it to her lips. "Steve here. Come in, Bart." Her voice was not quite steady. "One more time, come in, Bart!"

"Bart here. Come on." Even as a disembodied voice, the big man's strength and assurance were comforting.

"We're where the service road takes off," Steve said. "That's the avalanche site. Down below us there's a car and trailer. Maybe we've found your lost family. Over."

There was a pause. "Roger. Can you reach it? Over."

Jaime held out his hand and Steve gave him the walkie-talkie. "Affirmative," Jaime said. "A little rope work. We can handle it. We'll find out what the situation is and stay in touch. Over." This time there was silence that grew, stretched. "Do you read me?"

Slowly, "Roger. Maybe we'd better call in some help. You may need torches, litters—"

"Amigo. Suppose the car is empty? I think I'd better find that out first. Over."

There was another silence. Then, slowly, "Roger. Take care and keep in touch. Over and out."

Jaime handed Steve the walkie-talkie. She pointed upward past the head of the dark earth scar to the snow overhang. "I don't like that. It could go. This whole mountain—"

"*Guapa*. Good-looking." Jaime showed his white teeth in a smile. "What else is there to do? Do we stand here and think about it while more snow falls?" He shook his head. "A rope from the jeep, a little rappel, a quick look. If the car is empty, and the trailer, then you will move my belay away from the slide area, and I will come back up through the trees. Wait here, *guapa*. I will go back to the jeep for the rope. Fifteen minutes."

Warner pulled in the final stick of wood, and Ben crawled in after it, stood up and pushed back the hood of his parka. He brushed snow from his whiskery cheeks and his eyebrows before he took off his gloves and began to warm his hands at the fire. They all watched him in silence.

"I think the snow's tapering off," he said. He was breathing deeply from his exertions, and his lips were stiff from cold. "I'll catch my breath and then have a try for the airplane."

"To leave a message that we're here?" Lila nodded. "Anybody have anything to write with and on?"

83

"In the pack," Ben said. "Tell them how many we are, that we need help and we're in a cave on the north wall of the canyon. We'll try to put up smoke. Tell them too that we have an injury and will need a litter."

Billy, squatting beside the fire, said, "Is the snow drifting? That's what it does, isn't it?"

"It does, and it is."

Lila, thinking of the terrain she and Ben had struggled through on the way to the cave, shook her head. "Do you think you have a chance?"

"I won't know till I try."

"Because," Lila said, "if there isn't any chance, then it isn't worth the risk, is it? I mean, what if you clobber yourself in one of those deadfalls?"

"Do you think I'm doing this for the fun of it?"

"Here's your note," Lila said. "You can pin it to Joe's chest if you get there." She faced him, and spoke quietly. "I don't think you're going out there for the fun of it, no." She hesitated, shivering. "But—for better or for worse, you're all we've got. Remember that." She turned away.

Again the cave seemed suddenly cold and empty after Ben had gone. Lila stared thoughtfully at the wet spots on the cave floor where snow from Ben's parka had fallen and melted. Automatically she moved toward the fire. I almost accused him of heroics, she thought, and that—isn't it at all. I'm only afraid for him because he is all we have. Without him— She held out her hands to the flames and tried to put that thought from her mind.

Patty said, "The radio said that he, your friend in the plane, was a state senator." Somehow it had a hopeful ring in her young mind.

Slowly Lila nodded. "He was. And now he's dead and hanging upside down in his harness frozen stiff." She was probing the hurt as you probed a sore tooth, she thought, but it was more than that. Frozen stiff as we will be too, she told herself, when that new cold front moves in. Hopeless, helpless thought. "He was a nice guy," she said. Epitaph.

Warner had been sitting quietly, leaning back against the wall, staring at nothing. He said suddenly, "Smoke." He looked at Billy.

"If the snow stops they may be able to see it." Billy said in his quick way. "Indians used to use smoke signals. You could see them a long way." He was suddenly silent, thoughtful. "Unless there's a wind. If it's blowing, I don't think you could see the smoke from this fire any distance at all." He was silent, suddenly downcast.

"So what does that leave?" Warner said, his voice rising. It was pure anger growing in his mind now. He searched for a vent for his rage, and found none. "You're the bright boy with all the ideas," he shouted. "Let's have one now."

Billy shook his head in stunned silence. He had never seen his father like this before, a grown man suddenly throwing aside all adult restraints. The experience was terrifying.

In sudden decision Warner heaved himself to his feet. He pulled the Stetson down tight on his head and took the rifle that leaned against the wall. They stared at him as he crossed the cave and knelt at the entrance.

It was Sue Ann who said as calmly as she could, "What are you doing, dear?"

"If they can't see the smoke, maybe they can hear. Maybe somebody can!"

Billy cried quickly, "Oh, no! Dad! Dad!" The terror forgotten, he jumped to his feet, rushed across the cave and seized Warner's arm. "You can't! You can't!"

Warner shook his arm without seeming effort, and the boy was thrown loose to slam against the cave wall, where he dropped to his knees, stunned but unhurt. He crouched there motionless as in silence Warner crawled out through the entrance and disappeared into the snow.

7.

On the early morning statewide television news: "The light aircraft registered to State Senator Joseph Martin of Roswell is missing and believed down in the mountains behind Santo Cristo. Search efforts are under way. Governor Archuleta, contacted early this morning by TV-7, has announced that the full resources of the state will be thrown into the search, and that if possible National Guard as well as Civil Air Patrol aircraft will sweep the area where the Martin plane is apparently lost.

"State Senator Martin is a rancher, whose political career began . . ."

State Police Captain Lopez, still at his desk, read the fresh weather report his secretary brought him along with another cup of hot coffee. He thought of the mountain search and swore fluently and with feeling in Spanish. "It is what is called the sanctity of human life," he said to the secretary, "which means that when one damn fool gets himself into trouble, others who are not damn fools but foolish nevertheless have to go out and risk their lives to try to rescue him." He sipped the scalding coffee.

The secretary waited, uncertain whether to stay or leave. The captain was an odd one at times.

"Even if we knew or could safely assume that the man was dead," the captain said, "would we then do the logical thing, which would be nothing, relying on the cold to keep his body intact until conditions were much easier, and safer?" He shook his head. "We would not. Even dead, he would demand our effort

86

and risk." He sipped again at the coffee. "Does that make sense?"

"Yes, sir. I mean, no, sir. I don't know, sir."

The captain sighed. "I think that is the best answer. Keep me posted. The governor will want to know."

Traffic in Santo Cristo had almost stopped. City crews, bundled in heavy sweaters, hooded sweatshirts, reflective vests, hard hats, gloves and boots, plowed and sanded, and plowed again as wind whistled through the narrow streets piling more drifts and wiping out all signs of effort in a matter of minutes. A waste of time and taxpayers' money, but what else was there to do?

Nighttime temperature at the airport weather station had dipped to twenty-one degrees, and with what passed for daylight the readings, instead of beginning to rise, continued to drop as arctic air flowed south.

Chief meteorologist Brady Shaw drank more coffee and glared at the continuing reports. To his assistant, "When they laid out this continent," he said, "why weren't they smart enough to stick a mountain range across it like the Alps in Europe? Answer me that."

It was a joke, of course, the assistant thought, but underlying it was something in the old man's manner that was not at all light and humorous.

"Get on the horn to Corpus Christi and San Antonio," Brady said abruptly. "I won't wait for the satellite photos. Ask them what's doing with that front coming out of the Gulf." He saw the hesitation in the assistant's face. "Sonny," Brady said then, "there's an airplane down in the mountains right up there behind us. And some people are going in to try and find it. If they ask, I want to be able to give them the best guess I can about their chances."

"Chances?" The assistant was frowning. "Of finding the plane? But how can we—?"

"Their chances of staying alive while they look,"

87

Brady said. "Have you any idea what it's already like up there at ten—eleven thousand feet?"

Airport controller Joe Meems on the phone to Civil Air Patrol said, "Our best info is that the snow may stop by midmorning, but not for long. If you're going to put something into the air to see if you can get a better fix on Bonanza one-six-five-zero Bravo you'd better be ready to move fast."

He listened quietly, and then nodded. "It's always the same. It finally comes right down to the foot soldier slogging through the mud or snow. I feel sorry for those poor bastards up there. Volunteers, at that; nobody pays them a cent. I think they've got rocks in their heads, but if I ever get lost in the mountains, I'll be goddamned good and glad that they have."

Ben carried his compass in his hand as he worked his way from the cave entrance down into the canyon toward the ravine where the plane had crashed. With strictly limited visibility, it was dead reckoning at best, because frequently he had to detour around a drift too deep to go through, brush too thick to penetrate or places where the snow seemed to conceal rocks or small depressions where the footing might be dangerous. Lila of course had been right when she spoke of the danger of clobbering himself. So?

Just what the hell else did she think there was to do? Sit in that cave and wait for that predicted cold front to freeze them to death? Granted, there was firewood for the taking, but he had cleaned out what was above, and now all that was available was down here in the canyon, which meant climbing down and then climbing back up again with each armload, and while it would probably come to that anyway as a final resort, if there was any hope at all of getting help first, obviously the thing to do was give it a try. That kind of wood gathering would be a losing proposition. Eventually it would no longer be possible. And then, without that, they would be finished.

Lila hadn't come right out and said so, but she had

hinted pretty clearly that maybe he was doing this just for the heroics of it, like some kid on a dare walking the top of a picket fence. Well, goddamn it, if that was what she thought, to hell with her. He wasn't bucking for sainthood. If she didn't understand it now, she never would, but all he was trying to do was save his own neck as well as theirs.

They had survived last night, but if the weather reports were anywhere near right, and from the feel of things they were, their chances of getting through another night safely were no better than problematical. The simple fact was that unless they got help, and soon, they were dead, period, no matter what Lila or anybody else might think.

It was cold and getting colder. And here in the canyon the snow had drifted heavily and unevenly; in places it was knee-deep, in places which he tried to avoid but sometimes could not it reached his waist. Twice, despite all his care, he fell.

On one of those falls he had difficulty getting his footing again, and a wild fleeting thought passed through his mind almost with the force of revelation: snow is like quicksand, and I'm going down into it for good. The near-panic lasted only a moment, but he could still remember it.

He could only guess how far he had come one labored step at a time. Snow was light, light enough to blow at the wind's whim, but it clung to his legs nonetheless and weighted them down, robbing them of strength and of feeling. Compared to this, carrying Sue Ann up to the cave had been a breeze.

His first intimation that he was not going to reach the plane came with his third fall in what had looked like solid footing but turned out to be just what Lila had mentioned, a deadfall.

He had already shifted his weight to his forward foot and it was too late to draw back when he found no support. He pitched forward trying with his hands to break the fall, caught desperately at what felt like a branch of a fallen tree, felt the branch bend and somehow trigger a whipping motion that brought a larger branch out of the snow to crash down on his head.

He lay stunned, his face buried in snow, scrambling feebly and automatically with both hands until at last his head cleared and he managed to find support, and slowly, bit by bit, extricate himself from the tangle of fallen branches the snow had concealed. It was then that he realized he had dropped his compass.

He made himself stand quietly while the pain in his skull diminished, and the sense of despair at last fled. The compass was still here, somewhere within a few feet of him, that was certain. Finding it was something else again.

He began slowly, systematically, to search the trampled snow where he had struggled, the tangled twigs and dead leaves of the branch which had struck him, the snow beneath the branch where the compass might have dropped and by its weight buried itself in loose snow.

It was useless effort, and after some minutes he gave up reluctantly and tried to think through the situation.

He was not at all sure how far he was from the plane, and without compass guidance in the detouring he would have to make he could very well miss the plane and not even realize that he had gone beyond it. And each unguided step he took would add to the difficulty of finding his way back to the cave.

Project that, he told himself, and it comes out that you can easily get yourself lost down here. And then with that front moving in, you, sonny, are a dead duck. They might find you in the spring.

There was only one sensible choice, but for long moments he refused to take it. The plane could be just over the next rise, he told himself, and knew that he was talking foolishness. All he had had was a general compass direction; he might already have gone past the plane without knowing it—how about that, buster?

Okay, okay. There were times when you could not argue with logic and facts. He turned and began the slow, laborious process of backtracking, following as best he could his own rapidly disappearing footprints in the snow. Failure of mission.

At that moment of decision he was not quite two hundred yards from the plane, and less than one hundred yards from Bart Wallace and Carl.

Bart set the pace, one snowshoe ahead of the other in a steady, shuffling, wearing rhythm. He carried his compass in his hand to correct his course on mandatory, temporary detours; and he counted his paces automatically. As he moved, his head swung from side to side, eyes squinting, peering through the still falling snow in search of traces of plane wreckage. Carl was on a parallel course, fifty yards distant, just visible. They made no attempt to communicate.

It was monotonous, grueling work, and there was no substitute. In fine weather and open country either fixed-wing or chopper aircraft could cover hundreds of square miles in a matter of minutes. Here among trees, rocks, brush, snow cover and limited visibility, search coverage was measured in hours and yards—with no real assurance that they were even in the ball park area, not merely wasting precious time.

The trick was to put the pessimistic possibilities out of your mind and concentrate on the here and now, which, Bart was perfectly willing to admit, was probably easier for him to do than for others, merely because he was what he was, a plodder, content with the slow pace and the unspectacular progress. What he considered lack of brilliance in himself did have its compensations.

He reached an almost sheer canyon wall, stopped and beckoned to Carl to join him. Both men were breathing hard.

"If the son of a bitch crashed on top," Carl said, "CAP will spot him the minute they can get in the air."

Bart nodded in silence. There was temper in Carl's voice. He ignored it. He had the hood of his parka up, and his breath came like steam from its depths. He took the walkie-talkie from his pocket, and pushed back the parka hood to talk. "Bart here. Come in, Wilt." Of the pair CJ and Wilt, Wilt was always the leader.

"You got Wilt. Come on."

"We're at the cirque. We'll move north a hundred yards and start back."

"Roger. What's with Jaime and the *chica?* Over."

"Come in, Steve."

Steve's voice said, "Roger. Jaime's just back with rope from the jeeps. I've been watching the wreckage of the car and trailer. No sign of life. Over."

Carl was watching Bart. He said now, "You don't like it. Why?"

"A fresh slide. It'll be unstable. The whole area is unstable. Jaime could trigger more sliding." Bart shook his head and raised the walkie-talkie to his lips again. "Roger," he said. "They could be inside and hurt." They could be dead too, he thought. "Be careful on that rope." There was nothing else to say. "Over and out." He put the walkie-talkie back into his pocket and pulled his hood up again. To Carl, "Let's move out."

Carl hesitated. He looked at the trees, the rocks, the snow-covered desolation. "It's probably no use."

"Maybe not."

"What I mean, if he landed on top, like I said the CAP'll spot him. If he landed down here, he doesn't have a chance."

Bart was silent. From the depths of the parka hood he watched Carl steadily.

"I mean," Carl said, "we're covering how much, a hundred and fifty yards at a sweep?"

Bart's nod was almost imperceptible.

"At that rate—"

"What do you suggest?"

Carl took a deep breath, let it out in a sigh and shook his head. "Nothing. He's probably dead, and we're walking around freezing our ass off, but that's how it works, isn't it?"

"That's how it works," Bart said. "He may be dead, but we won't know for sure unless we look."

92

The big bastard was like a mountain, Carl thought, immovable once his mind was made up. "Let's go," he said.

The sudden sound like a shot was distant, muffled by trees and snow. It could have come from any direction. But this time there was no second sound and a following jet engine drone. Instead, there was another deep rumbling growing in volume, and the walkie-talkie in Bart's pocket came alive.

"Bart!" Steve's voice. "Oh, God, Bart, come in! Come in!"

"I read you, Steve."

"It's Jaime! Another slide! It caught him halfway down the slope! Over!"

Oh, Jesus, Bart thought. Aloud, "Roger. We're on our way. Come in, Wilt! Did you read that? Over."

"Roger. We're on our way too. Over and out."

They heard the sharp sound inside the cave too, and the immediate thunderous sounds that followed it, but what happened was too fast for comprehension.

The floor of the cave shook suddenly. Small pieces of the wall broke loose and rock dust filled the air. Patty screamed. Billy tried desperately to keep the fire from breaking up and scattering burning wood in every direction. Crashing sounds all around them seemed to go on for an eternity, and Patty screamed once more.

And then at last there was silence. And almost total darkness.

Billy coughed and then sneezed from the rock dust. He said in a voice that was not quite steady, "That's blown it." Strangely, what he felt was not panic but, rather, a paralyzing sense of calm robbing him of any power of decision. His father's sudden violence forgotten, in the near-darkness he went about gathering the fire back into its single place almost as if nothing had happened.

From the sleeping bag Sue Ann said quietly, "What's happened?" More unreality. Would it never stop? Her voice sharpened as she spoke to Patty. "Be

quiet! Stop sniveling!" And then again, "What's happened?"

Lila said, "Another snow slide." She dropped to her
knees and began to probe at the cave entrance. "This
one blocked the door." Without realizing it, she took
charge. "Billy, bring me a stick to poke with."

With Billy hunkered beside her, Lila poked and
probed and then sat back on her heels in silence. She
handed Billy the stick and watched him make a few
tentative jabs, stand up and walk back to his fire as
if in a daze.

Patty sat quiet, stunned. Sue Ann said, "Tell us."

Lila hesitated. She was in no hurry to put the facts
into words.

Billy rolled one burning stick from the fire and stifled
the flames in the dust. His movements were deliberate,
and his mind, released from its paralysis by Lila's command, was functioning clearly again. It was still not
panic that he felt; instead a feeling of inevitability had
taken over. Pop did it, he thought. He flipped. "It
isn't snow blocking the entrance," he said. "It's rock."
He rolled another burning stick away and carefully
put out the flame.

Patty said, "What are you doing? You're putting
the fire out and it's cold!"

"I think," Billy said, "that we'd better hang on to
what oxygen we've got in here. I don't think we can
afford a fire, not if we're going to keep on breathing."
The choice between freezing to death and dying of
asphyxiation, he thought. He looked at Lila. "Okay
with you if I explain the facts of life?"

He is no longer a fifteen-year-old boy, Lila thought.
Somehow in the last few minutes he's put on ten years
and he's beginning to sound like Ben. "Go ahead,"
she said. "We'd better know where we stand."

Billy nodded, "Pop and his elk gun," he said.
"That's what caused it."

Sue Ann said, "He was trying to help. In case nobody could see the smoke."

Billy looked at Lila, and then back at the fire. He
said nothing.

Ben was just struggling up from the canyon floor when he heard the sudden sound, and the beginning of the slide. Rocks hurtled down from the wall above, and automatically he dropped to his knees and covered his head with his hands.

Despite the snow and the cold as sometimes in nightmares, he was once again in Viet Nam, pinned down by enemy fire. What pounded on his back and his hands covering his head were not small rocks, but shell fragments, and the thunder that echoed above him was the rolling sound of enemy artillery that seemed as if it would never stop. He felt again that old bowel-watering fear while crouching, making himself as small as possible, waiting for the direct hit that would end it all.

When at last the bombardment slackened, and then died away entirely, he remained on his knees almost unbelieving for some moments before he got slowly to his feet, automatically brushed the snow from his legs and in an ecstasy of relief began to swear in a slow, monotonous voice.

Snow was still falling, and the air was perceptibly colder; the words he spoke emerged as steam. "As they damn well might," he said, thinking that steam expressed even better than words his reaction. To everything. He started once more for the canyon wall.

The ancient trail was heavily drifted now, here and there rocks of size had landed and stayed, and around these he had to work his careful way, slipping and sliding even at best.

He came around a shoulder of rock and there he stopped. Warner stood in his way, still clutching the rifle. The Fort Worth Stetson was gone, and there was a bloody gash high on Warner's forehead. Blood had run down his cheek. He seemed totally unaware of his hurt, and he stared at Ben as at a stranger.

Understanding came all at once. "You fired that thing," Ben said. "That's what caused the slide! You stupid son of a bitch!"

Warner's expression did not change. He stood silent.

"Just who in hell did you think was going to hear you even if you hadn't brought the mountainside down?"

More silence.

"Goddamn it," Ben said, reason beginning to replace the anger of relief, "we're all alone here. Can't you get that through your head? And I couldn't get to the plane, so God only knows what we're going to try now." He made a sudden angry grab to snatch the rifle from Warner's hand. "But you're not going to shoot this thing off again and bury all of us, that is for damn sure."

He was talking to a zombie, he thought suddenly; his words were making no impression at all. Warner's hands had not even tried to retain the rifle, and Warner's expression had not changed. All at once Warner's lips began to move, and Ben bent forward to catch the words.

"The cave," Warner said, mumbling badly.

"What about it?"

"It's—gone."

"Make sense. What do you mean?"

"I can't find it. There are rocks. Big rocks." He was silent.

Ben closed his eyes. He opened them again. He took a deep breath. "Okay," he said, and his voice was almost gentle, the anger suddenly evaporated, leaving only emptiness in its place. "Let's go see how bad it is."

8.

To THE WEST THE SNOW WAS SLACKENING, and overhead tiny patches of blue came and went. But the wind
had shifted, and from the north angry dark clouds
moved southward with deceptive speed, blotting out
first this mountain peak, and then the next; reaching
down to the mesa level and flowing along the ground,
dropping fresh quantities of wind-driven snow to pile
against buildings, fences and cutbanks in monstrous
drifts. The temperature continued to drop with ap-
palling speed.

State Police Captain Lopez, still at his desk, talked
directly with Civil Air Patrol and the National Guard
air arm. "All I want to know," the captain said, "is
can you or can you not get into the air for a search
of the area?"

"We've been standing by since first light, Captain."
The voice on the phone was weary with waiting and
frustration. "We can get into the air, yes. The question is whether we could get back."

"And?"

"I think we'd have just about the chance of a fart
in a whirlwind."

"They got two fixes during the night."

"Jet airliners, Captain, with pressurized cabins flying at thirty-five thousand feet above the weather are
one thing. We're something else."

"The governor—"

"Captain, if the governor wants to come out here
and try it himself—I'll attend his funeral. If they ever
find him, that is. You can pass that along."

The captain nodded wearily. *"Basta,"* he said,
"enough. I won't try to tell you your business."

"There's a switch."

The captain could even show his teeth in a weary smile. "Amigo," he said, "you don't even know what pressure is, and you are lucky that you do not. Keep me posted if there is any change." He hung up, and leaned back in his chair as his secretary came in. "More good news?" he said.

"Lieutenant Carter called in on the channel, sir. The S&R people have suspended their search for the plane. One of their men has been caught in an avalanche. It was their own fault, Carter says. He told them not to split up."

There were times, the captain thought, when things simply had to be ordained by mischievous minds. He could see no other explanation for the fact that every now and again an operation went wrong right from the start, compounding error and misjudgment and just plain bad break into a concatenation of small and not so small failures that could only add up to catastrophe.

And at times like that, when you saw the tragedy taking shape, the temptation was to rush to the scene and take over yourself, which was precisely the one thing he could not do. His place was here at this desk taking in reports and making decisions that affected roads, highway crews, police rescue operations and a dozen other problems throughout a state larger than all of New England, New York and New Jersey combined; and logically he simply could not afford to concentrate on one matter in one location to the exclusion of all others—pressure from above or not. But the sense of frustration remained, nonetheless.

"Get back to Carter," he said. "We want to know if there is anything, repeat, anything we can do to help —more people, equipment, whatever. Tell him that it is not likely that air search will be possible. Have him pass that along to Wallace." He stopped suddenly. "It wasn't Wallace who was caught in the avalanche?"

"No, sir." The secretary consulted his notes. "Jaime Leyba. He is—"

"I know Jaime," the captain said. "He carved the

98

doors for our new house." He closed his eyes briefly. At least it wasn't Wallace, but Leyba was a good man. It was always the good ones, he thought, and again that phrase ran through his mind: the sanctity of human life. It was a concept that sometimes devoured sacrifices like an ancient, insatiable god. "All right. Keep me posted."

The telephone on his desk buzzed insistently. The captain waved the secretary away and picked up the phone himself, spoke his name and listened. The call was from a village two hundred miles away. "Isolated and no heat?" he said. "So the roads are impassable, there are snowmobiles, aren't there? Use them. I don't care if they are privately owned. We'll straighten that out later. Get those people in before they freeze to death."

Billy still worked on the fire. He had reduced it to its smallest supportable form which would do little to heat the cave, he judged, but would also consume a minimum of oxygen. With the cave entrance entirely blocked, their only source of air was the chimney hole, and Billy was not sure how long the four of them could survive on that and what was already in the cave. He squatted patiently by the fire and tried to calculate the number of cubic feet involved. The trouble was, he didn't know how much oxygen one pair of lungs consumed at this altitude. But the speculation was something to do, at least. It was better than thinking about the increasing cold that was like nothing he had felt before.

The effects of Sue Ann's last pill were wearing off, and her foot and ankle were beginning to pain beyond her power to ignore. She closed her eyes and let the pain wash over her. It mingled with those night thoughts and the sense of this new calamity which was beginning to lose meaning. My fault, my fault, my fault—it was like a litany in her mind.

Patty had not said a word since she had upbraided Billy for putting out the burning sticks. She sat huddled now, arms around her knees, in the farthest corner of the cave, withdrawn, a picture of despair.

Lila studied the girl in silence tinged with contempt. A spoiled brat, Daddy's little angel, she thought, probably for the first time in her life being ignored and feeling very sorry for herself as a result. Well, let her. Other matters were compelling. Lila turned her attention to Billy. She spoke through stiffening and almost numb lips. "We could at least try to clear that rock."

"No way."

"Tell me why."

"You felt it with that stick," Billy said. "It's solid. All we can reach is the bottom of a pile of rocks, and the bottom rocks are too big to pull in through the opening, and with all the weight that's on them, they're too heavy to push away. You'd have to start at the top to clear it and we can't get there."

"You're just guessing."

Billy refused even to argue. "Go ahead and try it."

"All right," Lila said, "what about that smoke hole? Could you get through it? Maybe standing on my back to reach it?"

Billy looked appraisingly at the small opening near the top of the cave wall.

"If you were outside," Lila said, "then maybe you could clear some of the rocks, and I could help from in here. I'd try to get through the hole, but you're smaller than I am."

True. Obviously the hole was not large enough for her body. Billy stood up. She was doing her best, he thought, and he could do no less. He felt a small surge of hope. "We can try it."

Lila went down on her hands and knees. She braced herself against Billy's weight as he stepped on her back, and she tried futilely to turn her head to watch his progress, but her neck would not swivel far enough. She gave it up and concentrated instead on giving him as steady a platform as she could.

"My head'll go through." Billy's voice was muffled. "Maybe if I try one arm at the same time—" There was silence and his weight shifted as he struggled. "Nope," he said at last, panting from the exertion. "No way." His voice was dull with disappointment. He stepped down, and Lila freed of his burden could straighten stiffly to look at him in the dim light of the fire.

Billy's face was smudged from the smoke that had gathered on the rock, and there was a bloody scratch on one cheek. More important, his usual cheerfulness was entirely gone. "Okay," he said, "so now we know." He walked back to the fire and dropped to his knees beside its feeble warmth.

Lila said, "I'm sorry, Billy."

"Yeah." He did not look up, but continued to stare glumly at what was left of the fire. Beyond it, beneath a pile of rocks, the portable radio lay smashed beyond repair. Now they were wholly alone.

Lila got slowly to her feet and looked around the cave. Sue Ann lay unmoving in the sleeping bag, her eyes closed. And against one wall, Patty still huddled, looking exactly like pictures Lila had seen of deeply disturbed children withdrawn from the world. Unreal, she thought, and felt a sudden surge of anger. "We're still alive, aren't we?" Her voice was sharp.

It brought no response. Patty did not even look up. Lila crossed the cave and stood above the girl, glaring down.

The temptation was to take the girl's shoulders in her hands and shake her until her teeth rattled. She stifled it with effort. Instead, "What's the matter with you?" she said, and the tone of her voice surprised her. More surprising still she felt impelled to kneel and touch Patty's shoulder reassuringly. "The world hasn't ended yet. Not till the final whimper." A feeble joke, she thought, but the best she could manage at the moment.

Patty turned her head and looked at Lila's face without expression.

"Your mother's hurt, but she isn't complaining," Lila said, her voice suddenly pitched only for Patty's ears. "Your father meant well. Give him that. And Billy's

101

tried the best he can. Shall I tell you you ought to be ashamed of yourself for the way you're behaving?" She shook her head. "I have an idea you know it already better than I do. Am I right?"

Was there a glimmer of response in the girl's eyes? Lila could not be sure. Strangely, the anger in her mind had disappeared all at once, although nothing really had changed. Or had it? Somehow in this dark cave, silent, cold as a tomb and growing colder, she was seeing matters from a different perspective, that of responsibility, and maybe it was that which made all the difference. Maybe I am the one who ought to be ashamed, she thought, for taking less than a charitable view. We're all in this together.

Again her voice astonished her by the gentleness of its tone. "How old are you, Patty? Sixteen? Seventeen?"

Patty's nod was almost imperceptible, uninterested, and her face showed nothing.

How often, Lila wondered, has she heard that question asked? For the moment this was all that mattered. And how often has it been followed by something like a lecture on the responsibilities of young womanhood? Try to remember yourself how it was only ten years ago. And then, guilty thought: we forget too soon what it was like. There are other, worse pains than physical ones.

She left her knees and sank cross-legged to sit beside Patty on the cold floor, looking straight ahead at nothing, carefully keeping her eyes from the girl's face. And she kept her voice pitched low and almost uninflected as she began to speak. Why do I bother? She did not know the answer, but the compulsion was strong.

"I don't know about you," she said in an almost conspiratorial tone, "but hearing about other peoples' problems has never made my own seem any less important. I guess when you come right down to it, we're all pretty self-centered." Once started, the words came more easily. "Ten years ago when I was your age there were riots in the cities and on college campuses, people were concerned about all kinds of things—and I couldn't have cared less. I was only worried about one thing—me. Funny, isn't it?"

She allowed herself then to glance at Patty's face, but she could not be sure that she found in it any expression of interest.

"Boys that age," Lila went on, "have it easy. At least that was how it looked. They could play football or baseball, all kinds of things to make them something, somebody. But I couldn't think of anything that would make me important unless I wanted to spend my life in a swimming pool or on ice skates hoping I could make the Olympics. Otherwise all I could do was just wait around hoping somebody would notice me—and I didn't see why anyone would because I wasn't beautiful, I wasn't witty, I wasn't rich; I was just a mess."

There was a silence. Then Patty's voice came out with effort: "So what did you do?"

A gain? A breakthrough? Maybe. "What did I do?" Lila said. "Nothing much except feel sorry for myself and resent everybody else, but that didn't get me very far either." She smiled in memory; it was a grimace. "I wrote poetry too. Do you ever write poetry? It was something I could do all alone."

"Yes," Patty said, and that was all.

"I wrote one about why-am-I-here-and-where-am-I-going," Lila said. "You know the kind of thing?" Out of the corner of her eye she saw Patty nod as if she expected revelations. But I have none, Lila thought hopelessly. Then, because there was no way to turn back, "Well," she said, "you don't talk about little things in a poem, you talk about great big things and you ask great big questions. You don't know the answers, you just ask the questions, so I did: 'What if the world were to end in a moment?/ Would I then feel I had squandered my time?/ Or would I, through *caring,* have unlocked the riddle,/ Opened the door on the secret sublime?' " She was silent, vaguely shamed by the fact of revealing herself. "Pretty bad, isn't it?"

There was a long silence this time. Patty said at last in a new, quiet voice, no longer dull and uninterested, "I think it's beautiful. I really do."

From the fire Billy said suddenly, "Hey! Listen!"

Ben's voice, muffled and seeming distant, reached into the cave through the smoke hole in the front wall. "Can you hear me in there?"

Lila was smiling as she got stiffly to her feet and crossed the cave. She stood as tall as she could to shout back to the outside.

The scene, Bart thought, was utter desolation. The upper fifty feet of the service road were gone, carried away by the tons of snow, rocks, uprooted trees and debris that had thundered down the mountainside.

At the edge of the trees below, the slide had piled itself into a kind of jumbled terminal moraine, from which Jaime's climbing rope stretched taut to its belay around a standing tree by the main road.

Snow still fell, but to the west incongruously a single small patch of blue sky appeared and then was quickly gone. The mountainside was silent, forbidding, and the air was perceptibly colder.

"I'll go down," Steve said. "I—wanted you here before I did—just in case."

"You'll stay right here," Bart said. Wherever he was, without even thinking he took quiet command, and it would not have occurred to him to try to say why, because it had always been so. The mark of authority was in his size and his strength and his instant willingness to accept responsibility. Back in the Lockheed days this had been a constant source of friction. Only one of them, but somehow symptomatic.

Wilt hurried up on his long legs, stocky CJ right behind him.

"Back to the jeeps, you two," Bart said. "Another rope. Litter. And you'd better bring an ax too."

"And," Carl said in his sardonic way, "you might throw in the first-aid pack." He watched them start off and he turned to Bart. His tone lost its mockery. "You want me to go down?" Mocking, even critical, Carl might be, but he was rarely found wanting when there was work to be done.

"I'm going," Bart said. He was already taking off his parka. He had a quick, almost apologetic smile for Steve, whose mouth was open in protest. "You're probably better on a rope than I am, but I'm bigger than you are and it's going to take some muscle to get into that mess." He swung one leg over the taut rope, held it tight with both hands and step by careful step began to let himself backward down the steep slope. His breath was visible as steam through the falling snow as he moved away from them.

"At least," Carl said, "we know where Jaime is, somewhere along the rope. Or near it. Sometimes in a slide like this you can't tell." He studied Steve's face carefully, and his medical training took over. "You okay?"

"No, I'm not okay." Steve's voice was suddenly low-pitched, bitter. "And I'm not going to pretend I am. I'm sick. One of the finest people I've ever known is down there, maybe dead, because he felt he had to try to help some people he doesn't even know who probably aren't even worth it and maybe aren't even there." Her eyes were on Bart as slowly, laboriously he made his backward way down. "And there goes another." She looked then at Carl in sudden defiance. "And if you make one of your flip remarks, I swear I'll belt you."

Carl's solemn nod was uncharacteristic, and without mockery. "Fair enough." In silence they both watched Bart.

The slide area was raw, and each careful step Bart took dislodged rocks and dirt which started more small slides. He kept his eyes on the slope immediately above him, glancing only occasionally over his shoulder, never looking up to the top of the mountain, where snow still clung that could, without warning, come loose to trigger further, larger slides.

The trick was to screen out of your mind all thought of possible consequences, to concentrate on your hands gripping the rope and your feet moving with slow care as in a minefield. His shoulders and arms already ached from the strain, but mere pain could be ignored. Hang in there, Jaime, he thought; we'll find you and get you out.

And then? They were still searching for a downed aircraft with a man of some apparent prominence in it, probably dead, but until they found him they could not be sure, and so the search would have to be resumed.

And the smashed car and trailer Jaime and Steve had seen, now completely buried beneath how much debris? That too would have to be checked out to find if the people presumably still inside were also alive or dead.

We'll need more troops after all, Bart thought; some to work here, some to carry on after that aircraft—*as long as the weather permits*. Even with his exertion and his own great resistance to cold, he could feel the temperature plummeting as predicted. Would it reach forty below? Even twenty below with any wind was not to be endured in the open. But in the meantime, Jaime took precedence.

He reached the tangle where the rope disappeared. Gingerly, not trusting the solidity of his footing, he eased his grip on the rope, and finally stood free. He took a deep breath, looked to the top of the slope, where he could dimly see Carl and Steve watching, and waved an okay signal. Then he bent to work.

First these rocks, one at a time, two or three of them as much as even his great strength could shift. Now this uprooted tree. Legs widespread, knees bent, back straight, he gripped and heaved, grunting, even sweating inside his clothing while frost grew on his eyebrows and cold numbed his fingers, following the rope's lead down into the slide debris where, somewhere, Jaime, or Jaime's body, lay.

He lost track of time. The snow stopped, and he was unaware. He worked on, relentlessly, steadily, until Wilt's voice beside him said, "Move over. Let me at it for a while."

Bart looked up then, hesitated and nodded slowly. "I'll take five."

Wilt was already at work pulling loose a branch. "Carl wants you up top. He'll come down. They're going to need your heft to haul the litter up."

Logical, of course, even if it went against the grain. Bart moved his heavy shoulders uneasily. "Okay," he said. He hesitated. "Take it easy with Jaime. He—" At a time like this there were no words. He turned away then, made his way over to the second rope down which Wilt had come and took a few deep breaths before he began his slow hand-over-hand ascent.

Steve met him at the top. Bart shook his head. "Not yet. But it isn't packed solid. If he's able, he can breathe." He watched Steve's eyes close briefly, and a shaky smile appeared.

CJ said, "Word from the State cops. CAP can't get into the air." He pointed northward to the dark, fast-moving front. Within it clouds churned and swirled as if at a slow boil. "It's bad enough here, but if a plane got caught in that—" He shook his head.

Bart was putting on his parka. He nodded. "First Jaime, then for as long as we can, we'll pick up the search for the plane."

"The lieutenant," CJ said, "has reported that Jaime is all our fault. He told us not to split up."

Steve said, "That isn't fair!"

"Let the lieutenant think what he wants," Bart said. "We'll do it our way." There was a faint edge to his voice. "If he actually starts messing up the operation—"

There was a shout from below. They all turned to look down. Wilt stood tall and straight on his long legs, his right hand raised, thumb and forefinger in a circle, the other three fingers extended in a gesture of triumph. His voice reached them faintly. "Alive! Send litter!"

"Oh, thank God!" Steve said. "Now I'm going to bawl!"

Carl opened his mouth for a comment, caught the

look on Bart's face and said merely, "On my way." He strapped on the first-aid pack, walked to the second rope and started down. "Send the litter after me."

The walkie-talkie in Bart's pocket came alive, and Bart took it out and spoke into it. "S&R here. Go ahead."

"Lieutenant Carter. The governor wants to speak to you on the jeep radio. Over."

Bart's eyes were on Carl making his way down the slope, on Wilt bending and working now with great care at the mass of debris. Only the jeep radio would reach down to the city. The walkie-talkies were for short-range work. "When I'm free to walk back down to the jeep," Bart said, "I'll be happy to talk to him. Over."

"He wants to talk to you now."

"Then," Bart said, "tell him to come up here. I'm busy. Over and out."

9.

It was a subdued and still dazed Warner who stared at the rocks and snow blocking the cave entrance. He looked at Ben. "Can we clear it?"

"We have to. With all that weight of rock they can't do anything from the inside."

The words had to be spoken, but Ben was not at all sure that what they said was meaningful. An entire section of the canyon wall, no doubt loosened by the slide the sonic booms had triggered, had fallen from the shock wave of Warner's shot, and in falling shattered. Much of the rock had gone past the trail and down thirty, forty feet into the canyon itself, but what had caught on the ledge was better suited to the power of a bulldozer than to the puny strength of two men without tools.

"Let's get to it," Ben said, and bent to seize the nearest rock fragment, which weighed perhaps fifty pounds, straighten with it and toss it off the ledge down the steep talus slope to the canyon floor.

Maybe they should have stayed with the car and trailer after all, he thought; and knew that he was thinking nonsense. Open fire inside the trailer would have been suicidal, and without fire they would not have lasted the night. If the weather forecast is right, even with a fire we may not last this one, he thought; always assuming that they could use the cave again as shelter.

Well, maybe he could have rigged a different shelter with his heavy plastic sheet large enough for all of them to crowd beneath it, with a fire at the entrance. Maybe—

Goddamn it, he told himself, knock it off! The only sensible solution would have been for him to keep right on walking alone, over the hump to that deserted cabin, and he had rejected that. Now with drifted snow on the road and trail, it was too late. What they had done was the next best thing. They had lasted the night, hadn't they? So, okay, so far, so good, and we'll goddamn well keep right on one step at a time. Angry with himself, angry with the world, "Slow down," he told Warner. "We've got a long haul, and busting your puckering string right at the beginning isn't going to help."

Warner's breath was already coming hard as he attacked the rocks with a savage fury. "My fault." The words came in gasps. "My own goddamn fault!"

Ben bent his knees, kept his back straight, and with the full strength of his thighs, using his arms merely as connecting cables, he heaved a two-hundred-pound rock away from the pile, over to the edge and down. He was breathing deeply, but not hard. "Okay," he said, "it's your fault, but beating your breast isn't going to help either. Slow down, goddamn it!"

On the telephone to Captain Lopez, Jake Boone said, "So, okay, they've found the car and trailer, where are they?"

"On the side of the mountain at ten thousand feet buried beneath a hundred tons of rocks and trees and snow." The captain was being brutal, he knew, but pulling your punches with Jake Boone got you nowhere.

Jake's voice changed. "Are they—in it? Warner and Sue Ann and the kids?"

"We don't know. One of the S&R men was trying to find out, and he got caught in a fresh slide. They're getting him out now. Then they'll try again to see if anybody's in the car and trailer, and to find that downed aircraft." If there's time before the new storm closes in, he thought, and did not say it aloud. CAP did not shy at shadows, and they had made it plain that what was coming from the north was going to make last night's heavy snow seem like spring. And the reports the captain had been getting from the northern counties bore out the prediction. The weather was no longer an impersonal force of nature; it had taken on a malevolent personality of its own.

"I don't give a good goddamn about Joe Martin and his flying machine," Jake Boone said. "He's always been a pain in the ass. All I care about is old Warner and his family. What the hell were they doing up there, anyway?"

"They must have taken a wrong turn."

"They sure as hell did."

The captain could not resist. "Maybe your directions were a little confusing, Mr. Boone. Had you thought of that?" The light on his phone began blinking furiously. "I have another call. When we know anything more, I'll get back to you." He punched the button and spoke his name.

It was the governor. "That what's-his-name Wallace says he's too busy to talk to me on the radio. I don't like that."

"Right now," the captain said, "Bart Wallace and his people are getting out one of their own men who

110

was caught in a slide. Or they're trying to get him out." Despite himself, there was a note of impatience in his voice. "I don't blame him a bit, Governor, for not wanting to take the time to walk on snowshoes back to their jeeps just to talk to you, or anybody else, until they have that man out and on his way either to the hospital or the morgue."

There was a short silence. "I've got a waiting room full of press and TV people," the governor said. "We've got a lost airplane with a state senator in it, and a lost car and trailer with a whole goddamn Oklahoma family. We're beginning to sound like Lower Slobbovia. Visit us, and disappear. Damn it, Inny, tourism is our biggest industry—" The governor stopped. He sighed. "Okay, I'm beginning to sound like one of my own campaign speeches. I'll tell the press about the heroic rescue efforts under way.'"

"Yes, sir." The captain smiled wearily.

"But," the governor said, bitterness plain again, "will you tell me why these horses' asses have to go and get themselves lost in the first place? We have road signs, don't we? And radio beacons for airplanes? Why can't people use their goddamned heads?"

At the top of the slide Bart strained on the rope and behind him CJ added his stocky strength. Foot by foot, Carl and Wilt moving with it and adding their help, the litter crept up the steep slope with Jaime strapped into it, motionless.

Jaime's eyes were open, and he was conscious, just. The injection Carl had given threatened to carry him momentarily into total oblivion. But he fought off the temptation to relax and let the sedative have its way. It was agony to breathe, and his entire body felt shattered beyond mending. He tried to ignore that. Carl's words as he made his quick examination and then the injection had been soothing, optimistic—and quite probably meaningless, merely for effect.

"You're one goddamned lucky Chicano," Carl had said, "even if you don't feel like it. Everything's going to be all right, fine."

The words were probably bullshit, which made it all the more important that he, Jaime, resist the temptation to slip out from under the weight of the pain at least until he could tell Bart what he knew, or thought he knew. Once he went under, he thought, who knew whether he would ever come back? And so he hung on and endured the jostling of the interminable journey up the slope down which he had come so easily on the rope.

And all at once the litter came from its steeply slanted position to dead level, the agonizing jostling stopped, and Steve's face was only inches from his own, smiling despite the trace of tears.

"Hi, *guapa,*" Jaime whispered.

"Hi."

Jaime's eyes went beyond Steve to Bart, who stood a few feet away, hands hanging loose at his sides, breathing in great gasps from his exertions on the rope. "Tell him," Jaime said slowly, painfully, each word an effort, "that while I was buried I—listened, and didn't hear a thing. If there's anybody in the car and trailer, they're probably dead." A pause, and a final effort which took the last of his strength and will "Okay?"

Steve swallowed hard. "Okay," she said gently. "Now rest."

And then at last he could close his eyes and let the sedative have its soothing way to oblivion.

Brady Shaw, paper cup of coffee in hand, crossed the office and stood looking down at the recording devices relaying temperature, barometric pressure, humidity, wind direction and velocity from the instrument complex on the building's roof.

His assistant came up beside him, papers in hand, and for once stood silent, temporarily subdued.

Brady's eyes were on the steadily dropping temperature line on the revolving drum. "January '71," he said almost as if he were speaking to himself, "it hit twenty-one below zero at the Santo Cristo airport and thirty-three below up at Española. Some poor goddamn Indians froze to death out west on the reservation, and cattle froze all over the place."

The assistant cleared his throat. Brady ignored it. "That same January," he said "temperatures went up into the seventies—more than a ninety-degree swing within the month. I damn near decided to take up another line of work, something sure and easy like telling fortunes from tea leaves." He did turn then to look at the other man. "What have you got?"

"The latest satellite pictures." The assistant's voice lacked its customary assurance.

"And?"

The assistant shook his head in near-disbelief. "You were right. That pressure system from the Gulf seems to be moving north and a little west."

"In our direction?" Brady nodded.

"Yes, sir."

"At the risk of sounding like a typical male chauvinist pig," Brady said after a few moments, "do you know why they name tropical storms after women?"

"No, sir."

"Because you can't tell what the hell they're going to do next." It was a throwaway line. Brady was already looking at the temperature recorder again. "Down into the mid-teens here on the flat," he said. He pointed to the wind velocity record. "Crank eighteen knots of wind in for your chill factor." He had a long sip of his cold coffee, and wrinkled his nose at the taste. "Then," he said, "multiply that by a factor of thirty-five hundred, four thousand feet of elevation." He looked straight at his assistant. "That's what they're up against in their search up there now. And when little Gussie or whatever you want to call her comes romping up from the Gulf, you'll really see these instruments go wild." He shook his head slowly. "And those poor bastards up there on the mountain will stay just as long as they can—hunting for people who are probably already dead. Don't ask me why."

They built the pyramids by hand, Ben was thinking, but that was in another, warmer country, and they had more than four hands. His arms, shoulders, back and thighs were all one large ache now, and there were bloody torn places in his gloves where sharp rock edges had gone through the leather and into flesh.

Warner was in worse shape. He breathed through his open mouth with a harsh, asthmatic sound, and he staggered when he walked, but he would not rest, or even slow down.

The mass of piled rock was perceptibly smaller, but there still remained much to be moved before they could catch even a glimpse of the cave entrance. And, Ben thought, God only knew what was going on inside.

True, Lila's voice had sounded reassuring, but that was some time ago, and close confinement in near-darkness could do strange things to people already under tension. Panic—Ben had seen it—could be a contagion.

And in a sense, he thought, I feel a kind of panic myself because I have allowed my—command to be separated, and I cannot rest until we are together again. Foolish concept, maybe, but there it was. He lurched to the edge with a rock almost too heavy to carry. "Down you go, you bastard." It was a personal matter now.

They took turns working the litter back down the road to the jeeps—Wilt and CJ one team; Bart and Carl the other.

"Damn it," Steve said, "I'm not helpless! Let me have some of the work."

"You're going to get plenty," Bart said. "Carl will take Jaime down. You and I will take up where Carl and I left off, sweeping over near the cirque."

"What about the car and trailer?"

Bart had been thinking about it ever since Steve had given him Jaime's message. Whatever he decided was a gamble, that was the only certainty in the entire complicated equation.

"We were lucky," he said. He had his breath back now, and he spoke to them all. "You and Jaime warned us. That whole area is unstable. If we get more snow, and we're going to, we could have another slide, probably will, and I'd hate to have more people down there if that happened."

"Four people, a whole family," Steve said, "against one man if we have to choose." She closed her eyes briefly. "We need more troops."

"Carl can call Bessie on his way down and have her start phoning. It's going to have to be a loose operation at best because we just don't have the time to set up any kind of base. Have a look."

They all followed Bart's pointing arm. The sky to the north was dark dirty gray with lighter evil cloud streamers racing ahead of the main mass. The air was perceptibly colder, and the wind was beginning to rise. The chill factor, Bart thought, was going to go well beyond even his power to endure.

"Tell Bessie," he said, speaking directly to Carl, "to call in say six, that's enough. You get Jaime into Emergency, and then see what you think. If you need an estimate of conditions up here, call Carter on the radio. If you think there's a chance, come on back up, and see what you can do about the car and trailer. But be careful. Go down through the trees, stay as clear of the slide area as you can. One look inside the car and the trailer will tell you all we need to know. If they're empty, forget them."

"And if they're full of deados?"

Steve shivered.

"Get them out if you can, but if it looks too dangerous, leave them. We're not risking more lives on the dead."

Maybe that was the right view, Bart told himself, and maybe it was wrong. Maybe at almost any cost, if only from the standpoint of morale, they should attempt to get out any bodies there might be inside the car and trailer. *We bury our dead,* that kind of thing, which strictly speaking applied only to wartime and to your own troops, comrades-in-arms.

And yet there was a distinct parallel here. The forces of nature, and the mountains themselves, these sometimes became the enemies, and all men and women who strove against them were comrades if not kin. The difference of locale, city to wilderness, was a difference of kind, not degree.

People in cities were just that, people, faceless and characterless, painted all over with the dull gray of uniformity, ants scurrying no man knew where, nor cared. As it had been back in the enormous factory and the sprawling city he had lived in.

But on mountain trails and roads you encountered individuals, recognizable, usually friendly with at least a wave, a nod or a smile as you passed, and frequently a few words or at need an offer to help. You shared, even if you did not mention, a sense of the grandeur and the vastness and the power of the overwhelming forces around you, and it was this that drew you again and again into the wilderness if for no other reason than to refresh yourself in the silence and the mystery and the marvel of the unspoiled natural world.

"I will lift up mine eyes unto the hills" was a cry from the heart as ancient and as universal as man himself, and those who echoed that cry were strangers no longer.

"I'll leave it up to you," Bart said. "Do what you think best. Then let Carter know. He's our base." For better or for worse, he thought; Carter was a weak reed to lean on, a flatlander, but they had no other. The jeep Carter would guard and the radios he would monitor were their life support systems.

Lieutenant Carter saw them coming, and got out of the jeep to stand silent, watching as they gently maneuvered the litter in through the tail gate and made it secure. Jaime did not move.

Carl leaned in and took Jaime's wrist in his fingers. Carl's face showed nothing as he searched for the pulse, then after a brief time gently replaced Jaime's hand and forearm beneath the litter covering and straightened up, closing the rear of the jeep. "We'll be on our way," he said.

Jaime's eyes were closed, his normally olive skin

had lost its color, and its texture was that of wax, shiny, tight, inanimate. Steve's eyes searched Carl's face. "He'll be—all right?"

"The sooner I get him there, the better off he'll be."

It was no answer, but it was the best she was going to get, Steve told herself. She merely nodded.

Bart said to her. "You'd better go along with them." His voice was gentle.

"No." Steve had straightened to her full height. "That would leave only three. You need two teams." Never one alone, never.

"I think—" Bart began.

"I told you, no!" Steve looked at Carl. "Well? The sooner you get there, you said. What are you waiting for?" She turned away.

Carl, watching her, hesitated only a moment, then walked slowly to the driver's door, opened it, and before entering had a quick, appraising look northward at the dark mass sweeping toward them. "You'd better watch it," he said. "Luck." He got in, started the engine and eased the jeep into slipping, sliding downhill motion. They watched until the car disappeared around the first turn.

"Okay," Bart said, "let's move out. Stay in touch." His voice turned gentle. "Come on, Steve."

"I told you," Carter said, "that the governor wanted to talk to you."

Bart had completely forgotten. It had seemed unimportant, and was. But he nodded now. "See if you can raise him. Wilt, you and CJ take out."

"And," Carter said, "I don't want you to split up again. If you had listened to me last time—"

Bart had pushed back the hood of his parka. His vast patience exhausted at last, he said now in an oversoft voice, "Friend, don't push it. This is our country, and flatland dudes just get in the way. Get the governor on the blower and I'll talk to him. And then you stay right here while we go on about our business, which is trying to find a lost aircraft with a man in it."

Carter hesitated. Wilt and CJ were already moving

off, the tall and the short, awkward-seeming on their snowshoes but moving steadily, purpose clear. And this big man looking down at Carter merely watched, and waited, unyielding, immovable. Carter turned away, got into the jeep and began to fuss with the radio.

Steve shut away her thoughts of Jaime and watched Bart's face. It did not change. He locks himself in, she thought, and locks the world out. It was a sad concept, and she found herself thinking again of Jaime and his usual cheerful openness so different in all ways. Please, God, she thought; please see that he is all right!

They could not hear Carter's words, but the response through the radio speaker was clearly audible: "Frank Silva here, Lieutenant. The governor's busy at the moment. In twenty minutes, a half hour, he'll be able to talk. Over and out."

Carter hung up the microphone and got out of the jeep.

"We heard," Bart said. "Let's go, Steve." He turned away and started off, compass in hand. Steve put Jaime again from her mind, and followed.

Carter opened his mouth, thought better of speaking and closed it again in silence.

Inside the cave Billy said suddenly, "I saw this movie once on TV. It was miners, you know, down in a coal mine. There'd been a cave-in." The word for what he felt and could no longer ignore, he knew, was claustrophobia; he had looked it up once, and with his capacity for almost total recall, never forgotten: fear of closed or narrow spaces; only the dictionary called it abnormal dread, which made it sound like something loony, and his only problem now was that he was a little short of breath, *and he couldn't stop talking*.

"They were running out of air," he said, "and that was bad enough, but there was this one guy, he'd been in a cave-in once before, and he was beginning to flip.

Every time a little piece of rock fell, he'd get the shakes. He—"

"Billy," Lila said across the cold gloom of the cave, "I don't like this any better than you do and neither does Patty and neither does your mother. So forget the movie. They're getting us out." *I hope,* she thought.

The dust had settled inside the cave, and no rock fragments had fallen for some time, but the memory of that deep earth shudder was still vivid, the kind of thing you could not forget. If the earth itself was unstable, where was security?

"It was only a movie," Billy said, "but things like that do happen."

"Okay," Lila said, "they happen." Only a little while ago, she thought, the boy was suddenly a grownup. Now all at once he had reverted. It was that yo-yo behavior in the young that was so baffling to everybody, the young themselves included. Perhaps stimulated by her talk with Patty, she could remember now her own violent fluctuations between the poles of confidence and shyness, boldness and fear; the feeling that she was a person, attractive and personable, and that she was nothing at all, just a mess, as she had said, whom nobody would want around for even a second.

"There's a game we used to play," Patty said in the gloom. Her voice was quiet, even subdued, but in it there was determination. "You take a letter of the alphabet, and the next person has to say another letter, and the first one who finishes a word loses. I'll take *a.*"

Good for her, Lila thought; and felt a warmth growing in her mind. *"P,"* she said. "Billy?"

"That's a nutty game," Billy said. And then, unable to contain the thought, "What if there's another slide? How about that?"

"Another *p,*" Patty said. And, with no change of tone, "He used to wet the bed, too."

Sue Ann, in pain, heard the talk as if from a great

distance. Her ear was acute and she heard, too, faint but growing sounds of activity outside, a rattle of rock on rock as the men clawed at the pile of debris, an occasional grunt of effort and the whistling sound of breath expelled under pressure.

Even to her in the sleeping bag, the cave was perceptibly colder now that Billy had reduced the fire to a tiny flickering flame. That weather forecast they had heard on Billy's transistor radio had warned of severe cold and maybe outside the cave the temperature had already dropped alarmingly.

Then what?

Sue Ann tried to shake away the question and the implications it made plain. Think positively. That was all very well as a slogan, but until you tried it and failed, you didn't realize how hollow an admonition it was.

How did one die of cold? Slowly? Painfully? Or was it actually, as she had once read, more like going into a sleep from which there was no awakening?

However it came, death was the final experience, unless of course you had faith in an afterlife—and she was doubtful. When you were young, death was unreal; you were immortal, life stretched ahead endlessly and time dragged. But as you grew older time speeded up, and although you could not see an end, you became aware that it was there, and one day, you knew, you would come around a corner or walk through a door and find yourself quite suddenly face to face with extinction.

Like now, she thought. Lying here in this place where we have no business being, all familiarity left behind, I can almost reach out and touch the end, my end, the end of us all.

And paradoxically, although she had no desire to die, the temptation to relax and let happen what would was almost overpowering. At last she could understand the full meaning of the word *resignation*.

The sounds outside the cave were clearer now, and

120

it seemed to Sue Ann that the men were redoubling their efforts, working at frantic speed to clear the entrance. But why? As sometimes in that strange world between sleep and full consciousness, her mind drifted off in its own logical-illogical directions.

This cave could be our tomb. Sealed in like the Pharaohs we could lie here undiscovered through the ages, no fuss, no muss, no bother to anyone. Maybe one day someone would find the cave entrance, and our bodies, and wonder what strange chain of circumstances could possibly have led us to this last resting place.

Patty's voice intruded on these drifting thoughts. "A-p-p-l," Patty said. "I don't see any word but 'apple.'"

And Billy's voice sharp with disgust, "How about 'applicable'?"

It was hard for Lila not to laugh aloud in sheer pleasure that somehow, at least partly through her own small efforts, both Patty and Billy had climbed up out of that morass of despondency she had from time to time known so well. She felt stronger herself, uplifted. "Welcome back, Billy," she said.

And it was then, almost on cue, that a glimmer of gray daylight appeared at the cave entrance, and with a rattling clatter of rocks the entrance opened, and Warner began to squeeze through.

The blood on his forehead and cheek had clotted and was mingled now with sweat and grime. His hands were bleeding, but he seemed unaware. He breathed in great whistling gasps. Still on hands and knees, looking down at Sue Ann, "Are you all right?" The words came out with effort.

She could only nod.

Billy said, disgust again sharp in his voice, "They've been playing word games."

Warner looked around at them all. In his face there was no comprehension, only bewilderment, and his eyes seemed filled with surprise. His mouth opened, but no sound came out. And then, all at once, his arms collapsed and he fell forward on his face to lie

121

motionless in the cold dust and the dirt of the cave floor.

Patty screamed.

Carl had the jeep in four-wheel drive and low transmission for maximum traction and control. Normally the road was wide enough, well marked and well graded, but eighteen hours of snowfall and consequent drifting from the wind had narrowed the passage to a single lane marked only by faint depressions here and there locating the tracks the two jeeps had made struggling uphill early that morning.

The snow-laden tops of tall pines on the right side of the road indicated the drop-off. On the left it was not possible to tell exactly where blacktop ended and dirt bank began, but the trees and brush of the forest beyond were plain enough, thickly grown and to a wheeled vehicle impenetrable.

Carl drove slowly, carefully, using both accelerator and occasional brake with care, and steering as small as conditions permitted lest sudden overcontrol send the jeep into a slithering skid which could carry it over the drop-off.

Carl had grown up in the mountain country and learned to drive on mountain roads; his skills were automatic, and his basic thoughts now were on Jaime, still strapped to the litter angled inside the rear of the jeep body.

If there was still a pulse in Jaime's wrist, Carl's finger had failed to find it, but, admittedly, those fingers were cold almost to the point of numbness, so the failure was inconclusive.

Jaime looked like a dead man; Carl was prepared to admit that, and in his own way he was sorry that Steve had had to see it. But Carl had also seen patients who looked as bad recover with astonishing speed, and so he was making no final judgment.

He had heard once that years ago, at Bellevue in New York, he thought it was, any young medico who went out on an ambulance call and brought a DOA (Dead on Arrival) into Emergency instead of to the morgue automatically stood the Emergency staff to beer.

Well, that didn't apply in Santo Cristo, and even if it did, the hell with it. Jaime wasn't just another accident case; Jaime was a man Carl had worked with on rescues, a good man, one of the best Carl knew, and Emergency was where he was going just as fast as Carl could get him there, and unless or until examination under hospital conditions said different, in Carl's mind Jaime was still alive.

For the moment the road was relatively straight and the early morning tracks plain to follow. Carl took one hand from the wheel to switch on the CB, turn to Channel 9, the emergency channel, and pick up the mike. "Breaker on nine, breaker! Come on!"

"Go, breaker." The response was quick, and heartening, a flat, unexcited Anglo voice.

"This is Pipefitter and I'm coming downhill off the ski basin road with a injured man headed for hospital Emergency. Are the roads plowed and open?"

"Ten-four." Mere acknowledgment of the question. "The last we heard, crews were out and working, Pipefitter, but it's been snowing and drifting hard. That's our best info. Do you need assistance?"

So we're on our own, Carl thought. Okay, so be it. "Negatory. I got four-wheel drive and I'll go cross-country if I have to. Will you call hospital Emergency and tell them I'm on my way in? We'll need a medico standing by. My man was caught in a rock slide. Probable fractures. Maybe internal injuries."

Again that flat, reassuring, unexcited Anglo voice. "Ten-four Pipefitter. We'll have medical assistance waiting. Luck."

"Obliged. KZN nine-nine-eight-four; we're down." Carl hung up the mike. "Okay, Jaime," he said, "the best we can do for the moment. Just hang on." He was not heard by the inert body in the litter, he knew, but it made no difference. He drove on, concentrating.

Despite his skill and care the jeep suddenly slithered and swung. He corrected it with a touch of throttle, automatically avoiding the brake.

123

The tracks of the morning had disappeared. He steered by guesswork, midway between the drop-off, which he could see, and the imaginary line where he assumed the ditch on the uphill side would be.

It began to snow again gently, almost lazily at first, and then with astonishing speed harder and harder until what blew against and swirled around the windshield was a blizzard in intensity. Carl switched on the windshield wipers and their steady swish-swish mingled with the engine sounds to disturb the quiet.

So that pretty well settled it, he thought. Bart and the others could get downhill in the remaining jeep, but it would be some time before anything would be able to go up this road. The storm they had predicted from the north had arrived. "Snow, you bastard," he said. "We'll beat you anyway!"

In La Cantina Connie had the radio turned low, tuned to the program music of the local FM station. Only a handful of her regulars had turned up for breakfast, and since they had gone no one else had appeared. It was no wonder, she thought. Now, after a brief period of respite, snow had begun again, and the midmorning sky had turned dark as evening.

Bart was very much in her thoughts today. Last night was more than just an interlude; she knew that now. Something in her had reached out and touched something in him, and what might have been mere animal pleasure in mating had suddenly metamorphosed into a mystical communion between man and woman. The full implications were only now coming through to her.

She had no words for what she felt. Love, to her, had always been an intangible so battered around in song lyrics as to be almost wholly meaningless. And yet the feelings described in some of those same lyrics did actually exist and were with her now.

For the first time, she thought she understood what it was that impelled Bart and the others into their Search and Rescue operations, driving them in this kind of weather into mountain terrain to try to help people they did not even know and might very well not want to know if they had a choice. The word "humanity" was as close as she could come to summing it all up. It was a word that for her had never really had meaning before.

She had always been, she supposed, a loner, carrying her inner thoughts, and scars, in secret, exposing them for no man, no woman, and looking at the world through eyes that if not actually hostile, yet tended to view with suspicion those who would approach her closely.

Last night had somehow altered that, and almost without realizing it, with Bart she had let down the barriers that had always held the world out, flung wide the windows, as it were, and let the light and the warmth flood in.

She found that she was smiling now as she thought of the big, gentle man lying beside her, except for that single outcry sleeping as quietly, as peacefully as a child; and she, awake, in a sense guarding him while he slept. Could there be a lifetime like that?

The program music on the radio stopped abruptly. "We interrupt this program," the announcer's voice said, "to bring you a bulletin. It is reported that there has been an avalanche in the nearby mountain area where the search is under way for the missing aircraft containing State Senator Joseph Martin of Roswell. A member of the search team has been reported caught in the avalanche. Rescue efforts are in progress, but it is not known at this time whether the victim is alive or dead. When further details are available, KTFM will bring them to you. We now resume our scheduled program of music."

Connie closed her eyes. She opened them again and walked slowly to the coffee urn. She found that her hands were trembling as she half filled a cup and tried to drink from it. How do you pray, she asked herself, when you know no god?

Partially bent against the blowing snow, CJ trudged on in his stocky muscular way, swinging his head from

125

side to side searching each tree clump, suspicious mound and thicket for a sign of the downed aircraft. Wilt, on his long legs, was only dimly visible seventy-five yards off to CJ's right on a parallel course. It was silent, and colder.

CJ enjoyed solitude. At his easel or presiding over a hotel kitchen broiler, as now, he could be alone with his thoughts, or rather, with the almost kaleidoscopic visual impressions that crowded into his mind, left their imprint and faded into new forms and shapes and colors.

Here the world was white-on-white, the falling snow by its patterns and texture different from the shadows and brilliance of the snow already fallen; and the occasional sharp lines and angles of bare branches or rock facets contributed to the surrealistic scene, constantly changing.

Any picture of the scene would be a perfect bitch to catch on canvas, he thought, because unless you could somehow convey the cold that went with it, the cold that seeped through layers of clothing right into your bones, you would have merely somebody's pretty post-card, Currier and Ives, ho!, and that was not the kind of thing CJ gave a damn about.

Over and above the cold, or underlying it, however you wanted to look at it, he thought, would have to be something that conveyed the sense of urgency as well that had brought Wilt and himself and the others up here to try to find these lost pilgrims from car, trailer and airplane, and lead them by the hand back down out of the big bad mountains again into the safety of civilization; and just how could that be captured in pigment on canvas?

Jesus, it was cold! It was—

He stopped suddenly as new, sharp shadows in the snow caught his eyes, and he stared down unbelieving for a little time before he curled his tongue against his teeth and chilled lower lip and blew a single piercing whistle blast that brought Wilt up short. CJ waved his arm in a beckoning gesture, and watched Wilt come striding toward him, lifting his knees high like a trotting horse to clear his snowshoes at each step.

"What have you got?" Wilt's breath came out in steam quickly dissipated in the driving snow.

CJ merely pointed at the ground.

There were tracks, large tracks, human-like and yet not human, turned in, with claw marks showing— bear tracks, plain in the snow, and fresh.

Wilt pursed his lips and whistled softly. He lifted his head and almost seemed to sniff the air like a hunting dog as he looked carefully in the general direction the tracks pointed. There was only the falling snow to be seen.

CJ said, "What do you think? A big black?" He hesitated. "Not grizzly, for God's sake."

Wilt shook his head. He could even smile stiffly, without amusement. "What difference? He was probably holed up and one of the snow and rock slides woke him up and drove him out in the open, and I wouldn't like to meet him no matter which he is, but I think he's a black bear, big and probably with a short fuse after being disturbed." He got out his walkie-talkie. "Better tell Bart and *chica*. Wilt calling Bart. Come in, Bart . . . We're down below that north wall, and what we've got you aren't going to believe . . ."

Wilt put the walkie-talkie back into his pocket. He beat his hands together. "Let's get on with it. Keep an eye out for that bear."

CJ shifted his shoulders inside his heavy parka. He blew steam. "Jesus, it's cold!"

Wilt studied him appraisingly as he might have studied a pack-horse showing signs of fatigue on the trail. "You okay?"

"Hell, yes, I'm okay! For now, anyway. Let's find this goddamn airplane so we can go home."

Bart tucked his radio back into his pocket. He looked through the trees at Steve and waved his arm reassuringly as he started forward again. From the start to as far as they had gone, he thought, this entire

127

operation had been jinxed. And now this new factor to consider. A bear? Incredible. But CJ and Wilt knew their mountains as few did, Wilt in particular. And there were bears. And bear tracks were unmistakable. All right, Bart told himself, so now we've got a bear to watch out for too.

He waved again at Steve, and watched her answering wave of acknowledgment. That Jaime business had hit her hard, he thought, and probably he ought to have insisted that she go down the hill in the jeep with Carl to see what the hospital people said. On the other hand, she had been exactly right in saying that her going would cripple them, leave them with only one team of two, and so, being Steve, she had stayed. How many would have?

He leaned forward against the wind and snow and, like CJ, swung his head from side to side as he moved his snowshoes in steady rhythm. Cold, and getting colder; if it kept up like this he was going to have to make the decision in not too long to abandon the search until conditions improved. There was nothing else for it. You did as much as you could, and after that you did maybe a little more, straining to the limit, but sooner or later you reached the point at which you had to turn back at least temporarily, and that was all there was to it. Bitter thought. Particularly after last time and the dead hunter, bitter, bitter thought.

Warner was a dead weight, totally inert, his body and his limbs seemingly disconnected. Ben scrambled through the entrance as quickly as he could after hearing Patty's scream, sized up the situation, tried once to roll Warner over and failed. Then he set himself and heaved and the heavy body at last turned to lie face up, eyes closed.

Ben pulled off his torn gloves, grasped the big man's wrist and searched for a pulse. There was none. Nor did Warner's chest move in respiration. Oh, Jesus, Ben thought; now this. But which came first, breathing or heartbeat?

Patty said, "Daddy!" She was on her knees beside him. "He isn't breathing!"

"Goddamn it," Ben said, "I can see that. We've got to—" he began, and stopped in surprise.

Patty had rolled her father's head to the side, pried open his jaws and pulled out his tongue with her thumb and forefinger. Now, bending close, she closed his nostrils with one hand, and holding his mouth open with the other, pressed her own mouth tight to his and strongly exhaled a deep breath. Warner's chest rose a little. When Patty removed her mouth from his, Warner's chest fell again. She took another deep breath, placed her mouth again on her father's and exhaled with a strong, steady pressure.

Ben waited to see no more. Kneeling beside Patty, he placed the heel of his right hand flat against the left side of Warner's rib cage about a third of the way down, and placed his other hand flat on top of the first. He rolled forward on his knees until his weight was exerting pressure straight down on Warner's breastbone. Immediately he relaxed the pressure, waited only an instant and repeated. What was the rhythm? Once a second? Silently he began to count, one chimpanzee, two chimpanzee, three chimpanzee . . . pressure on the numbers, relax between.

If the books were right, it might work, he thought, unless whatever had happened—what was that ridiculous-sounding word, infarction?—had really torn it and the big heart muscle was ruptured beyond hope. Six chimpanzee, seven chimpanzee, eight . . .

Patty worked steadily, rhythmically at the mouth-to-mouth breathing. You would know when at last the patient could breathe for himself, the Red Cross lifeguard instructor had said; keep at it until you are sure. Now, in the emergency and activity, all of the doubts and self-worries had suddenly fallen away. Her mind was free of everything but this: I won't let you down, Daddy!

Sue Ann's eyes were closed, the pain in her foot and ankle forgotten along with those drifting thoughts of only a few minutes ago. Please, God, please!

Billy watched in fascination, while one part of his stunned mind immediately grasped the principle of Ben's pressure-and-release, and in an almost detached way examined it. Compress the heart, and push blood out into the arteries; relax the pressure and some blood theoretically would flow into the heart from the veins—artificial circulation. Neat. The wonder was that the rib cage and the breastbone were elastic enough—

"Let's build that fire up, Billy," Ben said. "We're going to need some warmth in here." We need to try for warmth, anyway, he thought. Even if it may be futile, goddamn it, we'll try. Twelve chimpanzee, thirteen chimpanzee . . .

Lila watched quietly. Quite a fellow, Ben, she thought. And Patty was showing that basically she was quite a girl too. In only how many short hours had she, Lila, come to know each of these people better than she knew most of her friends? Strange.

You went along your own way for years—what were the cant phrases, maintaining a low profile, making no waves?—in effect merely serving your time. She was beginning to see that now. You gave tit for tat, but no more, and called it even. But was that really the way to live?

Take Joe Martin, nice guy now hanging upside down, frozen. How much did she really ever know of him? He was good for lightness and laughter, liked to wine and dine well, liked their times together in bed. But we never went beyond that, never beneath the surface, never even asking the hard questions, let alone trying to put answers to them.

Her eyes were still on Ben and his steady rocking motion, which Lila vaguely understood had to have something to do with trying to start up a heart that had stopped. But why? It was a strange thought coming out of nowhere. When you came right down to it, what business really was it of Ben's whether Warner lived or died? Dead, Warner would be less trouble, a lot less, wouldn't he? Like Joe, out of sight, almost out of mind?

But what about me? she asked herself. Do I really care whether Warner lives or dies? If I could, would I walk out now and leave them, all of them, save myself and never look back? Would Ben? No, Ben would not; he's proving it further now. But would I? There was the hard question, and in honesty she did not know the answer. I know what I hope the answer would be, she thought; and suddenly seeing herself clearly, she added: and I guess that's something of a switch in itself. But I can't be sure, can I? And I am ashamed that I cannot.

One of Warner's feet stirred. His right hand opened and closed, and he waggled his head weakly against the pressure of Patty's mouth.

Ben stopped his rocking motion and bent to put his ear flat against Warner's ribs. In that cavernous chest he thought he could hear a heartbeat. He grasped a wrist and felt a pulse, weak, but detectable. He caught the girl's shoulder. "See if he can breathe by himself, Patty."

Patty straightened slowly to sink back on her heels, pressed the back of her hand against her mouth and held her breath while she watched. Warner's chest rose and expanded; fell as he exhaled. He took another breath, and another.

"Oh, God!" Patty said, and the tears began then, tears of pure relief.

"Hey," Ben said, "hey!" He caught her chin in his bloody, grimy hand, and turned her head to face him. He was smiling! "Good girl," he said. "You'll do."

Sue Ann closed her eyes again. Thank you, she said silently, oh, thank you!

Lila watched, unmoving, feeling somehow locked out.

10.

IN THE GOVERNOR'S OFFICE, Associated Press said, "That one Warner Harlow rings a bell: Wait a minute, wait a minute—Oklahoma U. in the glory days, Warner Harlow was a pulling guard, and the only reason Jake Boone ever got All-America mention. There'll be people remember him who never even heard of Joe Martin."

Great, the governor thought, ginger-peachy, a lost football hero!

UPI said, "Just what is being done to find these people, Governor? I mean, no air search—"

"Look," the governor said, "You've seen the weather. Light planes can't fly. That's exactly what happened to Joe Martin."

TV-7 said, "What was he doing here, anyway, Governor? His flight plan said Roswell to Tucumcari."

"When we find him, if he's still alive, you can ask him."

UPI said, "Let me get this straight, Governor. They haven't found the plane."

"Not yet."

"They did find a car and trailer. Or somebody saw one, is that right? Was anybody in it?"

"We don't know."

"Was it the Harlows' car and trailer?"

AP said, "If it wasn't, we've got somebody else lost too. Let's not louse it up any more than it already is. Why isn't that road closed to traffic, Governor? Shouldn't it be? I mean, it doesn't go anywhere."

"The men use it, hunters. There are picnic benches by the lake."

132

"What are the chances of getting this fellow Wallace down here where we can talk to him?"

"He's busy running the search operation. I'm not going to interfere with that. I've tried to talk with him by radio, but so far we haven't been able to get together."

"That avalanche, and the man caught in it, is he alive, hurt bad, dead?"

"We don't know yet."

UPI closed his notebook with a snap. There was impatience in his voice. "How can we get to the horse's mouth, Governor? I mean, no offense, but we get it from you, and all you know is what you got from Captain Lopez, and he got it from his secretary, who got it by radio—" UPI shook his head. "When a story goes through that many people it begins to get garbled. And people down in Roswell want to know. And there are probably people in Oklahoma who want to know too. What I mean, we want to get the facts as straight as we can, right?"

They were not the only ones, the governor thought; there was also Jake Boone beginning to talk about calling Washington and talking to the state's two congressmen and senators, and what the hell good Jake thought that would do was more than the governor could understand, but there it was. This thing was building into something that could explode.

In sudden decision the governor pointed a finger at his aide, Frank Silva, standing in the rear of the office. "Get on the blower, Frank. That man of Lopez's up there, Lieutenant Whoever-he-is. He won't be doing anything and they can spare him. Get him down here. He can bring us up to date."

Captain Lopez had had an hour's catnap, but he was not at all sure he wouldn't have felt better without it.

The weather reports on his desk indicated that things were going to get far worse before they even began to improve; despite all efforts, road conditions throughout the state were worsening, and one by one

133

all highways connecting Santo Cristo with the outside world had to be closed, and none too soon; there was a fourteen-car pile-up on I-25 north of Santo Cristo where the last cars to get through before roadblocks were set up had without warning hit glare ice on an overpass and skittered around like so many hockey pucks—no serious injuries reported yet . . .

The captain shook a fresh cigarette from his pack now as he answered his secretary's question: "That's standing policy. Leave the press to the governor's office."

"Yes, sir." The secretary had thought that would be the answer, but he had thought it prudent to ask anyway. "The gas company is shutting off gas to the Parque area. They say there isn't sufficient pressure to service their customers there *and* in Santo Cristo itself."

The captain took the news with a small glimmer of satisfaction. So others were having their problems too, were they? Parque was a wealthy community, the horsey people, and there were going to be screams. For once, he would not be the target.

"And," the secretary said, "there is a bear reported where the S&R people are working. They say they saw his tracks, Lieutenant Carter reports. He was monitoring their walkie-talkies."

The captain thought about it. It sounded unlikely. "Get me Cardoza in Game and Fish." While he waited, he lighted the cigarette and took three welcome drags. When the phone buzzed he picked it up and spoke his name. "Pete? What are the chances of a bear being loose around the ten-thousand-foot level near that White Peak road?" He listened quietly. "Wallace's people, Search and Rescue, say they saw tracks." He listened again. He sighed. "Okay, if you say so, Pete, thanks."

He hung up, and looked at his secretary. "Cardoza says if they say they saw tracks, there are tracks. They know their business. And there has been a bear seen in that area, a big one. Mean." The captain shook his head. "Problems come in litters sometimes,

134

like malevolent mice. Does Carter have a rifle? Just in case?"

"I don't think so, sir, but I'll try to find out."

Lieutenant John Carter was not an imaginative man, and he had long ago decided that his best approach to as much rank as he could achieve and an eventual comfortable pension was behavior by the book, and strict, unquestioning obedience to commands from his superiors. But there was no book to cover his present assignment, and he was not at all sure what he was supposed to do besides sit in the jeep monitoring both the UHF and the walkie-talkies Bart Wallace and his people carried with them.

It was cold, and getting colder, and the snow which had recently begun to fall in a tentative fashion was heavier now. And there was wind rising. Every few minutes, mostly for want of something better to do, Carter got out of the jeep and brushed clear the windshield and all the windows. He considered starting up the jeep's engine and turning on the heater, and decided against it until the temperature dropped a little further. Energy was precious, and gasoline was to be conserved wherever possible. There were department bulletins to that effect.

Since that exchange about the bear, for some time now he had heard nothing on the walkie-talkies, and it was easy almost to forget that there were four persons out there somewhere in the snow and the cold, slogging along on snowshoes for motives that were beyond the lieutenant's comprehension. Who knew how amateurs thought?

It was Carter's view that sooner or later, of course, Search and Rescue would be brought under some kind of official control, perhaps even as part of the State Police, and then matters would be handled in a more sensible fashion with regulations and planning and above all organization. It would no longer be a loose amalgam of garage mechanics and plumbers and wood-carvers and even female potters; it would be professional. Perhaps with this experience as an ob-

135

server, he, John Carter, would be qualified to take command—although he would not allow himself to think too far in that direction because it might never come to pass.

The walkie-talkie came alive. "Wilt here. Come in, Bart."

"Bart here. Come on."

"Negative on this sweep. We're heading east, toward you."

"Roger. Any sign of that bear?"

"Negative, thank God. I think he may be heading for one of those caves on the canyon wall to hole up again. In this weather if I had my druthers, that's sure as hell what I'd do. How's *chica* making out?"

Steve's voice said, "I can outwalk you any day in the week."

Wilt's voice held a chuckle. "That's the gung-ho spirit. Over and out."

In a professional organization, Carter thought, there would be none of this joking chatter. It would be strictly business. It—

The UHF came alive, and Carter took the mike from its clip to acknowledge.

"Frank Silva here, Lieutenant. The governor wants you."

"Yes, sir. Put him on."

"He wants you down here. Now."

Carter hesitated.

"Did you hear me, Lieutenant?"

"Yes, sir. I mean, affirmative. It's just that—"

"Then haul your ass down here. The governor's in no mood to argue. Over and out." The carrier wave hum ceased.

Sue Ann had worked her way out of the sleeping bag, and now sat braced against the wall of the cave, the injured foot and ankle straight out in front of her. "Warner needs warmth more than I do."

Ben nodded. There was bound to be shock, and warmth was essential. Getting Warner's mass into the sleeping bag, though, was going to take some doing. "Billy, Lila, give us a hand."

Warner's eyes were open, but comprehension came and went. Like a litany, a voice deep within his mind kept repeating a name, Warner Harlow, Warner Harlow, as if by mere repetition he, himself, the man who once had been, could be restored. And through it all was the tearing chest pain that would not stop.

He rolled his head and tried to bring his eyes into focus. There was the cave, and the flickering fire casting shadows on walls and ceiling, the smell of piñon smoke and the murmur of voices heard as if from a distance, hushed voices filled with concern.

There were shapes of people. He knew them, but through the pain it was difficult to remember who they were, which was ridiculous because they were his family, *his* family, and, sudden, painful memory, he alone was responsible for their being here.

A familiar voice, soft, gentle, said, "Just rest. Let them move you. It will be all right, and we'll have help soon." Sue Ann's face swam in the haze of pain, and smoke seemed to come from her mouth as she spoke. Strange; Sue Ann did not smoke.

Breathing was difficult and painful, but breath he had to have and could not get enough. And there was growing cold in his body and in his mind. He felt hands grasp his legs, his shoulders and his arms, and he felt himself being lifted and then lowered again, not ungently. A man's voice said, "Get his boots off and loosen his belt." That was the big man, the stranger, what was his name? Ben?

"Rest," Sue Ann said. "You're going to be all right. You're going to be fine."

"Let's get that fire built up, Billy," the man's voice said.

"We're almost out of wood."

"Use up what we have."

Lila straightened from her efforts and laid one of Warner's cowboy boots off to one side. Then, with Patty, Billy and Ben she helped arrange the huge, limp body in the sleeping bag.

137

"Hot-water bottles to warm him we don't have," Ben said in a low angry voice, rose and crossed the cave to his pack.

Lila followed and knelt beside him. She kept her voice quiet, for his ear only. "Now what?"

"It ought to be obvious."

Lila shook her head. "Let's say I'm a little dull. Spell it out for me."

"Goddamn it," Ben said, his voice as quiet as hers, "how long do you think he can last without oxygen, shots of some kind, God knows what-all? He's had a coronary and he belongs in coronary care, not here in this goddamned cave dying slowly. Or fast."

"So?"

"So what do you think?"

"You're going to have another try for help. How? Did you get to the plane with the note?"

"No."

Lila closed her eyes briefly. "So where do you think you can get this time?"

"Maybe the road. Maybe—" Ben shook his head. "Do you think I can just sit here and watch?"

"We lose you," Lila said, "and we're dead. All of us. Have you thought of that?"

"Maybe. Maybe I've thought of something else too. It's snowing again and the temperature's dropping. You heard that weather prediction. Sooner or later we'll run out of wood. We sit here and just hope, and we're all dead."

Lila was silent for some time. She said at last, "You really mean that?"

"I haven't been kidding for a long time." He started past her. "Now let me get at it."

"Tell me where you're going. Exactly where."

"Why?"

She stood silent, unyielding, but also unwilling to put words to the answer.

"You have some silly idea," Ben said slowly, "of coming to find me if I don't get back when you think I should?" He shook his head. "Uh-uh. No heroics. If

I don't get back, I don't get back and you do the best you can with the kids to help."

She was thinking again of Joe as she had seen him last, hanging from his seat harness in the shattered plane. "I'm turning into a jinx," she said. "If I hadn't been with him, Joe would have gone to Tucumcari instead of here. Now this—"

"That's silly too. If you look hard enough you can always find something to blame yourself for. What might have been, and all that jazz."

I wonder what might have been with you to make you angry with the world, she thought, and said nothing as she watched Ben cross the cave, pause to look down at Warner, at Sue Ann, and nod to them both. Then he dropped to his knees at the cave entrance. "Luck," Lila said in a voice that carried. She hoped no one heard the tremble that was in it.

It was slow, slogging work searching the area, and it was made more difficult now by the fresh falling snow. And the cold. From time to time Bart looked carefully at Steve as she mushed along on her snowshoes, fifty, seventy-five yards away, no more, but scarcely visible in sudden snow flurries.

She looked all right, and once she saw him watching her, and she waved without slackening her steady pace. Quite a girl. Somebody to go along with. Connie came to mind too. Neither of them at all like one he tried not to remember.

Despite himself he felt rare anger growing at their apparent ineffectiveness. And in his mind there grew a sense that time was running out. You would have thought, he told himself, that in an area as limited as this, something as large as an airplane could not be hidden—and he knew that his thinking was without foundation.

In the first place, they were in effect simply guessing that this was indeed the area. A fix from only two bearings, if not always suspect, was frequently undependable; a third bearing would have narrowed the margin of error considerably. And anyway quick bearings from high-flying aircraft at near-sonic speeds taken from a ground signal that in these mountains could have been reflected any which way—guesswork was a flattering name for their search premise.

The odds, of course, had been against them from the start. What you needed in an operation like this was a base established with a communications center and teams working out on predetermined sweeps, constantly in touch, combing the area—but there simply had not been time for that kind of organization, and that was that.

They would have to do with what they had as long as they could before the weather drove them back down to Santo Cristo, and that would not be long. In the sub-zero cold that was predicted and he knew in his bones was coming, there was no way the search could be continued. Either they lucked out now, or they waited for another day.

He looked again at Steve. She waved and plodded on.

The Emergency entrance to the Santo Cristo hospital was through the new parking lot, and the wooden arm across the roadway was supposed to rise automatically when you came in. (When you tried to leave, the arm rose only after you inserted either $.25 or a properly punched plastic card.)

The arm, its mechanism frozen, did not rise when Carl swung the jeep in from the snow-covered street and checked its skidding swing with a touch of the throttle. The hell with the non-functioning arm; the jeep's sudden forward surge shattered the wood, and in four-wheel drive they plowed a double furrow across the empty lot. Carl pulled up at the Emergency dock, swung and backed neatly into position before he jumped out to open the tail gate.

A stretcher and two attendants appeared, and Carl followed them and the litter inside. To the waiting doctor, "He's all yours. He—" The words stopped. Carl took a deep, unsteady breath. "He's a—good man, Doc. A friend."

"I think," the doctor said, "that you'd better catch a little rest yourself. You look as if you need it." He turned away then and followed the rolling stretcher into the examining room. The door closed.

Rest, Carl thought, as he plumped himself down on one of the straight chairs and loosened his parka in the welcome warmth. Sure, sure. But what about the others up there on that goddamned mountain? When do they get rest?

At least the trail down toward the road was free of trees and brush and, unlike that tangle down in the canyon where Ben had floundered around looking for the plane, easy enough to follow despite the fallen rocks. With the canyon wall on one hand and the drop-off on the other, there was no place else to go.

The snow, though, was knee-deep and a bitter wind was blowing. Ben kept his head lowered, and used his staff with constant care lest a loose rock beneath the snow trip him up and cause a bad fall.

He had no illusions about his inability to walk all the way down into Santo Cristo for help: he might make a few miles, but far short of any help the attempt would inevitably end from cold and exhaustion, and he had no intention of becoming merely another snow-covered hummock, a body to be discovered after the first big thaw.

And not even a statistic, he thought, because nobody would miss him except the people back at the cave. And who but those same people would care that he was missing even if they knew? It was a strange, disquieting thought.

In a matter of no more than eighteen hours, through a combination of circumstances he would not have believed, he had met and become inextricably tied to five persons he had not even known existed. Or cared. And those five now constituted his entire world of humanity.

It was only a temporary relationship—unless, of course, it was the ultimate permanent relationship

141

ending in oblivion, but that was a thought he was not prepared to deal with yet.

He had seen too many apparently deep attachments and interrelationships dissolve like smoke once the immediate bond was removed to believe any longer in permanence.

Dangers shared in jungles or in rice paddies too easily faded in memory, and he could not now even recall names of men he had been sure he would never forget.

And then there had been his one real attempt at intimacy, with Madge, who, in the phrase, had shared his bed and board, and sworn eternal fidelity. But when they shipped him back from Saigon and turned him loose in the outside world again, Madge was gone, and he never knew where, without even so much as a Dear John note. So long, baby, it was nice knowing you.

He was still not sure why he had made his decision to go back down the road to see if Warner, whom he no longer thought of as the dude in the Fort Worth Stetson, had been able to turn car and trailer around; but once the decision was made, he could have done no other than what he had. That much was obvious.

On the other hand, lest Lila or anyone else get the idea that he was busting his ass right now in this growing blizzard just for the sake of five people back in the cave, he wanted it clearly understood that he was trying to save his own skin every bit as much as theirs and probably a whole lot more.

What he had was only a forlorn hope that if a search team *was* in the area looking for the plane, they just might stumble on the car and trailer as Warner had hoped, and since he, Ben, had failed in reaching the plane to leave the note, he might just as well leave it at the car, which he was pretty sure he could reach. Hope mounted on conjecture based on faint possibility. But what else was there?

His feet were cold, and even in down-filled mittens his fingertips were beginning to go numb. No danger yet; he had been colder than this before without real harm. But it was no time to twist an ankle or a knee. It would be a long crawl back up to the cave.

He kept his head bent against the driving snow, and he carefully probed each step with his staff before he shifted his weight.

In his concentration as he reached the bottom of the ancient trail and started off down the road, he passed unknowing within twenty feet of the bear whose tracks CJ and Wilt had seen.

It was a large, male black bear, and Wilt's guess had been correct—the two snow and rock slides had exposed and made untenable the den in which he had settled down for his long winter sleep, and brought him in a rage out into the open to search for another wintering place.

He weighed perhaps four hundred pounds and now at the beginning of the hibernation period he was in prime condition, his pelt thick and glossy, ample protection against even bitter cold.

The bear watched Ben quietly until he was out of sight, and then started, unhurried, up the ancient trail. There were caves which would serve. He had seen them in his wanderings.

Ben came around the bend in the road to the place where the car and trailer had been, and as before, stopped short to stare.

Snow covered much of the destroyed area, but signs of destruction were still visible, and it was clear what had happened to car and trailer. Ben walked as close to the edge of the slide area as he dared and looked down.

Car and trailer were not visible, but there was no doubt that they were there in that huge pile of debris. As we would have been, Ben thought, if we had stayed. Inwardly he shivered, but not from cold.

He shook his head, turned away and then began to stare again. There were tracks not yet buried by the new snow, unmistakable tracks of snowshoes and cleated boots, and, yes, twin tracks that had to have been made by runners of some kind. They headed down the road.

Ben crossed the slide area almost at a run, floundering in the snow, caution discarded now. There were searchers, snowshoe-equipped, which meant that they were part of an organized unit. They would have transport and the means to call in more help to get Warner out, and Sue Ann, all of them. He began to shout as he ran.

Lieutenant Carter did not know Frank Silva, the governor's aide who had talked to him on the radio, but he did know the governor, who in only a year in office had shown himself to be on occasion both mean as a scorpion and unforgiving.

Under him there were no more hour-and-a-half lunches around the capitol, no more joyrides in state vehicles, no more goofing off when there was work to be done.

It was Frank Gomez, the State Police man assigned to the governor, who had told Carter, "He says 'frog,' he expects to see some hopping. When he doesn't, he damn well wants to know why."

There was that, and there was one thing more, in Carter's experience and belief an immutable fact: you didn't get your ass in a sling by obeying orders.

That big fellow Wallace had told Carter to stay put, of course, and monitor the radios, but in Carter's view there was no real need for that since all he had heard was non-essential chatter. Besides, far more important, it was not Wallace's prerogative to give orders anyway; it was his, Carter's, and Wallace had deliberately ignored or disobeyed each order that Carter had given him. Carter would not have said right out that Wallace deserved a lesson, but the thought did lurk in the back of his mind.

There was, then, no hesitation in Carter's movements or thoughts as he started up the jeep's engine, gave the instruments a quick check as department driving regulations required and then in low transmission and four-wheel drive began the slipping, sliding descent toward Santo Cristo.

The road was more treacherous than he had

thought, and so, concentrating on his driving, he did not bother to look into the rear-view mirror. He neither saw nor heard Ben coming around that last turn in the road at a lurching run, shouting and waving his arms.

For Jake Boone, inactivity was no longer possible. He was a proud man, and Warner's disappearance, with his family, was a blow to his vanity.

"Goddamn it," he told his wife, "it makes us look bad, like we're the ass end of the universe, somebody comes here, gets lost and then we can't find them."

Ethel agreed. He was a big, sometimes violent man, this husband of hers, and although on occasion she could, and did, stand up to him, she was careful to pick her circumstances. A sportswriter's description of a pro football player Ethel had read once fitted Jake to a T: agile, mobile and hostile.

"More snow," Jake said, as if it were a personal affront. "Look at it." He gestured toward the huge picture window through which normally you saw a breathtaking view of diminishing mesaland and sudden, towering mountains. Now the view extended only the width of the *portal*. The snow came in slantwise, wind-driven; from time to time a heavy gust buffeted the north wall of the room and wailed through the TV antenna on the roof as if attacking a house under siege.

In sudden decision Jake turned away and walked toward the phone extension. Ethel said, "What are you fixing to do, honey?"

Jake shook his head, picked up the phone and dialed a ranch number. "Johnny? Have you got chains on the flatbed? Then put them on. And load the big snowmobile on it. We're going to take us a little ride." He hung up.

Ethel hesitated. "There was a man hurt up there, honey."

"Goddamn it, I know it."

She could ask him what he thought he could do that experienced search people could not, but all she would get would be argument. Ethel sighed. "Have it your way, honey. Just be careful."

Jack grinned suddenly. "Miss me, would you?"

"I would." Simple truth. Ethel's smile matched his. "You're no bargain, but you're all I've got."

Carl got up wearily from the straight chair and waited in silence when the doctor came out of the examining room.

"He's going down to X Ray," the doctor said; "then we'll know better where we stand. I've called Carling. He's coming down." Carling was one of the local orthopedists. "He's taken a bad pounding."

"A good piece of a mountain fell on him."

The doctor shook his head. "People will take chances." He missed the sudden protest in Carl's expression, quickly stifled. "It will be some little time," the doctor went on, "before we can make a sensible prognosis. There could be internal injuries. The human body isn't designed for the kind of punishment he has taken." The implied rebuke was plain.

"He couldn't help himself," Carl said.

The doctor smiled. "It's never their fault." His gesture dismissed the matter. "There is no point in your staying around. There is nothing you can do. In a few hours perhaps we'll know more." Dismissal.

Buster, Carl thought, if I didn't have things I had to do, you wouldn't have enough people here to throw me out. Aloud, deceptively mild, "I'll check back later."

He came out of the hospital, got into the jeep, picked up the microphone and called Bessie. "Jaime's in the hospital and I'm on my way to the firehouse." He stared at the falling snow and let some of his anger emerge. "But we haven't got a chance in hell of getting back up there and doing any good until we get a break in the weather. Any word from Bart?"

"Negative."

"Okay. Over and— No, hold it! For God's sake what's *he* doing down here? I'll get back to you later, Bessie. Over and out."

He had just seen Carter, alone at the wheel of the

146

second jeep, headed around the loop toward the capitol, even here on city streets slipping and sliding as he went. Carl started up his engine, wrenched his jeep around in a skidding U-turn and followed, muttering to himself.

He was a hundred yards behind Carter into the capitol parking lot. He narrowed the gap into the building and up the stairs. Carter turned into the governor's outer office. Carl followed at a trot. The governor's inner door was open and Carter was already inside. Carl went in too.

There were half a dozen people, and the governor behind his desk. Carl ignored them all and spoke only to Carter in an angry shout. "Just what in the goddamn hell are you doing down here with that jeep?"

In the sudden silence, "What's this all about?" the governor said. His voice was sharp. "I sent for him."

"Did you tell him to leave four people up there without transport and without any communication in this kind of weather? Because if you did, by God—"

"Simmer down," the governor said, "or I'll have you—" He stopped. "Repeat that," he said.

The room was silent. "Seven of us went up there in two jeeps," Carl said, his voice a little quieter, but not much, "six of us to bust our asses trying to find a missing aircraft and maybe a car and trailer too." His voice altered. "One of us just to make noises and get in the way." He jerked his thumb toward Carter. "Him."

No one stirred.

"Jaime Leyba's hurt," Carl said, "probably bad. I drove him down in one jeep. He's in X Ray now." He had not realized before how deeply Jaime's injury had affected him. And now, with Carter standing there, proof that the rest of the searchers were abandoned, trapped up on that pitiless mountain, the fury in Carl's mind could scarcely be contained. "Now," he said in a voice that was no longer steady, "this horse's ass has come down in the other jeep, just—leaving four better people than he'll ever be up there to freeze to death."

147

His voice climbed uncontrollably. "Was that what you intended, Governor?"

AP said softly, "Jesus!"

"No," the governor said, "that wasn't what I intended at all. We want information—never mind. We'll send the jeeps back right away."

"Will you now?" Carl said. "Will you just? I had one hell of a time getting down. Ask the horse's ass. He had trouble coming down too. He had to. No car's going up that road, four-wheel drive or not, until this weather lets up and we can get the road cleared a little."

In the silence the governor looked at Carter, and waited.

"I was ordered to come down," Carter said.

UPI said almost inaudibly, "What was his name— Good Soldier Schweik?"

"I didn't even think about getting back up," Carter said, "I had my hands full getting down, like he said. But I don't like being called a horse's ass, and—"

"You are a horse's ass, in spades," the governor said. "And suppose you think now about driving back up. Can it be done?"

Carter was silent, his negative reply plain. The office was still.

AP said, "Offhand I would say that the stuff has hit the fan, Governor. Would that be a fair assessment of the situation?"

The governor looked at Frank Silva.

"You told me to get him down here, Governor," Frank said.

The governor took a deep breath and let it out slowly. "Okay," he said at last. His voice sounded weary. "My fault. The question is, what do we do now?"

Interlude

WIND STRAIGHT OUT OF THE NORTH brought the predicted frigid air to settle over the city and its environs like an army of occupation. At noon the temperature at the Santo Cristo airport had fallen to ten degrees Fahrenheit, and was still dropping.

Most inhabitants of the city stayed indoors, but those who did venture out scurried along, heads down and shoulders hunched, their faces contorted into masks of discomfort scarcely distinguishable from expressions of fear.

As the afternoon crept on, the cold deepened, and to those like State Police Captain Lopez who were accustomed to anticipating trouble, certain results became inevitable:

By morning there would be pipes frozen that had not been affected by winter weather since that January 1971 record cold.

Telephone and power lines, contracted by the cold beyond their limits of strain, would snap, cutting communication, light and heat.

Range cattle and sheep by the tens of hundreds would be caught out on the open range beyond saving.

Road crews would struggle on, fighting massive drifts, sanding areas of glare ice, extricating trapped cars and trucks and near-frozen passengers, fighting their best fight; but while they might win some skirmishes against the weather, until a warming trend came to their assistance the war was completely out of control.

And there was more:

To the south the storm system from the Gulf moved erratically, a restless gigantic mass, sometimes in haste, sometimes almost with hesitation like an invading army on a slow, plundering march.

Its progress was always north, and as it rose in obedience to the rising contours of the land, its warm air cooled and surrendered some of the water vapor it had collected in its travels over the sea to fall torrentially as rain on the parched land, producing flash floods known locally as "gully washers."

When the land beneath this mass reached the foothills of the great mountains and the rising air cooled still further, the rain it released would turn to snow, adding to the already heavy drifts, trapping more cattle, and even in places herds of deer and antelope unable to reach shelter.

The energy released by this condensation powered winds which churned at the farther boundaries of the storm and even reached ahead, driving cloud streamers like outriders with banners flying to warn of the main army's approach; and when these winds reached the stationary front of the arctic air mass settled over the Santo Cristo area, the battle between these two gigantic forces would be joined. What the outcome of that would be, no man could know.

In the meteorology office Brady Shaw studied his photos, charts and reports, and understood their implications. As he watched the confrontation approach, it almost seemed to him that some insane celestial joker had taken over the controls—and who now could forecast what would happen next, or when?

PART
TWO

II.

BEN FLOUNDERED BACK UP THE ROAD, the sight of that disappearing jeep still vivid in memory. Footprints—Bart's, Steve's, Wilt's and CJ's—led away from the spot, but in his anger, he failed to see them. His fault, his own goddamned fault, he told himself. If, instead of wasting time trying to reach the plane, he had come looking sooner for the car and trailer, he would have walked right into the rescue team, wouldn't he? Well? So why hadn't he done it that way?

Cut it out! he told himself angrily. It's done, and they're gone, and that's that. Still a part of his mind refused to accept the verdict. The whole thing didn't make sense.

Obviously the rescue team knew there was a car and trailer down in that tangled mess. Why else would they have tramped around, both on snowshoes and without, at least three or four of them and maybe more? He did not fancy himself as a super tracker, but any fool with eyes could see the differences in the tracks, some larger, some smaller, so an entire team had gathered on the site.

Okay. Either they got to the car and trailer or they didn't. If they did, they would have found them empty. And that meant, goddamn it, that there were people up here somewhere, didn't it, almost certainly in need of help? Then what the hell were they doing just driving off as that jeep had?

On the other hand, if they hadn't reached the car and trailer, then they couldn't know that there weren't people inside, maybe hurt, isn't that right? So, again, why aren't they still here doing their thing?

And you might as well cut that out too, he thought,

153

because you can't know the answer and it doesn't make a goddamn bit of difference anyway. There's only one thing to do now, and that's to get back to the cave in a hurry, haul up as much wood as you can for the fire and see if you can keep people alive through the night. Yourself included. With the falling temperature, the chance was minuscule, but never mind; there was no chance at all if he didn't give it a try.

He crossed the slide path quickly as he could, and not until he was beyond it did he let himself look up to the great ugly scar where part of the mountain had torn away. It looked as if it might fracture again given any kind of stimulus.

Thank God Warner was in no shape to fire off that rifle of his a second time, although Ben had an idea that Warner had learned his lesson, and right now was learning even more about himself and his mortality. Poor bastard.

Ben's own tracks in the snow were plain, but blurring rapidly. He kept his eyes on them as he floundered on, like the chicken following the chalk line, he thought. Well, big brain, clever hands and all, we humans aren't realy a goddamned bit better equipped than that silly chicken once we're confronted with what we can't control. Any animal in the woods is better off than we are huddled shivering in that cave just trying to stay alive. A fur coat and a bushy tail—

His legs automatically stopped their motion, and he stood quite still staring disbelieving at the tracks beside his own, but leading up the trail instead of down. They were blurred by new snow, but unmistakable, and they could add up to only one animal: bear.

No, God help us, Ben thought, a grizzly? Grizzlies were supposed to be extinct in this area, but there was always the chance, the bad chance, that there was still one left, and one was all it would take.

He stared at the tracks and tried to remember what he had read. Grizzlies had longer claws on the forepaws. These claws didn't seem overly long. And grizzlies were larger than black bears and presumably

154

their tracks would reflect their size. And black bears were not uncommon in these mountains. Probably a black bear.

Okay, it was still damned small comfort. Granted that grizzlies had notoriously short tempers, that they were a law unto themselves, that a full-grown grizzly could outrun a horse, with a single blow of his paw kill a steer, could without noticeable effort flip over a rock that two men together could not lift—granted all that, a black bear was no bargain either.

All bears were unpredictable; that was the rule. If you met one in the mountains, you gave him a wide berth because while he might take alarm from your scent and flee, he might just as easily feel threatened by your presence and decide that attack was the best defense. And if you encountered a female with cubs, you not only gave her a wide berth, you got the hell out of the area just as fast as you could.

And black bears were smaller than grizzlies, true, but not all that much, and the result of a personal encounter with either four hundred pounds of black bear or eight hundred pounds of grizzly was likely to be the same—disastrous.

He was already moving up the trail automatically, like that chicken, he thought, hypnotized by the tracks. But where else was there to go? The cave is now my home; it has become home for all of us. A strange concept, but entirely true. Home was where you were sheltered from a potentially hostile environment, where you were enclosed in the sense, if not the reality, of security; home was a concept, and when you had said that you had said it all.

The cold, he thought, was getting to him. It had moved from his feet up his legs to his thighs, which were now numb, and his hands in the down-filled mittens no longer seemed to belong to him. No danger yet. The cave was only a hundred yards more, and although the temperature in the cave was probably near freezing, it was far warmer than the air this north wind was bringing down upon them.

But he was not at all sure that he was thinking

clearly. Hypothermia did that. Okay, so at least I know where I am going, and know full well that I will get there. Then I can rest a bit and warm up by what is left of the fire, and—

He saw the bear. Through the blowing snow it was at first a flickering illusion, perhaps only a dark rock or simply a trick of vision. But then it was plain and clear, and it looked big as a barn, strangely motionless, without a head—until Ben realized that its head was in the cave entrance. Faintly Ben heard Lila's scream. Floundering and shouting, he began to run.

It was the kind of a story a newsman could bear down on. "Events," the radio newscaster said, "have taken a bizarre and possibly tragic turn in the search for the missing aircraft carrying Senator Joseph Martin of Roswell. Besides the senator, in the mountains behind Santo Cristo there are now eight other persons caught in the extremely heavy snow and intense cold, and at least for the present beyond the reach of outside help.

"Four of the missing persons are Warner Harlow of Oklahoma City, his wife and their two children, Patricia, aged seventeen, and William, aged fifteen. The wreckage of their car and trailer has been seen at the ten-thousand-foot elevation below the White Peak road. Apparently car and trailer were caught in one of the avalanches that have occurred in the area within the past few hours. It has not yet been possible to reach the wreckage to see if the family is still inside, and if so, if they are still alive. Warner Harlow will be remembered by sports fans as a star lineman on the great University of Oklahoma football team in the 1950s. It has been learned that Harlow and his family were to have been guests of the John Boones at their large ranch near Santo Cristo. Their presence on the White Peak road is unexplained.

"The remaining four persons unaccounted for are all members of the local Search and Rescue team. Their last known location is near the avalanche area. Due to what is described as a misunderstanding, they have been left without transport and without any means of communicating with their base in Santo Cristo or with Santo Cristo authorities. Their names are: Bart Wallace . . ."

Connie turned off the radio. The single customer at the counter said, "Hey." And then, "Bart Wallace. The big guy? Runs that foreign-car garage? You know him?"

"I know him." It was hard to keep her voice steady.

"I thought I'd seen him in here. How do you suppose they got themselves hung up?"

Connie shook her head.

"What I mean, this is no weather to be playing games in. It's supposed to go way down below zero tonight down here, and up there—" The customer shook his head. "Rather them than me."

"Yes." The one word was all she could manage.

"I know that White Peak road," the customer said. "I've hunted up there. Got me a deer once, eight points. But when the weather turns bad they ought to close that road. Too dangerous. Rock slides. And I don't know how they're going to get anything up there before the next warm spell either." He slid from his stool and stood up. "Well, I'm warmed up now. Back to the grader. See you."

Connie merely nodded. She did not trust herself to speak.

As with Ben late yesterday afternoon, it was the red color where no red ought to have been that caught Steve's eyes. She hurried toward it, taking the walkie-talkie from her pocket as she went. No doubt; it was the shattered plane fuselage, almost but not quite completely snow-covered, upside down.

She raised the walkie-talkie to her numbed lips and her voice was not quite steady as she spoke. "Steve here. Come in, Wilt and Bart. I've found the plane. Repeat, I've found the plane."

"Roger." Bart's voice. "Good girl. Stay where you are. I'm coming to you. Wilt, you and CJ join us.

About a quarter mile from the north wall, near the cirque. Over."

"Roger." Wilt's voice. "Nice going, *chica*."

Bart, Steve thought, looked like a great bear looming through the falling snow and through the trees as he made his way toward her. Like a bear too, he did not seem to hurry, but his shuffling strides carried him to her with astonishing quickness. He wore a smile of approbation vaguely visible through the steam of his breath, but he said nothing, and together they approached the plane's fuselage.

The cockpit windows were snow-covered. Bart brushed one clean with his mittened hand and bent to peer in. Slowly he straightened. "Now we know," he said, "and I suppose we could have stayed home and saved ourselves the trouble." Stayed with Connie, he was thinking. She had not really been far from his thoughts all morning.

Steve said slowly, "He's dead?" Anticlimax.

"Dead, and not very pretty to look at."

The term was dependent lividity. Bart had seen it more than once but never quite like this: the huge, angry, bruised-looking area of a dead body where blood had drained after death through gravity to the lowest spot. Upside down, Joe Martin's face was purple now, his open eyes protruded, and from one corner of his gaping mouth the tip of a swollen tongue lolled out in idiotic fashion.

"We'll wait till Wilt and CJ get here," Bart said, "and then see about getting him out. If we can." He took out his walkie-talkie again. "Bart here, calling Carter at the jeep. Come in, Carter."

There was silence.

Steve had bent for her look. She straightened now and swallowed hard. Not very pretty is right, she thought, and said nothing. And then, new thought, "One jeep. Five of us. And—him too?"

Bart had the walkie-talkie again at his lips. He lowered it slowly. "You have a point."

"Couldn't we just—leave him, and come back later? I mean—"

Bart's voice was gentle. "I know what you mean." He raised the walkie-talkie again. "That Carter," he said. "Bart here, calling Carter at the jeep. Come in, Carter!"

"Bart!" It was CJ's voice.

"I read you. Come on."

"The jeep's gone!"

Bart said slowly, "Give me that again."

"I tell you, the jeep's gone! And not long. Wilt says the tracks are fresh! That son of a bitch drove it down, and he sure as hell isn't going to get it back up again the way the road is, either! Do you read me?"

In a kind of reflex action Bart slowly lowered the walkie-talkie until the hand holding it hung loose at his side. He stared unseeing into the falling snow. In all the world there was no sound. Slowly he raised the radio again. When he spoke his voice held nothing. "I read you," he said. "We're coming over. Stay where you are. Over and out." He was conscious that Steve watched him, wide-eyed. He avoided her glance.

That jeep was, as he had said, their life support system. Without it they had the clothes they stood in and what each might have carried in his pockets, a map, a compass, probably a pocketknife, maybe even some matches, but that was all. The specter of that dead hunter came unavoidably to mind.

Oh, they were dressed for the weather as the hunter had not been. But the cold was already getting to them, even to him, nonetheless, and clothing alone would not suffice. They would need shelter, if possible a fire. And then, when nighttime came and with it the predicted arctic cold? One step at a time, he told himself; remember that.

Steve looked around in bewilderment at the falling snow, the dim shapes of trees, the huge piled rocks at the side of the ravine. The mountains are all around us, she thought, and suddenly they are no longer friendly; they seem to be closing in. She looked again at Bart's face in the shadow of his parka hood. His expression was inscrutable. Against the mountains and the weather, she thought, even he is—helpless. "We're —stuck, aren't we?" Her voice was quiet.

Bart put one big arm around her shoulders and squeezed gently. "We aren't through yet. Let's go."

Lila's scream brought Billy to his feet in a single jump. She was pointing at the cave entrance, where the bear's snow-covered muzzle protruded into the cave. His nose was working, and his little eyes seemed filled with fury. He growled. The angry sound echoed from the cave walls.

Patty said, "Daddy's rifle!"

"No!" Billy's voice was almost a scream. He seized a burning stick of wood from the fire and crossed the cave in two long jumps waving the brand before him.

The bear growled again, and his great jaws opened and clashed shut with a fearful sound as the burning stick came closer. His shoulders were constricted by the narrowness of the cave entrance, and he was at a distinct disadvantage.

When the burning stick made sudden contact, the growl turned to a roar of pain and rage that filled the cave. The sharp smell of burning hair mingled with the piñon smoke from the fire. The bear roared again and backed away from his tormentor, out onto the narrow trail.

He brushed once at his face with a forepaw, and then turned suddenly at a new sound. A man emerged from the falling snow coming toward him at a shambling run, shouting and waving his staff. It was too much.

The bear rose on his hind legs, roaring again. He brushed Ben's staff aside as if it were a twig and swung one forepaw in a sideways swipe that had it landed cleanly could have crushed Ben's ribs. Instead, even with a glancing blow, the force was sufficient to throw the man backward, stunned, automatically fighting to regain his balance.

The bear roared again, and Ben's shout was cut off short as he threw up one arm for protection, stumbled, felt himself falling and, clawing desperately for support that was not there, went over the edge and disappeared. There was a brief clatter of rock, and then silence.

The bear rubbed twice more at his painful muzzle before, unhurried, he shambled off down the trail to find another, less inhospitable den.

Inside the cave Billy still stood with the burning stick in his hand. His knees were shaking now and it seemed that his bowels had turned to water. There was an emptiness that was almost nausea in his chest. He tried to speak, but no words came out.

"Nice going." Lila's voice.

Warner had seen, and dimly comprehended. He lay quiet now, breathing painfully, while wild, flickering thoughts chased one another through his hazy consciousness.

Patty said, "You were—wonderful, you really were!"

It was Sue Ann who said, "There was somebody out there. I heard him. I can't hear him now." She was almost afraid to put the question. "Could it have been Ben?" Please, God, no! We can't lose him!

Lila said, "I didn't hear anything."

"It's Mom," Patty said. It was a family joke. "She can hear the grass grow."

Lila got slowly to her feet. She looked at Sue Ann. "Sure?"

"I'm afraid so."

Lila took a deep breath. "Okay." There was resignation in her voice. She crossed the cave, knelt beside Ben's pack and began to paw through its contents. Gloves, a billed cap, heavy wool socks which she pulled on over her shoes and trouser bottoms, a sweater far too large, a scarf which she wrapped around her throat.

Sue Ann, Patty and Billy watched her in silence as she stood at last and looked around at them all. "Okay," she said, once more unconsciously assuming command. "Behave yourselves." She started for the entrance.

Sue Ann said, "Maybe he's—dead!" There, it was out.

"Maybe he is," Lila said. "I'll be back when I find out." I hope, she added silently; crawled out of the entrance, looked both ways at the empty trail and, rising, followed the bear's clear tracks toward the place where he had attacked Ben.

Bart, Steve, CJ and Wilt stood close together and stared at the jeep tracks. "I tried to raise him on the walkie-talkie," CJ said, "but the son of a bitch was already out of range, or else not listening." He took a deep breath. "If I ever lay eyes on him again I'm going to kill him." From his dual occupations he even picked his weapons. "I'll either use a dull palette knife or a cleaver."

"*If* you ever see him again," Wilt said. He looked at Bart. Tall as Wilt was, he had to look up. "Well, governor?" From his packtrain experiences, and his lonely walks, of them all, he was the one who knew the mountains best. "We've got two choices, and they're both bad."

Bart nodded. It was better, he thought, that the explanation and assessment came from other than himself. It would be well to hear opinions and if possible reach a consensus. "Go on."

"I make it fifteen miles," Wilt said, "maybe a little more down the hill. In this snow, on webs, we couldn't hope to make it in less than five hours—if we made it, that is, and still had some toes and fingers left."

Bart merely nodded.

"On the other hand," Wilt went on, his voice light, almost unconcerned, "we can stay here and maybe freeze to death the easy way."

Times like now, Steve thought, it had often seemed to her that men, even these whom she knew so well, behaved like children at make-believe, treating matters of utmost gravity as if they were trivial.

Now, all at once she was looking at it differently, probably, she told herself, because any decision affects me, my actual survival, just as much as it affects them, and suddenly I too want to keep facts at a distance to make calm judgment possible, instead of immediately enbroiling myself in the situation emotionally. CJ had the temper tantrum for all of us. It was strange how clearly she understood that now.

Bart said, "Any suggestions?"

He stood there in the driving snow, Steve thought, like a giant tree, one of the redwoods back in California, unmoved, immovable and always alone, until his mind was made up. You could take comfort, and strength, from a man like that. But what help could he find? Strange, new questions, and again that sense of sadness. "I pass," she said, and, turning, walked a few paces away merely because immobility was impossible. I'm scared, she thought, and I don't want them to see. I've never been scared in the mountains before, but I am now.

CJ said, "I'll go along with what you two decide. Only thing, I think we'd better all go, or stay, together."

"That," Bart said, "is for sure. Wilt?"

Wilt said, "I don't think we could all make it down —and I'm not just talking about Steve. You might." He spoke directly to Bart. "But the rest of us— uh-uh. And then you'd probably try to carry us and nobody would make it." He shook his head. "There isn't any choice. We're here, and we'd damn well better stay here and hope for the best, find some shelter, do what we can. Goddamn it," his voice rose in sudden anger, "the son of a bitch didn't even leave us what we'd normally be carrying in a backpack! It's all in that jeep. I've got a compass and matches and a knife, and that's all, and in this weather—"

"Bart!" Steve's voice was sharp, urgent. "Wilt! Come look!"

She was pointing at tracks in the snow, blurred but identifiable. "Where do those come from? Somebody's been here, a man, isn't it? No snowshoes, so it isn't one of us."

CJ said, "The son of a bitch Carter?"

"No, son," Wilt said. His voice sounded easier now.

"Carter's prints are here, and here, walking around the jeep, see? Different size? These are another man, a big man."

Bart said, "From the Harlow family?" And then, answering his own question, "Why not? But it doesn't really matter, does it?" He was thinking back to the dead hunter they had found, and to his tracks in the snow proving that he had survived the storm. "Whoever he is, he had to have made it through last night, no?" He was looking at Wilt.

Slowly Wilt nodded. "Had to. That means he almost had to have shelter."

"So let's find him," CJ said, "and just drop in for an indefinite stay." His voice turned grim. "He'd better be hospitable."

They all looked at Bart. They were in agreement, Bart thought, and that was good. So was he. He nodded. "Let's go. Wilt, you're the best tracker. I'll take the rear." He made himself smile at Steve. "I told you we weren't through yet. Not by a long shot."

She could have cried. Always, she thought, always he *gives* help and comfort. *But who helps him?*

It was cold; God, it was cold! Lila thought. Already in only these few yards, her feet were hurting and her toes were beginning to turn numb.

Here were the bear's tracks. She didn't know anything about such things, but any fool could see that these tracks had claws and certainly weren't made by anything human. Yes, and here were a man's tracks, coming up the trail and—oh, God!—going backward right to the edge!

She was afraid that beneath the snow the footing might be slippery, and she was unsure that in their condition her feet would do what she ordered them to. She had always disliked even moderate heights, and so she approached the edge of the trail now with great caution, to look down.

There was something perhaps twenty feet below, something dark against the white of the snow, only dimly seen through the falling curtain. She could not tell if it was moving, nor could she even be sure that it was a man. But what else would it be?

"Okay.'" She whispered the word aloud. "It's my turn now." She turned away and floundered down the trail, looking for a place to get safely down the steep slope.

There were rocks and trees and unexpected resistance from brush and branches, all of which she remembered vaguely from last evening. But then she had had Ben's arm to lean on and his strength at times almost to lift her bodily when she faltered. She had only herself now, and a wonderment in her mind that she was even forcing herself to make the effort.

Maybe now I know the answer to that big question, she thought. I hope so. I am not turning my back and walking away. There was a measure of warmth and comfort in the concept. She floundered on in what she hoped was the right direction. Where are you? she cried silently. Where?

And all at once here he was, lying in a heap of snow and exposed brush and branches which had somewhat eased his fall. Snow was already beginning to cover him, his clothing, even his whiskery face. But his eyes were open, and there seemed to be understanding in them. He moved one arm weakly, and tried to roll on his side.

"Let me give you a hand." Lila bent, grabbed an arm and heaved. Slowly Ben got to his knees, got one foot beneath him and began the long effort to rise. He stood erect at last.

"Okay," Lila said. She was panting from exertion. "Let's go." She got his arm around her shoulders. "You've got to help. I can't do it all myself."

"I thought I told you to—stay in the cave."

"That," Lila said, "is something we can argue about later." And then, with rare profanity, "Now walk, damn it! Walk!"

12.

THE GOVERNOR SAT BEHIND HIS OWN DESK, presiding in shirtsleeves, his collar and tie loosened, a fresh yellow legal pad in front of him. "Okay," he said, "we've got nine people up there now, nine, goddamn it! And I've had two phone calls from Washington asking what the hell kind of circus we're running out here—one call from the House and one from the Senate, guess who. They say it's bad for the state's image."

State Police Captain Lopez in a chair against the wall could not have cared less about the state's image. A slow fire with Carter turning on a spit above it would be just about right, he thought; the *conquistadores* had a number of sound ideas. "No, sir," he said now, "we don't have any vehicles, and neither does the Highway Department, that could get up that road under present conditions."

The district forest ranger said, "It's drifting as bad as I've ever seen it, and temperatures are predicted to go down to January '71 levels tonight, that's maybe thirty below zero, maybe colder. Only thing is, in '71 we didn't have heavy snow to contend with too."

The state health officer said, "We don't know about the Harlow family. Maybe they came prepared with adequate clothing. Let's hope they did. *If* they're still alive. The Search and Rescue people will be adequately dressed, but that isn't going to be enough in the kind of cold that's predicted."

Game and Fish said, "They know their mountains, but they were left without any of the things they'd normally have—sleeping bags or blankets, an ax or a saw—" He shook his head. "Damn it, this is a sur-

166

vival problem under the worst possible conditions." He glared around the room.

Civil Air Patrol said, "We're grounded until this storm passes." He looked questioningly at Brady Shaw, the meteorologist.

"Maybe until the next one passes too," Brady said. Again that feeling was strong that they were at the mercy of irresponsible and unpredictable forces. "Anybody's guess," he said.

The state engineer coughed before he spoke. He was normally a cautious, peaceable man, but events were coming close to home and he wanted his department's position made clear. "Ever since the blasting when that service road was built," he said, "we've wanted the main road closed off. I have correspondence in my files—"

"Why?" the governor said sharply.

The state engineer was uncomfortable, but he stuck to his position. "Because it's unsafe." Probably never in his professional life had he ever made such an unqualified statement, and with the words spoken he suddenly felt almost reckless. "That entire canyon wall is like a honeycomb and the blasting weakened it. We've already had two snow avalanches that triggered rock slides. Another one could collapse the whole structure. And if those people are in the area—"

The district ranger said. "We had to have that service road."

"Oh, cut it out," the governor said. "Nobody's trying to hang you federal people. We're trying to figure out what to do, not who to blame."

There was silence. The governor studied the notes he had made on his pad. He looked around. "Any ideas?" He looked at Captain Lopez. "What about snowmobiles?"

Privately, the captain put snowmobiles in the same category with trail bikes, which he did not like either, but he had to admit that at times they did have their uses. "We can try," he said, "but up that road under present conditions, I don't think there's a chance. In open country, maybe, but—" He stopped. "Wait a

167

minute. Just the other day I saw one of those things, I think it's called a snow-cat, or something like that, a big red affair with an enclosed cab, on tracks, not wheels, high clearance—"

"Now," Game and Fish said, "we're getting somewhere. Here in town, Inny?"

"On a flatbed trailer in somebody's yard. I wondered what he had it for." The captain popped his fingers. "Over on Via Vista. I remember now."

"Get it," the governor said. And then a new thought. "Do we have any dog teams around here?"

The district ranger had served his time in the north country. "That snow's too deep for dogs, Governor, and I don't know of any, anyway."

"Okay," the governor said, "the snow-whatcha-macallit it is. Get on it, Inny. And make sure it carries a radio to keep in touch."

"Yes, sir," Captain Lopez said.

Jake Boone drove the ranch flatbed truck with the big snowmobile securely lashed on it.

Juan Ortega rode on the right side of the truck seat. Juan was uncomfortable about this entire operation.

"As far up as we can go, Johnny," Jake said, "then we'll unload and go on in the snowmobile."

Now that he was doing something, Jake's spirits were higher. Just plain waiting was always a drag, like times in the locker room before the game began, or just sitting on the bench waiting for the defense to get the ball back so you could start moving it again. "You wait for the bureaucrats to do something and it never gets done," he said. "That's what's wrong with Washington, and it applies right here too."

"Sí, señor," Juan said.

"How far do you think it is up that road, four, five miles? I never went up, but that much oughtn't be too hard."

"I think maybe more far than that, Mr. Boone."

"Well, we'll see." Jake had the truck in bottom gear. "We're going fine so far. Those chains, and that weight on the bed."

"The road gets narrow, Mr. Boone."

"Okay, we'll still have plenty room."

Slipping and sliding, the truck engine howling with effort, they scrambled on. The snow was falling heavily, and visibility was poor. Occasional gusts of wind drove snow flurries across the road so thick that Jake could see no farther than the truck radiator, but he kept the accelerator against the floorboards and steered by guesswork.

"Maybe we better slow down a little, Mr. Boone?" Maybe we better turn around and go back right now, *pronto, de seguido,* Juan thought, but did not venture to say aloud.

"Warner Harlow's an old friend of mine, Johnny."

"Sí, señor."

"I don't let my friends down."

"No, señor."

"You know about football, Johnny? Sure you do, only I don't mean local high school football, I mean college. Old Warner and I played together. That's something you don't forget."

"No, señor." And this is something I don't forget, Juan thought. When we get back—he changed that—if we get back, I will see that Teresa burns a candle, maybe two candles—

The truck lurched and swung, slowed suddenly. Jake bore down hard on the accelerator, let up and bore down again. The rear wheels whined as they spun and the truck swung farther, bumped a few feet, struck something solid and stopped.

"Son of a bitch," Jake said.

He slammed the shift lever into reverse and bore down again on the accelerator. The engine howled, for a moment the truck did not move, and then all at once it jumped rearward swinging as it went, slammed into another obstruction and stopped with a jar.

Slowly Juan opened his door. "I will see, Mr. Boone." He got out, was gone only a few moments and returned. Standing outside, almost waist-deep in drifted snow, "I don't think she will move, Mr. Boone. We are like this—" He held his hands crossways.

"And there is a tree, and a big rock." And how we managed to get between them, he thought in Spanish, only *Dios* could say, but there we are, and there we stay.

"Son of a bitch," Jake said again. Reluctantly he shut off the truck engine and got out on his side to stare at their predicament. "Okay," he said at last, "the hell with it. Let's get the snowmobile unloaded." He started forward and sank immediately up to his thighs in the snow. "Goddamn," he said, "I didn't realize it was this deep."

"No, señor."

"Think the snowmobile can take it?"

"No, señor."

"You may be right." Jake stared thoughtfully as far up the road as he could see through the falling snow. "You may be right," he said again.

"Which side do we unload the snowmobile on, Mr. Boone?"

Jake turned. Jesus, it was cold! He hadn't realized that, either. "What's that? What difference does it make?"

"If we unload here," Juan said, indicating the up-hill side, the road disappearing into the falling snow, "then we cannot go down because the truck is in the way."

Jake thought about it. Slowly he nodded. "I see what you mean." He had one last look up the road. "Okay, the other side it is. We'll go back down. The hell with it. We tried."

"Sí, señor. And the truck?"

"Why, hell, we leave it. We couldn't get it out if we tried, and anyway, nobody's coming up this road for a long time to come. Let's go."

There was sudden lightness in Juan's mind together with a vast sense of relief. "Sí, señor."

Where the trail up the canyon face began, Wilt stopped for a careful study of the blurred tracks in the snow, recent enough to show vague details. He was under no illusion that as a tracker he was anywhere

170

near the class of some he knew from the Jicarilla Apache reservation who seemed to be able to tell at a single glance what the quarry they were trailing had eaten for breakfast and when; but he considered himself reasonably competent, and anyway what he was looking at now was as plain as print.

Bart, CJ and Steve gathered around to listen. "Our man came down here," Wilt said. "There, there and there are his early tracks. And here comes that bear after the man had passed. See his track here on top of the man's? He went on up the trail, probably looking for a den." He pointed.

CJ said, "Is he still there?"

"Nope. Here he comes back down. Recently, but *after* our man has gone back up.

"So," Bart said, "maybe they met?"

They stood silent in the falling snow. Steve shivered, only partly from cold.

"All right," Bart said, "let's get on and see what we find. We're looking for shelter, remember?"

And, he thought with rare profanity, we'd damn well better find it. And soon. Cold affected him less than it seemed to affect others, but even through multiple layers of clothing it was beginning to get to him now. None of the others had complained, but it was safe to assume that they were well beyond the merely uncomfortable stage. "Push along, Wilt."

"And God bless Carter," CJ said. He spoke over his shoulder as he trudged along on his snowshoes. "I suppose he had some kind of reason, but I'll be goddamned if I can think what it was that was good enough to leave us up here like this, the bastard."

CJ, Steve thought, is our safety value. Through him, without even thinking let alone saying aloud ungenerous thoughts ourselves, we can vent our collective anger, our sense of helplessness and, yes, actual fear. Because we know, as few do, precisely what the loss of that jeep can mean. We found and carried in that dead hunter last time. Others have been brought in, here and in other places throughout these mountains, alive, but no longer whole, with toes and fingers to be

171

amputated because of frostbite and gangrene most people probably think belongs in the Dark Ages. Why did people allow themselves to be caught in these situations?

There were many reasons, and not all of them were out of sheer stupidity, but frequently rather out of a blind faith that the elaborate support systems of civilization, artificial warmth, easily obtained food and comfortable shelter would always be near at hand. When we leave those behind, deliberately or by accident, Steve thought, we are suddenly thrown into a pitiless, primitive world for which without careful planning we are totally unprepared and without defenses.

That bear will find a den and curl up, his metabolism will slow, his thick fur will keep him warm enough and he will exist comfortably in an almost suspended state through whatever winter may bring until he emerges, thin and gaunt, granted, but healthy nonetheless, when spring finally arrives. Man in the same situation would be long dead.

She watched Wilt's long legs in their steady rhythm and followed automatically.

We have a chance for survival, she told herself, because we are four healthy, strong, experienced people, clothed for this weather. And because we have Bart as our focus, our basic strength. We will use what we have and try to improvise. But the line separating survival from extinction was a very thin line, she thought, and only one careless mistake could send you across with no possibility of return.

She wondered if Lieutenant Carter understood that, and decided that he probably did not. His was a world of rules and regulations, of highways and people and instant communication across hundreds of miles. Had he considered, or did he even understand that we, here, now in this snowstorm, are as remote from Santo Cristo only fifteen miles away, and any possibility of assistance, as if we were in the middle of the ocean? Incredible, both that it was so and that so few people understood.

Wilt called suddenly, "Hey!" And his long legs began to move at a faster rhythm. "Hey!" he called again.

Steve too speeded up her pace. She could not see yet what it was that had caught Wilt's attention, and then all at once she could.

On the trail ahead was a man almost but not quite on his knees, and another, smaller figure covered with snow, shapeless in an odd variety of clothing, struggling to hoist the man to his feet. They seemed oblivious to Wilt's calls.

Wilt reached them. He grabbed the man's arm with one hand, held him up, almost lifted the smaller figure with the other and passed it back to Steve, who caught it and held it erect as one holds a large, limp doll.

From somewhere in the depths of the snow-covered clothing Lila's voice said indistinctly, the words slurred, "I don't believe it!"

By contorting her stiff lips, Steve could smile. "We're real, cold but real."

Lila's eyes rolled back in her head as she fainted.

"Here." This was Bart. He picked Lila up as if she were weightless. "CJ, give Wilt a hand."

Wilt said, "There's a cave. That's where they're trying to go." His voice took on an odd tone. "He calls it home."

13.

THE SNOW-CAT PERCHED IN REGAL SPLENDOR on its own flatbed trailer in the graveled drive of the Via Vista house Captain Lopez remembered. The captain had the district ranger with him, and they both got out to walk around the machine, admiring the wide caterpillar tracks, the high clearance, the large engine obviously packed with power.

"She's a beauty, isn't she?" A man, Anglo, in a parka with a fur-rimmed hood, wearing heavy fur mittens, walked out from the house to stand beside them. He squinted into the falling snow and studied the car they had driven up. "State fuzz," he said. "What's up? There's a law or something?"

"None that I know of," Captain Lopez said. "We need your help. My name is Lopez, and this is——". .

"My name's Craig." And then in the tone of one whose grievances lie close to the surface, ready at any moment to emerge, "One of your State guys wasn't so damn friendly when he gave me a ticket on the Interstate for doing sixty, sixty, goddamn it, only five miles over the limit, and there wasn't another car in sight! How about that?"

Inwardly Captain Lopez sighed. He wondered how many times Craig had driven at seventy miles an hour, seventy-five or more, and not been caught. Now this once—no matter.

The district ranger said, "I'm from the Forest Service. We've got nine people stranded up in the mountains. That's why we need your help."

"We need this," Captain Lopez said, and nodded toward the machine and trailer. "Nothing else can get up to those people."

"Just like that?" Craig said. "I'm supposed to say, 'Why, sure. Here are the keys. Help yourself'? You know what these things cost?"

"We'll see that you're reimbursed," the captain said.

Craig seemed only slightly mollified. "Nine people," he said. "What're they doing up there in this kind of weather, anyway?" He shook his head suddenly. "Okay. It's probably a long story. Where are they?"

"Near White Peak. There's a road——"

"I know that road," Craig's voice had altered again. "It's where every winter they have rock slides." He looked at the district ranger. "You people, blasting away up there, and loggers going in, lousing up the country—" He stopped. "Okay, okay. I suppose I'm not bastard enough to say no." He gestured toward the snow-cat. "But if Besty here goes, I go too. This isn't any U-Drive operation."

Captain Lopez nodded. It was as much cooperation as they could expect, he thought. Fair enough. We'll pay you for your time." Probably through the nose, he thought, and did not say. So be it.

Captain Lopez and the district ranger walked together back to the State Police car. The captain got in, picked up the microphone of the car radio and called the State Police. "Get hold of that fellow Carl What's-his-name at Search and Rescue. Tell him to call me on this frequency. Over and out." He sat quiet with the mike in his hand.

The district ranger said, his voice heavy with irony, "A real public-spirited citizen, Craig. He'll go, but only if he's paid. And paid well."

The captain nodded wearily. In the past thirty-six hours he had had one hour's sleep. He saw the world now through a thin haze of unreality, or perhaps it was a new clarity, all usual illusions stripped away. What did the Forest Service-type expect, anyway? Instant, for-free, wildly enthusiastic cooperation? Because that wasn't how the world worked. He said obliquely, "In my business we see all kinds, and maybe you can't blame them for what they are. I don't know. I've heard too many explanations to believe any of them. The Craigs of this world, and worse, are the result of underprivilege or overpermissiveness or they sucked their thumbs when they were babies or they didn't suck their thumbs—" He shook his head. "But he's going, and that's what counts." There was satisfaction in that thought.

The radio speaker crackled. Lopez lifted the mike and spoke his name.

"Carl here. They told me to call. Over."

The captain explained about the snow-cat. "Enclosed cab," he said. "You can probably crowd three, four in besides the driver. Over."

"On my way," Carl said. "Over."

175

"Do you need any gear? Over."

"First-aid pack and walkie-talkie. Once we get close enough I can raise them on that. Over."

"Roger," the captain said. "We'll wait here. Over and out." He hung up the mike, got out a crumpled pack of cigarettes and lighted one slowly. He blew out smoke and looked up at the district ranger. "Do you ever wonder how things manage sometimes to get out of hand—just as if they were planned?"

"No comment," the district ranger said.

The captain managed a weary smile. For the first time in two days there was a sense of relaxation in his mind. "Maybe at last we're back on the track."

To Bart the cave seemed crowded. Stooping to clear the roof, by his size and presence already dominating the scene, he pushed back his parka hood and shook himself like some primeval beast while he concentrated on what had to be done. "Steve, you take care of the girl." He pointed at Ben. "Wilt, you see about him." His voice was gentle, but it carried authority.

"I'm okay," Ben said. "Just let me sit down, warm up, rest." With one hand he undid the drawstring of his parka hood, and with effort pushed it back from his head. Slowly, painfully, he lowered himself to the floor, leaned against the rock wall and closed his eyes.

He was not okay, but maybe the weakness and the sense of confusion would pass; the pain he could endure. Once as a boy he had suffered a brain concussion from a fall, and all he could ever remember of the entire happening was a sense of bewilderment, as if a piece had been taken out of his life and could never be regained, the events of that time of unconsciousness forever remaining at best unclear, and at worst a total mystery. As now.

He opened his eyes again. Wilt was squatting close beside him, watching his face intently. "Anything you want?" Wilt said. "Anything to do?"

Ben waggled his head faintly in negation. He saw Lila lying on the floor, shaking with cold, and somehow she was mixed up in what had happened to him, but the brain within his aching head could not immediately bring memory back. He closed his eyes again.

Bart looked around at the others: Sue Ann was propped against the wall, her splinted leg extended stiffly. Her attention was on Warner beside her enveloped in the sleeping bag. Warner's face was gray, his breathing shallow and labored; his eyelids fluttered as if from a tic. A bad scene, Bart thought; very bad.

To the boy beside the fire, "Use all the wood you've got," he said, his voice gentle, kindly. "We'll get more. Wilt, stay here with Steve and mind the store. Come on, CJ." He knelt and squeezed his bulk out through the cave entrance.

Steve was kneeling beside Lila. Patty bent to touch her shoulder. "Can I—help?"

"We just have to get her warm. It's what they call hypothermia."

"I've heard about that." But never expected to see it, Patty thought. "What can I do?"

Steve looked up at the girl. "Warm her with your body."

"Okay." No hesitation. "Show me how."

Steve smiled once more through stiff lips. You never knew where you would find the good ones, she thought; they sometimes turned up in the most unexpected places. "Help me get these wet things off her," she said. "Then if we can find a blanket of some kind . . ."

Outside, starting back down the trail in the cold and the falling snow, "A goddamn mess," CJ said. "That guy in the sleeping bag is on his way out if I ever saw one. The woman with the splinted leg. And that big guy, what's with him?"

Sheer accident piled up on improbability, Bart thought. From the start of this operation it had been so. "He met the bear," he said. "It was trying to get in the cave."

"Jesus! He's—"

The sound they had heard twice before began again, a low heavy rumbling, growing in force and volume. Rocks rattled off the face of the canyon wall above them, and they both bent immediately and covered their heads with their hands for protection. Beneath the snow, the ground moved perceptibly, a deep shudder.

It stopped at last, the rumbling died away, a few more rocks fell and then there was silence.

Bart straightened. He looked as far as he could up through the falling snow to the wall face. "God only knows," he said slowly, almost as if in prayer, "how long it will be before one of those slides brings down the whole cliff." He looked at CJ. "Jaime warned us."

CJ nodded in silence. He was standing again, his stocky legs widespread in an attitude of defiance.

"But," Bart said, "where else do we go for shelter?" Because out in the open we're dead, he thought. CJ understood that too, and there was no point in saying it aloud. "Let's gather wood. As long as the cave holds up, we're going to need it."

Back again in his office, Brady Shaw stared down at the weather map and the most recent satellite photos. There was no relief there, he thought, and said as much aloud. He added: "I don't go around preaching Murphy's Law: that if anything bad can happen, it will. On the other hand, if various bad things are possible, then there is always a finite chance that a whole lot of bad things will happen all at once. And that's just what we're watching here."

His assistant said slowly, tentatively, his voice no longer filled with assurance, "That Gulf system still could veer off."

"Sure it could. Hell could freeze over too. But I'm not betting on either one." Brady was silent for a few moments. He said at last, "I hate to say it and maybe jinx everything, but there are a couple of things to watch, and hope."

The assistant shook his head, uncomprehending.

Brady touched the cloud mass in the photo centered over Santo Cristo. "This arctic system *is* moving. Not much, but some. It's sliding southeast." He gestured with his forefinger. "And this Gulf system coming up

178

at us is moving in spasms, not at a steady pace." He looked at the assistant. "You've noticed?"

Pride and honesty struggled briefly. Honesty won. "No, sir, I really hadn't." But now that it was pointed out, the assistant could see that it was so.

There was hope for the boy yet, Brady thought with some satisfaction. "Okay," he said. "If the arctic system keeps on moving away, and if the Gulf system hesitates a few more times—" He paused and mentally crossed his fingers. "Then," he said, "there just might be a gap between them, maybe even a big enough gap to get something into the air, one of the State choppers, maybe." He sighed. "Let's hold that thought, anyway."

Jake Boone was back in the huge living room of the ranch house standing, legs widespread, in front of the roaring fire. He had a stiff drink of bourbon in his hand. "Cold out there. Freeze the tits off a brass virgin," he said. "Fact. We got as far as we could and got stuck. Just between us, we had one hell of a time just getting back. Johnny kept mumbling in Spanish. Prayers, I'll bet."

I could say I told you so, Ethel thought, and knew that she would do nothing of the kind. "Warner and Sue Ann—"

"Goddamn it, don't you think that's just what I'm thinking about? And the kids, whatever their names are."

"Patty and Billy."

"Okay. I'm thinking about them too."

"It isn't your fault."

"Maybe I gave them wrong directions."

"You didn't. I heard it. It was perfectly clear. They couldn't miss the road."

"But they did, sweetie pie, they sure as hell did." Jake raised the glass and drained it. The bourbon burned pleasantly in his throat.

"You've done all you could," Ethel said. "Nobody could do more."

Jake set the empty glass on the mantel. He

179

was tempted to have another, but he told himself that he would wait a little. He thought about what Ethel had just said. "Yeah," he said at last, "there's that. We gave it a try."

Ethel got up from her chair. "I'll fix another drink," she said. "Then lunch will be ready. Hungry?"

Jake could smile then as he handed her his glass. "Nothing like a little romp in the snow or in the hay to work up an appetite. Baby, you don't know how cold it is out there. Old Warner and—"

"They'll be all right."

All at once the smile was gone, and his voice turned solemn. "I hope so, honey, I purely do."

Captain Lopez watched from his car as the big snow-cat trundled up the road, engine roaring, wiper blades swishing back and forth. Carl and Craig were just visible through the rear window of the cab.

Craig, the captain thought, was a reluctant ally, but once his demands had been agreed upon, he was all business, and it was clear that he knew what he was doing. During his preparations, he had mumbled something about the Alaska pipeline, which, the captain thought, probably made sense. If Craig had worked up there, deep snow and intense cold would be nothing new to him. It was a comforting thought.

The captain told himself that he belonged back at his desk, and made no move to start the car. There was luxury in just sitting, relaxing for a bit now that this one crisis seemed on the verge of settlement, and before the next one arose.

Nine people, he thought, and Carl and Craig made eleven. Say four could squeeze into the snow-cat's cab besides Craig; that would mean three trips. Okay, it was going to take some time, but it looked possible. The sanctity of human life—again that phrase ran through his mind.

Of course, he told himself, he was assuming that all nine people were gathered in one place, which was by no means certain or even likely. The last word they had, the S&R people still did not know where the downed plane was, or whether the Harlows were still in their car and trailer, and if so, whether they were alive or dead. But the essential thing was that the S&R people themselves could now be reached, and they at least could be brought out. As for the others—

The car speaker crackled, and Carl's voice said, "Calling Captain Lopez. Come in. Over."

The captain picked up the mike and pressed the button. In his mind an alarm bell was tolling clearly. "Roger. Lopez here. Over."

"No go," Carl's voice said. His tone was heavy with angry disappointment. "You won't believe it, but some son of a bitch has got a flatbed truck jammed crossways blocking the road. We can't get through the trees, and the road drops right off on the downhill side. No way. Over."

The captain let his breath out in a weary sigh. "You're sure, dead sure? No way? Over."

It was Craig's voice this time, his original irascibility plain again. "You better believe it," he said. "Until you can get some heavy equipment up here and lift the son of a bitch right out from between a big rock and some trees, she's here to stay, and there's no way around. Wait a minute. The other guy's taking a look."

The captain sat quiet. Once again he had the feeling, unmistakable, that malign forces had planned this entire operation from start to finish, which was, of course, a silly notion. Still—

"Captain?" Carl's voice again, and this time the anger in it was almost uncontrollable. "The truck has a brand painted on the door. The brand is JB. Over."

The captain closed his eyes. Jake Boone, he thought, it would be. Maybe trying to help, but only fouling things up for fair. "Roger," he said in a tone of resignation. "Come on back. Over and out."

He hung up the mike and started the car's engine. All at once the familiarity of his office seemed best as the place from which to report to the governor.

Failure.

14.

BILLY KNELT AS NEAR THE FIRE AS HE DARED, while the exposed side of him was warm, almost toasting, the other side felt as if it was freezing; and as far as his hands and feet were concerned, there seemed to be no way he could keep them from going numb.

He wore his new wind jacket, silver side in, black side out, which was the way it was supposed to absorb and contain heat, the advertisement had said, adding that this jacket would probably be the only jacket one would ever need. Well, Billy had news for the ad writer: when it was really cold, like now, what you wanted was good, old-fashioned insulation like goose down or fleece such as Ben and all these new people wore, and that was that. He moved infinitesimally closer to the flames.

Billy's reaction to the encounter with the bear had almost disappeared; the feeling of nausea was gone, and the weakness from his legs. It would be nice to tell some of his contemporaries about the incident, if the opportunity ever arose, but for the present the cold occupied the center of his thoughts. Robert Service's "The Cremation of Sam McGee" suddenly came to mind; it now held new meaning.

He felt the sudden earth tremor and heard the deep rumbling of the fresh slide that bombarded Bart and CJ with rocks, and for a moment he was afraid again that the whole cave might collapse, but nothing more happened, and that too passed.

Across the cave he saw his mother put her hand comfortingly against his father's cheek, and it occurred to him that he could not recall ever seeing her make a gesture as intimate as that before. She said something, too, but only the faint tone of her voice, no words, reached Billy's ears.

There seemed to be between his parents now what Billy could only think of as a sense of peace, acceptance of what was, resignation toward what might be, just the two of them, the rest of the world locked out. It was a change, and in a way he envied them.

Patty too seemed to have changed her spots. Billy had watched in awe while she gave Pop the kind of mouth-to-mouth resuscitation he had only read about —and it had really worked. Even when Patty burst into tears after it was all over and Pop was breathing again, Billy hadn't been able to find it in him to feel superior as he always had. And now look at her.

Patty was swathed in the space blanket, which was something like Billy's jacket, but heavier, and Billy remembered from the night that it had really trapped their body heat as he and Patty clung together until almost immediately he was warm, and then hot and sweating. He couldn't see Patty's arms, but from the closeness of the two heads it was evident that Patty was holding Lila close and warming her with her own body. It was not the kind of, well, unselfish thing you would expect from the Patty Billy had always known, and despite the incident of the bear he felt somewhat put down. He concentrated on the fire, and tried to forget how cold it was.

But something else was running around in his mind, and he could not bring it into the open. Once sitting in his own room at home, reading, a motion had caught his peripheral vision, but when he looked he could see nothing. It happened several times again, and at last he saw what it was—a tiny field mouse somehow inside the house, scurrying around behind the floor-length window curtains. He had that same feeling now as he tried to pursue whatever it was that lurked in the shadows of his mind.

Something somebody had said? Done? The questions produced no response, no glimmer of recognition.

Shivering, Billy poked at the fire with numb hands while he considered the matter.

He was sure it was important, or at least might be, and he frowned in concentration as he tried to figure it out.

Wilt squatted on his hunkers near the fire, carefully not screening its puny warmth from anyone else. He could almost at will efface himself and retire into his own lonely company with his silent thoughts. Bart had left him in charge, but there was nothing to do but think.

That third snow slide followed by rock vibrations was a warning, that was for sure. Throughout these mountains, and few knew them as well as he, there were canyons like this one, many of them pocked with caves large and small. In many caves there were still signs of ancient habitation, smoke stains, carved petroglyphs as here, even at some, as over in Bandelier or Tsankawi, man-made depressions above the cave entrances where the ends of poles had been anchored extending out to posts to form the framework of rude porch roofs.

Inevitably piled against these canyon walls beneath the caves there was fallen rock, some of it small, but some of it huge pieces, ten, fifteen feet across, rock which, perhaps weakened by weather-caused expansion and contraction or merely by centuries of weathering from wind and snow and rain, had finally broken from the canyon wall. And in many of those large pieces too, there were signs of habitation that once had been.

Now add to those natural destructive forces, he thought, sonic booms such as they had heard and felt today, and shock waves from hunters' gunshots, and, most important, blasting when those two roads were built, and it was a wonder that the entire honeycombed canyon face had not collapsed long since.

It was no longer a question of *if,* but simply *when* the collapse would occur, either burying them beneath hundreds of tons of rock or, if miraculously they were spared that, leaving them stripped of even the feeble protection of this cave and exposed to increasing cold and wind which they could not possibly survive. We are living on borrowed time, Wilt thought, and was surprised how calmly he accepted the fact.

Bart understood it too, of course. Wilt looked around the cave. But nobody else did, which was just as well because it would only have added to their fright, and God knew the situation was bad enough without that.

Steve squatted beside him, and Wilt smiled faintly in greeting. "Getting warm again?"

"Fine." But the way she pronounced the word with still numb lips told the true story. Steve's eyes were on Lila, wrapped in the space blanket, her body tight against Patty's young life-giving warmth. Because I was dressed against the cold, I was only chilled, Steve was thinking. But she was already over the edge and on the long downhill slide which only ends one way unless it is interrupted: hypothermia with its mental vagueness and its violent shivering, to frostbite, to unconsciousness and eventual death. It was close, too close. If we hadn't come along—never mind, Steve told herself almost hysterically, close only counts in horseshoes. We *did* come along.

Lila's eyes were open now, and showing comprehension; some color had returned to her face; her fingers and toes were hurting badly with the return of circulation. The uncontrollable shivering had diminished and then stopped altogether as the warmth of Patty's body spread strength throughout her own, reawakening her mind. She stirred in Patty's arms, and spoke indistinctly, "Okay. I'm okay."

Patty's arms did not loosen their tight hold. "Better wait a little."

Lila's head waggled a negative. "I could wait forever, but I won't." Her voice was stronger. "You know, like you lie in bed in the morning and try to put off getting up when you know you have to?" She could even smile faintly. "Thanks."

Patty hesitated and then unwrapped the blanket. She sat up and slowly got to her feet. Her face was damp, and she could feel the tickle of sweat between her breasts. Her eyes had not left Lila's face. "Maybe you'd better go sit by the fire." She held out her hand and helped Lila to stand. Together they walked the few feet to the cave wall where Ben sat leaning.

Lila sank weakly to the floor beside him. "My joints creak. Are you okay?"

Ben nodded in silence. He did not need to look to know that his chest and shoulder were one huge bruise where the bear's paw had stunned him with unbelievable force, and who knew what damage might lie beneath? It hurt to breathe, which possibly, maybe even probably, meant cracked ribs, but there was nothing to do except endure.

One by one, he thought, we're succumbing to forces we can't control. As it had been sometimes from sniper and mortar fire in Nam. And now fresh troops had arrived. Good? Or simply more bodies committed to a lost cause?

Wilt was watching Billy across the fire. The kid was shivering, but he was also scowling in thought, and Wilt wondered why. A strange, quiet kid, withdrawn like himself, but apparently standing up well to what was at best a harrowing experience.

You never knew, Wilt thought, just how you would react when the familiar props of civilization were suddenly snatched away and you were left on your own to improvise. He had seen it before, even helped prepare for it in survival training. But you never knew until it actually happened. And by and large this entire group was reacting well. They were still alive; there was the proof.

Patty crossed the cave and knelt beside her mother. She spoke quietly. "Okay?"

Through numbed lips, "I'm fine, dear."

"No." Patty shook her head. Tears were close again. "You're not, but you're—doing fine." She took a deep breath. "I'm—proud of you. Of both of you. And I'm proud of Billy. I—just wanted you to know."

Sue Ann sat quietly studying the girl's face. How long has it been, she thought, since we have been like this, mother and daughter close, women together in a male world? She said slowly, carefully, as she held out her hand, "I think we can be proud together, dear."

Lila was watching Patty and Sue Ann. There had been a chasm between mother and daughter. Was it closing now? God help me, Lila thought suddenly, I am involved with all of them, they have become a part of my life too! Silently she sent her thoughts and hopes across the cave.

Ben said, "I think I owe you a big one." For a moment he thought the words had not been heard.

Then Lila turned her head slowly to look at him. Owe? she wondered; was that the word? She shook her head in silent answer to her own question.

"You were the one who found me," Ben said. "I seem to remember that. And being pushed up to the trail." Strange, there was sense of neither shame nor embarrassment at this confession of his own weakness. Maybe he had gone beyond that. "Thanks," he said.

Lila looked across the cave again. Sue Ann and Patty were no longer talking; they were just sitting, side by side, both of them looking down protectively at Warner. The family finally closes ranks, Lila thought; and where had that concept come from? No matter; it was a warm thing to see. She turned her head toward Ben once more. "I threw you a lifeline," she said. "You did the same for me. Isn't that how people are supposed to behave?"

He had said his thanks, done what convention required. He could retreat again now into his own shell which kept the world outside. "So they say. But it doesn't always work out that way. Not always, not even often."

Lila watched him steadily. I'm tired, she thought, and confused, or I wouldn't be like this, suddenly angry. But the words would not be stilled. "I don't know what soured you on—everything," she said. "But it did a good job. What I don't see is why you even bothered to keep the rest of us alive until now. There wasn't anything in it for you."

It was slow work gathering wood, poking through

snow for suitable fallen branches, breaking them loose, piling them at the foot of the trail, tramping back through the snow and the fallen rocks to gather more.

"Enough," Bart said at last. He was breathing deeply, but not hard. He was feeling the cold more than he cared to admit, so it was safe to assume that CJ was close to his limit. "You might start hauling it up. I'll gather more." At least on the trampled trail CJ would not be coping with the heavy snow that lay, and was still building, on the canyon floor. "There's a cable saw in the cave."

CJ merely nodded. He was a strong man with pride in his strength and endurance, and yet he was almost beat and Bart showed no signs of fatigue. The big bastard was inhuman, and if he wanted he probably could just go on indefinitely while others dropped like flies. That would have been bad enough for the ego, but what really galled was that Bart always seemed to know when others had had all they could stand, and then, like a watchful teacher with a bunch of kids, *he* would call the rest stop. So, okay, as a leader Bart was admirable, but, by God, CJ retained the right to resent the hell out of him. Still, Bart's mild order made sense.

CJ trudged dutifully up the trail with his first load, bent into the snow and wind, reached the cave entrance, squatted on his snowshoes and began to pass wood inside to Wilt. "More coming," he said.

Wilt studied him. "You okay? I can take over."

CJ shook his head. "You mind the store. Like he said." He took a kind of perverse pride in obeying orders as he rose and shuffled back down the trail.

Wilt carried wood across the cave. He had already seen the cable saw, and he set to work with it now, stacking cut pieces in a neat pile, handy to the fire.

Billy still wore his worried frown. His fire-tending movements were automatic, and his attention was obviously far beyond the cave walls.

"It isn't the end of the world yet," Wilt said. His voice was gentle with encouragement. "It's a rough deal, but—"

"I'm trying to remember something," Billy said. His

teeth chattered. He ignored them. "You know how it is?"

"Sure, kid." Wilt formed his own words with some difficulty. He picked up the saw again.

"It's important," Billy said. "At least I think it is." He stared at the flames for a few moments. "What's our elevation here? Ben said something over ten thousand feet."

"Just about right," Wilt said. "The canyon rim above us is ten-five. Why?"

Billy shook his head. He was not sure he knew why, but the figures seemed important. "And how high is the top of this whole big mountain?"

"White Peak? Twelve-four."

"That's what I thought. I read about it."

A strange kid, Wilt thought, with a mind that went off on tangents. "Thinking of climbing it?" he said. "It's a fair haul, especially in wintertime."

Suddenly Billy's face cleared. He shook his head in slow wonderment. "That's it," he said. "That's what I've been trying to think of."

"Are you all right, kid?"

Billy was shaking his head again, but this time without enthusiasm. "But maybe it wouldn't work anyway. I mean, how would you know?"

Wilt put down the saw. Either the kid was off in some kind of dream world which cold, altitude and lack of oxygen could induce, or he had something that ought to be settled before it really bugged him. "Maybe you'd better tell me what's on your mind," Wilt said. And he added, "No matter how far out it is."

"Okay," Bart told CJ, "take up that load, get inside the cave, warm up and get some rest. I'll be along." From the depths of his parka hood his breath emerged as a cloud of steam in the cold, snow-filled air. His feet were numb, and he was beginning to give his hands visual rather than automatic internal orders.

"If this snow keeps up," CJ said, "this is going to be our last chance to get wood." It was angry pride speaking now. "We'd better—"

189

"I'll get another load or two," Bart said. His voice took on a tone of command. "Split. You're dragging, and we don't want another casualty." He turned away then and plodded off.

CJ stood hesitant, watching Bart's immense bulk move off into the falling snow at its steady, inexorable pace. There the big bastard went again, playing the teacher, do-this-do-that-because-that's-all-you're-capable-of, as if a man couldn't think for himself. Defiance was tempting, but CJ put it aside reluctantly. The hell of it was, the big son of a bitch was right again, as usual. I've reached the end of my tether, he told himself; face it, I'm beat, and damned near frozen. He turned away and started clumsily up the trail as he had been told.

The thought of the cave and its comparative warmth was tempting to Bart too, but it would have to wait. Unlike CJ, he had not yet approached the end of his endurance; and CJ was right, they had better gather all the wood they could now before the snow was too deep and the still dropping temperature, *and* the wind, made working outside impossible.

Bart was aware that CJ resented being told what to do, and it was probably his own fault, Bart told himself, a basic lack within him that it was so; merely one more instance of his inability to communicate on an equal-to-equal basis.

It was not that he was particularly heavy-handed, as some were, or that he carried a perpetual chip on his shoulder, or that he could not control his temper; it was none of these things. And he rarely found it difficult to see the other fellow's viewpoint, even though however firmly, but almost always mildly, he might disagree with it.

Nor was he tongue-tied or even shy in social gatherings. He could be outwardly as gregarious and conversational as the next man. But always there was, and had been as long as he could remember, a sense of difference, of not really belonging, of being totally unable to achieve the ultimate feeling of relaxation that would make him a part of the group, one of the boys.

Maybe it was his size, maybe it was a variety of other things; he had never spent the effort or time required to try to pin it down. It was there, and that was that, and he had learned to live with it, which was one of the reasons, probably the main reason, he was far happier and more comfortable working alone in Santo Cristo than he had ever been in the vast California corporation.

Until last night.

Last night—God, it seemed a long time ago!—had been not only an exception, it had been *the* exception. Connie, asking nothing, not even trying to break through that invisible barrier, merely accepting him, and *liking* him in intimacy *just as he was,* there was the miracle. And this morning when she had gone to the door in the pre-dawn with him, and said that last night was not something to forget, but rather something to think about, there was the miracle extended freely and without strings. It was a memory treasured in his mind, to be brought out and examined with care at a later time.

He shuffled up the trail now with a penultimate load, pushed the wood through the entrance and started back down again, moving his feet by force of will. He stumbled, almost fell, righted himself without annoyance and plodded on until he reached the bottom of the trail. There he paused for a brief respite before he gathered up the last load.

He had cut it pretty fine, he thought, closer to the limit of his endurance than he had realized. The temptation was to sit down, rest for only a few minutes even here in the open with the snow falling heavily and then get up to struggle the final time up the trail— and he knew that that temptation was a blueprint for extinction, a siren call to inevitable oblivion.

The human body was a marvelous thing, and as an engineer he could appreciate its finely tuned, self-adjusting, built-in systems of control and defense.

His hands and his feet were numb and the numbness was spreading up his arms and legs simply because the regulatory mechanisms of the autonomic nervous system were limiting the supply of warming blood to expendable extremities, withdrawing the body's lines of defense against cold to the vital torso area which had at all costs to be defended. Eminently sensible.

He faced the upward trail again, took a deep breath, the deepest, bent forward and began the steady climb. The trick was not to look up the trail, which then would stretch endlessly, but rather to keep your eyes on the trampled snow immediately ahead and concentrate on moving first one foot and then the other, if possible emptying your mind of all considerations of time and distance. Think of something else.

Okay, how long would the wood CJ and he had gathered and carried up to the cave last? And when it was finished, what then? I don't know the answer, Bart thought, but when the time comes we'll think of something. We'll have to.

He was unaware that he had stumbled again and gone down to his knees. He shook his head now as if to clear it, took another deep breath, tried to rise and failed. All right, he told himself with no sense of surprise, now we crawl.

He shifted the precious load of wood to one arm, placed the other hand flat in the snow and began to hunch himself forward. How far was it to the cave entrance? Never mind; there were no longer dimensions or distance; there remained only the will to go on.

Carl came back into the cleanliness and the quiet bustle of the hospital, taking off and shaking gloves and cap as he walked down the corridor. The doctor he had seen before was not around, but he found a nurse he knew, a square, no-nonsense, middle-aged woman, her absurdly tiny nurse's cap perched squarely on her gray head.

"It's you," she said. "At least you had the sense to bring him here where we can patch him up. Oh, he'll live and probably be good as new one day and go out and do it all over again. No, you can't see him yet. They're still reducing that fractured shoulder. Then—" She stopped to glare. "What did you say?"

First Carter, Carl thought, and then the unnamed son of a bitch who had gotten the truck stuck crosswise. Now this. The sense of relief in the contrast was palpable. "You won't believe it," he said, "but I love you."

On the telephone to Jake Boone the governor let some of his frustration come out. "For your information, Jake, there is a truck stuck sideways across the road. Lopez turned up a snow-cat that might have gotten up, but the truck's in the way and it can't be moved."

There was a long silence. Jake said at last. "That's my truck."

"I know. It has your JB brand painted on the door."

"I thought—" Jake's voice stopped. When he spoke again his voice had changed. "I blew it, Manny."

"Yes, Jake, you did."

"Son of a bitch," Jake said, and hung up.

There was the cave entrance. On knees and one hand, Bart lifted his head and stared at it, almost unbelieving. Then, still clutching the armload of wood, he began to squeeze his bulk through.

Inside, Wilt crouched in earnest conversation with the boy who tended the fire, and Steve knelt beside them, listening.

CJ sat slumped against the wall, his head back and his eyes closed.

Ben and Lila sat unmoving, unnoticing, gathering their own strength; and the three other Harlows, mother, daughter and recumbent father, were closed into their own private world.

No one even knows I've come back, Bart thought, and had an insane urge to laugh. Instead he dropped the wood on the dirt floor, crawled to the nearest area of cave wall and leaned back against it, breathing in great gasps, his eyes closed, and waited for the inevitable pain of returning circulation. He had no idea how long it was before he heard Wilt beside him speaking in a quiet voice filled with concern.

"You okay? You look beat, almost as bad as CJ."

Bart opened his eyes. The cave came slowly back into focus, and Wilt's words took on meaning. "Okay," Bart said. His lips were stiff, and his voice was scarcely audible. He tried it again. "Okay," he repeated. "What's up?"

Wilt said, "Maybe you'd better just sit here, take it easy. You worked getting Jaime loose, and hauled that litter up, and now this wood gathering—"

"I said I'm okay." His voice was stronger now. Bart made himself sit straight. There was the pain of returning feeling in his arms and legs now, and the numbness was beginning to leave his hands and feet, which would mean more pain, much more. But pain he could endure, and the fact that there was pain proved that his extremities were still alive. And his thoughts, if not yet quite clear, had lost that deceptive sense of euphoria. "What's doing?"

It was a measure of the respect they all had for the big guy, Wilt thought, that he had felt it necessary to break into Bart's deserved rest. But the fact of the matter was that judgment was needed, Wilt did not want to make the evaluation entirely on his own and even a less than whole Bart was better than most men at their peak.

"Okay," he said. "The kid has come up with a wild idea I think you'd better hear." He was squatting beside Bart now, and he kept his voice low. "We've been thinking about getting back down to the city. What about going up? At least some of us?" He raised one hand. "I know, I know, it sounds crazy. But the ski basin is up there, only a couple of miles, up to the rim and around the shoulder of the mountain. The kid had read about it and he saw the sign for the ski basin road when they were driving up, and he asked me where it was. That started me looking at the map."

Bart gathered himself. He rubbed his whiskery face with one big, still faintly numb and increasingly painful hand. He was not at all sure he was thinking clearly, but the idea had to be considered because any idea deserved attention. Glancing briefly around the cave, he thought: we can't be any worse off than we are, or will be when the wood runs out, or when the next avalanche triggers another rock slide and this whole cave comes down on us. He said slowly, "Suppose a couple of us could get there, then what would we have? There's nobody in the basin this early in the season. And we couldn't get these people up there anyway."

"The telephone," Wilt said. "It might still be connected. Then at least we'd have communication."

True, and obvious, or ought to have been. It would not be much, but it would be better than nothing. Bart brought the map into his mind and studied it. It was, as Wilt had said, only a couple of miles to the basin. He held down any sense of enthusiasm. "Those are a couple of cold, hard miles."

Up on the rim without protection the wind would be blowing the snow horizontally like harsh driven spray. Footing would be treacherous. The higher you went, the colder it would be. And maybe when, or if, you did reach the cluster of buildings at the base of the ski lift, the phone would not be connected after all and the entire labor would have been for nothing.

"No more than two hours," Wilt said. "Probably less." He had thought that he was almost prepared to make the decision on his own. He knew now that he was not. He wanted, he needed, Bart's approval.

"A gamble," Bart said.

Wilt nodded. He could not deny it.

Bart looked around the cave again. Ten people, he thought, one in critical condition, two more injured, all of them now his responsibility. Their numbers, their condition and their location were all unknown down in the city, where, presumably, at least thought was being given to rescue operations—when weather permitted. And so even the possibility of a telephone was worth almost any risk, wasn't it? Well? Make up your mind.

Wilt said slowly, "A gamble, like you said." Steve had joined them. She bent low to hear. "But what we've got here," Wilt went on, "is a sure thing—

the wrong way. We stay in this cave and just wait and hope—and we're dead. If the roof doesn't fall in, sooner or later we'll run out of wood, and either way it's all over." He glanced up at Steve. "Sorry, *chica,* but that's how it is."

"I'd already figured it out for myself," Steve said. Her face was set. "I say we go." Wish us luck, Jaime, she thought, but save some for yourself, too.

So in the end it decided itself, Bart thought; big decisions frequently did, which was something too many people did not comprehend. He spoke to Wilt. "Give me a few minutes. I'll go with you."

"You're beat."

"You're not going alone." Never alone on a venture such as this; too many things could happen, all of them bad. And CJ—"

"I'm going with him," Steve said. Her voice was firm. "Don't argue, damn it. You've been going easy on me all day and I'm as good on a trail as Wilt is. I—"

Wilt squeezed her arm. He was smiling; the decision made, he felt immediate relief. "Let's go, *chica.*" And then, to Bart once more. "Two hours. We'll be back. This time you mind the store."

15.

THE OFFICIAL REPORT ESTIMATED that sixteen inches of snow had fallen on Santo Cristo. "The figure," Brady Shaw said, "doesn't mean a damn thing; averages seldom do. Some houses are blocked to roof height by drifting, automobiles are completely buried, the highway people report six-foot drifts in places— six foot in the open!—and in other places the roadway is almost clear because of the wind. Why, just outside town a big semi, what they call an eighteen-wheeler, with a full load, hit glare ice and was blown sideways clear across the road and off into an arroyo. They're still trying to cut the driver out with torches. Sixteen inches, hell! That doesn't begin to tell the story." He gestured around the office at the instruments, the teletypes, all of the paraphernalia of modern meteorological science. "You know what this reminds me of?"

His assistant shook his head. There was simply no following the old man's thoughts. "No, sir."

"There was this king," Brady said, "who sat in his tent while a big battle was being fought outside, moving little pieces around on a board and giving orders for his generals to follow. Finally he leaned back in his chair and said, 'There. We've won. They are competely destroyed.'" He looked at his assistant. "You know what happened next?"

The assistant shook his head again although this time he could have guessed the answer. How often had he heard the old man say, "Before you say it's a fine day according to your charts, you'd damn well better have a look out the window. It may be raining like hell."

"Some of the victorious enemy walked into the tent," Brady said, "and cut the king's head off."

The assistant was silent. It was all very well for the old man to carp about the questionable accuracy of weather forecasting; everybody else did too. But what did he suggest they might do about it?

"I'll tell you what," Brady said, as if he had been reading the assistant's mind. "In not too long that telephone over there is going to ring and somebody, probably the governor, is going to want to know exactly when the snow is going to stop and how long it will be before it starts up again so they can plan to get a chopper into the air because those poor damn people are still up there on the mountain, and there comes a time when you can't just sit any longer with your thumb up your ass waiting."

"But," the assistant said, "we can't give them that kind of precise information. No one can."

Brady nodded. "You know it, and I know it, but they don't know it, or at least won't believe it. They're going to give it everything they have, even if it doesn't work. And you know what? So are we."

Up the ancient but now almost hidden trail to the rim, at least partially in the lee of the canyon wall, was the easy part—if you could call it that. Wilt was in the lead, and his lungs ached from the climb against the sometimes gusting wind, and from the cold, which was no longer a negative as they said in textbooks, the simple absence of heat, but rather a force of its own with the power to drain your muscles of their strength, your body of its fearlessness and your mind of its will. The cold was inescapable.

You could bend into the wind and by this much shield your face from its searing force, but there was no way of evading the cold which was everywhere, coming from all directions, sucking out your living warmth and leaving only the husk.

Wilt reached the top of the trail, came into the open and was almost blown over sideways. He steadied himself, leaned against the wind and the biting snow and looked back at Steve.

Deep in her parka hood her face was almost invisible, but by a trick of the light her eyes seemed to glitter angrily, as if she took the wind, the snow and the cold as personal affronts, threats of malign forces of nature before which she refused to cower.

Wilt had to shout to make himself heard. "Okay?"

"Go on! I'll follow!"

Wilt had never worked on a team with Steve before. Always her partner had been Jaime, who alone could match her special talents for rock climbing and skiing. "You don't have to worry about *guapa*," Jaime had said once out of Steve's hearing. "When you get where you're going, she's right there with you ready to lend a hand if you need it."

Still. "Look," Wilt shouted, "it's going to get worse going around that shoulder!"

"We're going to the ski basin, aren't we?"

Wilt nodded briefly.

"Then let's get at it!"

It was a warm thing to work with someone who displayed such determination and confidence, and there was a smile in Wilt's mind as he turned away, bent into the wind and began his steady, painful, plodding shuffle, one snowshoe ahead of the other in a relentless rhythm.

There was no need for his compass. The map had been clear enough, and his own sense of the terrain could be depended upon to fill in the minor gaps. Their trail lay across the head of the cirque in the howling wind, and then on a long climbing slant around the mountain's shoulder into the ski basin itself.

He did not harbor even a faint hope that there would be anyone there when they arrived. The chair lift had long since stopped running for summer visitors who wanted to admire the almost limitless view; the crews who had worked during the summer clearing the slopes were back in school or college; and the skiing season was at least a month away. Or, Wilt thought, ought to have been, and probably still was. This storm was a freak, a once-in-a-hundred-years storm, as the records would show, and after it was over, a sudden thaw, maybe even a chinook, could erode the snow almost as fast as it had fallen.

Which, he thought, is no help to us now. Head down he plodded along, ignoring the torment of the driving snow and the cold, occasionally glancing over his shoulder to see Steve right on his heels.

Quite a girl. He had often wondered if there was anything between her and Jaime. It was none of his business, of course, but it was sometimes pleasant to speculate. For all her toughness on a trail, a rock face or on skis, Steve was distinctly feminine as well when she chose to be, a fact Wilt was sure had not escaped Jaime's notice. Jaime always called her *guapa,* which meant not only good-looking, but also sexy, for whatever that might mean.

Here on the wind-scoured open rim the snow was not deep, a mere six or eight inches, and they would probably have done almost as well without webs. But once they came around that shoulder into the basin it would be a different thing, as it had been down in the canyon drifts. Snowshoes had their purpose, of course, but on them your progress was excruciatingly slow, totally unlike going on skis, either cross-country or downhill.

Skis! "Oh, my God!" He said it aloud, almost as a prayer, as the new thought struck him. And he held the thought in his mind as a fragile thing, almost afraid to look at it straight on lest it shatter. "Be there!" he whispered. "Be there!" It was difficult to keep from breaking into a shambling, stumbling trot.

Sue Ann's hand rested against Warner's cheek. His cheek was cold, and every shallow breath he took seemed to Sue Ann as if it would be his last, but the breathing went on and on and on, bringing pain into her chest too, but also strength to fight the aching cold and the fear that had seeped into her inner being.

Because Warner was a fighter. He had always been. He expressed himself largely in clichés, which were always suspect, but the difference between Warner and most who used the same clichés was that what he said, he meant. "It's never over until the final whistle." How often had she heard him say that? Or, "Quitters never win, and winners never quit." Warner's creed. It had always been; something to rely on.

It was of course both a strength and a weakness, this total refusal to give up. There were times when the sensible course was to take your losses and walk away. Billy saw that, as Warner did not. Maybe it was because Billy did not care enough about things like winning or losing, although Warner had seen it differently.

"The kid hasn't any guts," he had said once when Billy had backed away from Little League competition. And that wasn't fair because who could fault Billy's performance right here in the cave with the burning stick against that horrible bear? Maybe Billy's courage was simply of a different kind.

Warner applied his own standards to others, too, there was the trouble. And yet would she change him if she could? The answer had to be no. It was his creed that was keeping him alive right now supporting her too, and although it was a losing battle he was waging, of that Sue Ann was sure, he was fighting on, one shallow breath after another, and would continue —until the final whistle blew.

She began to talk, softly, steadily, letting her thoughts seek their own direction. It was that, or open tears. She neither knew nor cared whether Patty sitting close could hear her words:

"Do you remember that week we spent in Mexico with Jake and Ethel? All those ruins and the flowers on the lake, the buses out on the highways always blowing black smoke, and that Saturday market where you bought me that beautiful embroidered surplice?

"We didn't see the mountains because of the smog, but they are even taller than these, and I didn't think of it before, but Mexico City is almost the same elevation as Santo Cristo, isn't it? Jake did mention that. Jake was in good form. He didn't lose his temper once. He even joked about Montezuma's revenge, remember? He called it the Aztec two-step.

"You have always worried that we have never gotten to Europe. I don't care, Warner. Other things are far more important, and you've given me those. Our home, Patty and Billy, all the friends anyone could ask for, far more than we ever thought we would have when we began.

"You've always worried that we didn't have as much as Jake and Ethel, and I don't care about that, either. I don't think they've enjoyed themselves a bit more than we have, or even as much.

"You have been working too hard and I should have seen it. My fault. I am sorry. I'm afraid I have missed other things too, not because I wanted to, believe that, please, but rather that other things, things that are not important, have a way of becoming habit before you realize it and all at once you find your days and your thoughts—*cluttered* is the word, with nonessentials.

"When Patty and Billy were little, yes, and we, you and I, had less, things were simpler. You had the business, and I had the children. It was as easy as that, do you remember? But Patty is a—young woman now, almost able to live her own life.

"And Billy is, well, Billy. But you will be proud of him, dear, that I know. You and he are different. He admires you. He has told me so. But the difference is there, and his way is not your way, but that doesn't mean that it is not a good way, too, please try to see that.

"When this—nightmare is over, and we are home again—*home*. I don't think the word has ever meant so much. You'll have to rest, and there'll be time to talk, to do some of the little things we used to do— how long has it been since we played cribbage, and kept the running score and couldn't wait until the children were in bed to get to our game that didn't really mean a thing except that we played it together?"

Her voice changed suddenly. "Oh, Warner, we've let too much slip by! We'll make it up! I promise!"

The words stopped then. She stifled the tears and sat quiet, her hand against Warner's cheek, drawing strength from the contact even as she listened to the painful, shallow breathing.

Patty had listened to the monologue, at first with embarrassment as if she had been caught listening at a keyhole, but then with growing understanding, a sudden sense of warmth and pride, and a feeling of family solidarity that had been lacking before. Even toward Billy, carefully tending the fire, annoying as a little brother though he sometimes was, who came strongly now into her affection. Who would have thought that Billy would turn suddenly, well, heroic, driving away that horrible bear? Or that he would think of something, whatever it was, that had obviously impressed these new people and sent the man and the big strong girl out again into the snow?

The warmth Patty had generated beneath the space blanket with Lila was dissipated now, and she was shivering again. She wondered if she could take the blanket again, just for herself, and rejected the idea as too obviously selfish. For the first time, she was beginning to feel hope that the ordeal would somehow end. Ben was hurt, but he had carried them this far, and just when he could carry them no longer these new ones had appeared, the huge man who had taken charge, the other two men and the big girl who dealt on even terms with the men and was clearly respected by them. They would find a way out somehow.

Her mother's voice had stopped, but the inner warmth, pride and sense of family had not left Patty. *I am proud of you, Billy. I am proud of all of us—yes, even now of myself. I did help Daddy. And Lila.*

She glanced at her mother's face and then again at her father, and listened to his shallow, painful breathing. Words formed soundlessly in her mind. "You mustn't die, Daddy! You mustn't!"

Leaning against the cave wall, ignoring the pain of returning circulation in hands and feet, Bart watched the girl's face, tried to guess what thoughts were behind it and finally gave up. Slowly he gathered himself and got to his feet, bending low to clear the cave roof. It occurred to him that those who had originally used this cave must have been small people—and the thought merely reminded him how easy it was in fatigue to let your mind wander. He brought himself back to the present with effort. Standing above CJ, "How's it going?"

I quit before he did, CJ thought, *and I've had longer to rest, but he's the one who's up and around, taking charge again.* His hands and feet were painful too, but his earlier resentment and anger were forgotten. "I'll live."

For the fourth time they heard the sudden distant

rumbling, and then felt the movement of the cave floor beneath them. A piece of the wall dislodged itself and fell clattering. Outside, they heard other rocks crashing down the canyon wall. Then there was silence.

"That snow keeps building up," Bart said for them all to hear, "and down it comes." His voice was unconcerned. He shrugged. "A lot of noise, that's all."

Ben raised his head and looked up at Bart. He said nothing, but his eyes were eloquent. He knows just as well as I do, Bart thought, that it's a great deal more than a lot of noise; that the next slide or the one after that could be the one that will collapse this entire rock structure and kill us outright or drive us out into the open where we might last a little longer, but not much. He said without inflection, "How's the shoulder? Want me to take a look?"

Ben shook his head. "Nothing to do. Maybe something's bent, that's all." He was near the end of his endurance. "There are some pain pills in my pack—"

"I know where they are." This was Lila. She got slowly to her feet, and stood for a moment looking at both men, so different in make-up and approach, Ben almost perpetually angry and Bart quiet and gentle, and yet basically similar if not identical in that imponderable quality called leadership which could accomplish miracles. We are lucky, she thought; and then corrected herself: we are *alive* only because of the two of them. Aloud, "Now we just wait, is that it?" she said to Bart. Her breath was visible when she spoke.

"We just wait," Bart said. And hope, he added; and knew not for what.

16.

FRANK SILVA CAME AGAIN INTO THE GOVERNOR'S office, but this time almost on tippy-toe. He waited with uncharacteristic patience until the governor noticed him and leaned back in his chair. "Yes, Frank?"

There was nothing in the governor's tone to indicate that he still held against Frank that direct order that had brought Carter and the S&R jeep down the mountainside. The governor had accepted the blame, and that was that; there would be no further recriminations, but neither would the matter be forgotten, and Frank had damn well better not screw up again soon. "Uh," Frank said, "these." He held up a sheaf of papers. "Phone calls, telegrams." He shook his head. "From all over the country! Ideas, real, far-out ideas, you wouldn't believe!"

The governor was silent.

"And the TV," Frank said. "It isn't the local stations now. It's networks. And phone calls from the New York *Times,* the L.A. *Times,* the Chicago *Trib,* the Washington *Post* . . ."

"Okay," the governor said, and held out his hand. "Let's see what we have."

He read steadily for a time and then again leaned back in his chair and stared at the ceiling. What they had, he thought, was one of those stories that could get completely out of hand, and then all at once be dropped, leaving only vague memories and entirely too strong an impression that the New Mexico mountains of which they were so proud were the hell of a place to visit because God only knew what might happen if you so much as took a wrong turn on the road. But what was there to do to counter those impressions? Nothing.

And some of the suggestions well-meaning people had sent in were, as Frank had said, clear out of sight. Laser beams or an atomic bomb to melt the snow; tunnels beneath the snow; search dogs carrying brandy and lifelines; guided missiles to carry lifesaving supplies; cloud-seeding to shorten the storm . . .

A number of the messages mentioned prayer, and an almost equal number demanded severe punishment for those responsible for the plight of the trapped victims. Obviously two different ways of looking at the same situation, the governor thought: faith versus vengeance; New Testament versus the Old.

There were offers of help, from individuals, from other Search and Rescue teams . . .

"CBS," Frank said, "wants to film an interview with you for the evening news."

Just as I wanted Bart Wallace to leave what he was doing and go back to the jeeps to talk to me on the UHF, the governor thought. Strange, how different it looked when you saw it from the other end. "No interview until we have something to report," he said, "and probably then they won't be interested. What's the weather? Any sign of a break?"

"No, sir. And Washington has been on the phone again. Senator Baca—"

The frustrations he felt simply had to have release. "Tell Joe Baca for me to go screw himself," the governor said.

They were around the shoulder of the great mountain now and into the shelter of the trees on the floor of the ski basin. Wilt slogged on steadily, half frozen, head bent, only occasionally glancing over his shoulder to see Steve right on his heels. He paused to orient himself.

Snow had drifted unevenly, and identification was not simple, but here was the lower parking area, flat and open, and there the road that led to the buildings hidden now in the falling snow. Beneath that mound

206

of snow was the bench where one bright afternoon just about this time of year, he remembered, he had sat for a couple of hours doling out sunflower seeds and watching the behavior of Steller's jays, Clark's nutcrackers, camp robbers, gray squirrels and one bold chipmunk, panhandlers all.

Beside him Steve said indistinctly, "The closest building? If any phones are connected, they'll all be."

And vice versa, Wilt thought; they may all be dead. He refused even to look at the other possibility that was in his mind as he started across the parking field.

Here, looming suddenly through the snow curtain, was the building housing the machinery that drove the chair lift, and there stretching out of sight was the doubled cable, the chairs themselves like beads on a necklace facing downhill on one strand and uphill on the other, silent and motionless, patiently bearing their burden of fresh snow.

Wilt turned left, across the foot of the nursery slope toward the small building where they sold soft drinks and candy and hot soup, so welcome after a cold run down one of the intermediate or expert trails. God, how good that would taste now!

There would be a phone inside the building, but with the new idea strong in his mind, Wilt did not pause, and Steve followed him in numb, wondering silence to the larger building, which housed the restaurant, the bar and the shops, shuttered and now empty of merchandise.

Wilt clumsily unfastened his snowshoes, stood them against the railing and lurched up the steps. Steve waited, her back to the wind. Automatically Wilt tried one door and then a second. They were locked, of course. He shook his head at Steve and trudged around the broad porch out of her sight. She stood in stolid patience, ignoring the snow and the cold, at last letting her thoughts turn where they tended to go, toward Jaime.

She had wanted desperately to go down the mountain with Carl and the injured man, to see for herself

207

that they reached the hospital safely, to know that Jaime's injuries were not grave, or even, God forbid, fatal. She had not realized before how deeply she cared.

But it was essential that Carl go because he was the one with para-medical knowledge and skills, and for her to join him, although she was sure Bart would have allowed it, would have been to leave only three to carry on the search, and an uneven number was no good. It took two to make a team; one was never allowed alone.

And now there was no way of knowing how Jaime was, whether he would ever again flash that smile at her, call her *guapa* in that soft voice, call down encouragement to her from a rock face that looked impossible to climb or lead her down an unbroken field of powder snow in long, swooping curves of sheer exhilaration.

Before today it had been a long time since she had been even vaguely tempted to tears. But she had been scarcely able to contain them as she watched Jaime being loaded into the jeep; and they were very close again now. If the telephones were connected, a call to the hospital, or a talk at least with Carl—

The door at the top of the steps opened and Wilt looked out. His voice reached her faintly. "No phones! But come up anyway!" He turned away and disappeared.

No phones, no possibility of word, nothing. Steve's mind felt suddenly dead. She bent automatically to fumble with her snowshoe harness. There were no tears. She was beyond that.

She straightened at last, stood the snowshoes beside Wilt's and trudged clumsily up the steps. It took a moment for her eyes to adjust to the dim light inside where Wilt stood waiting.

"No phones," Wilt said. In the absence of wind, his voice was overloud.

"You said that." But there was something in his voice beyond disappointment. "So?"

"I'm a breaker and enterer," Wilt said. His tone

208

was almost exuberant. "Never mind how. We experts don't give up our secrets."

"Wilt! What is it?"

"The ski shop, *chica*. I was hoping. No new skis, but racks of rental skis. And boots. And the rescue sled is there. We wouldn't last in this cold getting down the mountain on snowshoes, but on skis, downhill, even with somebody on the sled—" He shook his head in happy wonder. "We can do it. We've got to. Come on. Let's get ourselves fitted."

Carl, summoned, sat in Captain Lopez's office and ignored the blue haze of stale smoke. The third man, whose name was Pete Benjamin, left most of the talking to the captain.

"Pete here," the captain said, "is one of our chopper pilots." He raised a hand to forestall Carl's comment. "I know, I know, we can't put a chopper in the air now. But sooner or later this snow will stop, and what we want to know is where can a chopper land then?" He opened the map on his desk. "You've been there. Show us."

We're just going through the motions, Carl thought, because we can't get a chopper up now, and God only knows when we will be able to, and we don't even know where anybody up there is anyway, so what the hell good is this kind of foolishness? He and Jaime were down and Jaime would live, but the others were beyond help. It was a dismal concept.

The captain read Carl's thoughts without trouble. "When you're all through finding reasons against," the captain said wearily, "maybe you'll tell us what we want to know." He lighted a fresh cigarette, took two long drags and dropped the cigarette into an almost empty paper cup of coffee with an air of finality. "Okay. Are you through sulking?"

Carl took a deep breath and bent over the map. So okay, we go through the motions. "This canyon wall is almost sheer. You can see that. And down in here—" He moved his finger over the canyon floor where he and Bart had searched for the plane. "Trees and rocks. No way to put down there."

Benjamin put his finger on the open area where the service road led downhill. "That looks possible."

"Forget it. That," Carl said, "is where the rock slides came through. There isn't anything there any more." Except the raw slide, the wreckage of a car and trailer, and Jaime's climbing rope still taut to its belay.

The captain too was studying the map. "That leaves this area up here." He touched the rim above the cirque. "It looks flat enough. Are there rocks, trees?" He bent closer to read a contour marking. "It's below timberline."

"No," Carl said, "it's open. And it's flat."

The captain studied his face. "You're still dragging your feet. Why?"

"I don't know much about choppers," Carl said, "but I've seen them throw up a lot of dust when they land even before they touch ground." He looked at Benjamin. "They throw down quite a blast, no?"

"That's what keeps them in the air."

"So?" the captain said.

"A sonic boom set off the first slide," Carl said. "I don't know what kicked off the second. You put a chopper down there and start throwing snow around, and God only knows what kind of a slide that will start. Or what it will do."

Lila had given Ben the Demerol pill, and taken another across the cave to a grateful Sue Ann. Now, back against the cave wall, as close to the fire as she could get without shielding its puny heat from others, she sat shivering quietly and watched Ben's face, his closed eyes, the slow relaxation of his body as the pain-killer took effect. She waited until his eyes opened again. "Better?" It was a silly question, but continuing silence was unendurable.

Ben nodded almost imperceptibly. "Thanks."

"I'm sorry I said what I did. It was no time to pick on you."

"Forget it."

"Anything I can do?"

"No." And he added slowly, almost as an after-thought, "Thanks." The Demerol had eased but not eliminated the pain of his chest and shoulder; but more than that the drug had produced in his mind a sense of near-euphoria, almost wiping away the vague anger he seemed to have been carrying like a burden these last many months. Strange.

"I've been thinking," Lila said. Her voice was pitched low, only for his ears. "We aren't going to make it, are we?"

Ben's eyes went to Bart standing, head and shoulders bent, in the center of the cave, seemingly impervious to the cold, his face expressionless, his slow, even breaths clearly visible in the still air. "Ask him."

Lila shook her head. "I don't want command oratory. I want the truth. You and I wouldn't have lasted much longer outside. I know that. And all we're waiting for in here is for the roof to fall in and either bury us or push us back outside again. I thought the roof was coming down when the entrance was blocked. I've thought so every time there's been a slide since. And sooner or later it will happen, won't it?"

"I'm tempted," Ben said, "to say, 'How the hell should I know?' "

Lila nodded. "I wouldn't blame you. It isn't fair to lean. I know that too." She closed her eyes briefly, opened them again and stared straight ahead, avoiding his face. "Okay. You've given your answer." She was silent for a few moments. "You know the funny thing?" She turned then to look at him. "I don't think I'm afraid any more. I just don't want it to happen. There's a difference."

17.

STEVE LED, choosing the course, the front rope from the rescue sled fast around her waist. Wilt followed the sled, braking at need, steering from behind as a rudder steers a ship.

Here was no place for graceful parallel skiing; stem turns, sideslipping and snowplows were the trick, but their progress nevertheless was to laborious trudging on snowshoes as running to crawling on your belly. On occasional short straight runs they could let it out, and the snow hissed beneath their skis.

Here on the rim above the cirque, unprotected from the wind, it was unbelievably, painfully cold, and speed merely added to the agony. Once they started down the trail, Wilt thought it would be slower, and better. He hoped.

The sled they guided so carefully was fitted with a mummy-type bag in which an injured person could be securely contained with only part of his face exposed. Piled on the sled now were their snowshoes and extra skis, poles and boots.

Wilt was under no illusion that the guided run down into Santo Cristo was going to be easy. And the more he thought about it as they made their painful way now, the more difficult it looked.

Cold was the force to be reckoned with. Given the wind, which in no way seemed likely to abate, and the constantly dropping temperature, the chill factor was probably going out of sight. What was that awesome formula? In thirty knots of wind at thirty degrees below zero, human flesh freezes in thirty seconds? Pleasant thought.

Equipment was something of a problem too, strange boots, and strange skis; but this was merely a minor difficulty they could surmount.

No, it was the cold and the fifteen or so miles of drifted, and possibly in places blocked, road they would have to negotiate safely with a heavily loaded sled that posed the challenge. It would be an obstacle race against the cold, a gamble, with at least three lives at stake: Warner on the sled, and Steve and himself. And in the race, there would be no second place; either they won, or they lost. So be it.

Billy waited until Bart prowled again toward the fire, stopped and began to turn away. "I've been thinking," Billy said. He watched the big man turn back, hesitate and then hunker down beside him to listen. "I mean," Billy said, "I've been trying to think of, you know, something."

"I know," Bart said. There was only patient interest in his voice. "And?"

"Well, I mean, nothing works out. You read about all kinds of things you can do, and I've thought of some others too, but—" Billy shrugged.

"Let's hear them," Bart said. The ski basin was the kid's idea. You never knew who might come up with something.

"Well," Billy said, and hesitated. Probably this big guy knew all the things he'd been able to think of, and a lot more besides. On the other hand, he had asked. "Like trampling in the snow," he said, "messages. Up on the top where we gathered wood last night. I read that from the air messages like that in the snow look black. Shadows, I think."

Bart nodded solemnly. "They do. It's a good thought, and if they can get something in the air, and the snow stops, we'll try it. What else?"

"Mom has a mirror. Patty probably has one too, girls always do. If the sun ever comes out we could send signals."

"That's another good one," Bart said. "We'll remember it." There was no mockery in his voice.

213

"Then there's smoke," Billy said. "Ben thought of that. And there's one more thing. It sounds funny, I know, but that's what it said in the ad."

"What, Billy?"

"This jacket of mine. See? It's like they say reversible, one side is black and the other side is silver-colored, like metal?"

"I see," Bart said gently. "Go on."

"Well, it is metal, if you see what I mean. And they say it reflects radar. They might even be able to spot it through the snow."

Bart took his time. He said at last, "I didn't know that, Billy." He rose to his feet. "And we'll be sure to keep it in mind."

"It might not work," Billy said.

"No, it might not." Bart's voice was grave. "But you keep on thinking anyway, and if you come up with anything else, I want to hear it. You're doing fine, better than the rest of us." He turned away to resume his prowling.

A very bright kid, he thought, in this helpless situation thinking hard instead of simply sitting feeling sorry for himself. An admirable kid. Oh, he probably wouldn't come up with anything that would solve their problems, but he was trying, not giving up, and that was what counted.

Bart paused in his prowling to smile down at Sue Ann and tried not to listen to Warner's painful breathing. "You should be proud of Billy," he said. His words emerged in a cloud of steam.

"I am." There was a faint smile touching Sue Ann's lips, despite the tremble in her voice. "I'm proud of Patty too, and of Warner. I guess pride is all we have left. Pride, and love."

"We'll see." Bart turned away.

Pride, and love, he thought. That was quite a bit when you came right down to it. Could he say as much? Pride, yes, always that, in doing well whatever he did, not because of what others might think, but simply to satisfy his own standards. Nothing

214

noble in it; it was just the way he happened to be. But love?

He doubted if he had ever really known love, and maybe that was just the way he happened to be too, but he was beginning to doubt it. Maybe despite the poems and the songs to the contrary, love wasn't something that just happened; maybe it was something you had to involve yourself in consciously. Like Sue Ann and Warner. He had never thought of it like this before, and now, he told himself, was a ridiculous time to start. Or was it?

That sudden distant rumbling sound began again, and he could feel the floor of the cave trembling beneath his feet. He made himself continue his prowling as if nothing had happened, conscious that CJ, Ben and Lila all watched him; he pointedly ignored them.

A piece of rock broke loose from the cave wall, and another. They rattled down to the floor and were still. The sudden silence seemed loud.

"In Norse mythology," Ben said unexpectedly, "I think it's the Ice Giants who shake things. Or maybe it's that wolf they tied up with magic cord."

Billy said, "In 'Rip Van Winkle,' isn't it the little men bowling?"

Good for both of you, Bart thought; good for everybody in this cave. It was with a different kind of pride that he viewed them all now, pride tinged with affection. Maybe I am beginning to learn to belong, he thought. Maybe—

On hands and knees Steve crawled through the entrance. There was snow on her parka, and she was shaking with cold, but there was a smile on her face, and triumph in her eyes. "Skis," she said, "and the rescue sled. Wilt found them." She looked at Sue Ann, and at Warner. "As soon as we warm up a little we can get him down the mountain now," she said, "where he can get the help he needs."

Jaime was under sedation, but conscious. He lay quiet in the hospital bed looking up at Carl's face.

215

"They found the plane?" His voice was weak, but clear.

"I don't know." Carl hastened to change the subject. "Anything you want? Need?"

The white teeth appeared in a shaky smile. "Some new ribs, and a shoulder, and one or two other minor parts." The smile disappeared. "Why don't you know whether they found the plane, amigo? Haven't you talked with them?"

"You better relax," Carl said. "They told me I could see you for only a few minutes. Is there anybody you want me to call?"

"Amigo." The dark eyes searched Carl's face. "What has happened? Another slide? Someone else is hurt? "¡Dígame! Tell me!"

"Now don't get excited. They'll throw me out of here."

"And I will go with you if you don't talk! What has happened?"

"You're a stubborn goddamned Chicano."

The teeth flashed briefly. "Okay," Jaime said, and the smile disappeared. "But they are my friends too. Had you forgotten that?"

In a way he had, Carl supposed, or at least he had ignored it, which was the same thing. "Okay. I'm down here, and they're up there, and we can't get to them or talk to them. That's the picture."

Jaime said slowly, "The second jeep? It—"

"It's down here too." Carl went through the entire stupid story, his anger near the point of explosion. When he had finished there was silence.

"Bart," Jaime said slowly, "CJ, Wilt—and *guapa*." He looked through the window at the driving snow. "And it is getting colder, no?"

Carl nodded in silence.

"I will have that man Carter's *cojones*," Jaime said, "and then I will have his heart."

"You'll have to stand in line."

"No." There was finality in the single word. Jaime rolled his head to look up at Carl. "If anything happens to *guapa,* he is mine. That is not a threat, amigo; that is a promise."

Warner waggled his head. His lips formed the word, "No!" but little sound emerged. Through the haze of pain, and consciousness that seemed to come and go, he tried desperately to make them understand what was so clear in his mind.

From the beginning, all my fault. Everything. It is because of me that we're here, all of us, and I have been nothing but a useless burden.

The voices he heard he had heard before, but their meanings had been unclear. Now in sudden, undependable lucidity, he managed to understand, and he wanted to shout his refusal of what they had in mind, but the shallow painful labored breaths which were the most he could manage allowed no extra air, and all he could do was survive. Barely. And that was part of it too. He was on his way out. He knew it. And so what they had in mind was wrong, all wrong. Like voices from another room, another world, he could hear the talk going on and on discussing him.

Bart said, "Take him in the sleeping bag. There's no warmth in that bag on the sled. And when you get into the trees, take some small boughs and pile them on him too. More dead air space for warmth."

The sound from Warner was not loud, but it commanded attention. He tried to form words, and failed. The best he could do was waggle his head in weak sideways, protesting movements.

All at once in the silence Sue Ann's face was close above his, and she was smiling in understanding and shaking her head too. Her eyes were very bright. "I want you to go. We all do. Please. For me." She looked up at Bart. "Take him in the sleeping bag. I'll be all right. We'll all be all right." And speaking again to Warner, "You have to believe that. We all want *you* safe! That's the important thing. We'll be all right here." Once more to Bart. "Won't we? Won't we? Tell him!"

217

Bart's voice was quiet, but decisive. "He goes down in the sleeping bag. Wilt, you, Steve and CJ—"

"Now, wait a minute," CJ said. He heaved himself wearily to his feet. "They brought enough skis and boots—"

Bart looked at Sue Ann. "You can't ski on that foot."

"I don't know how to ski anyway."

Bart nodded. He looked at Patty, "Do you? Or you, Billy?" He watched both shake their heads.

"Skip me too," Lila said. "I'm a flatlander."

Bart looked at Ben, who shook his head slowly, in silence.

"So," Bart said, "that's it. Wilt, Steve and CJ, with the sled."

Steve said, "How about you?"

There was silence. It was Wilt who broke it. "Let's get going."

Warner waggled his head again. Sue Ann said, "Hush. It's settled." She bent to kiss him, a long kiss. She straightened quickly to lean back against the wall, her face carefully expressionless. "Take care of him." Her voice was not quite steady.

Steve wore a gentle smile as she bent down and put one hand on Sue Ann's shoulder. "We'll take care of him. I promise."

Bart crawled out through the entrance to watch the sled preparations. Snow fell on Warner's exposed face. Bart said, "Put some pine boughs over him, like I said. They'll keep the snow off." He looked at them all. "Luck."

CJ said, "You're the one who needs it."

Steve slid close on her skis. "You're quite a guy." Her voice was quiet, for Bart's ears only. "I only hope that somehow, someway you can stop living all alone. You deserve a lot better." She stretched high, and poles dangling from her wrists, pulled his head down for her brief kiss. Then she turned away and started down the trail, the sled rope as before fast to her waist.

Wilt nodded and followed on his long legs.

CJ hesitated. He lifted his solid shoulders and let them fall. "See you," he said, and skied away, short and almost square in the falling snow.

Bart squinted skyward. No break that he could see. And it was colder now. Already Steve, Wilt and CJ had almost disappeared down the trail. They were not going to have an easy time of it, Bart thought, but he would have to hope that they would make it. And then?

Well, the results would be positive, if not conclusive. If Warner survived the journey he would, from the look of him, go at once into coronary care, and from there on it would be up to the medicos and Lady Luck.

Steve would be able to see what had happened to Jaime, be with him if he was still alive, at least no longer ache with the uncertainty she had been trying to conceal.

Wilt and CJ could report that Martin was dead, that there were six persons left, two of them injured, and that they were all together in the cave which either Wilt or CJ could pinpoint on the map against future rescue efforts.

Not all that much on the plus side, but what else was possible?

Nothing.

The cave was only temporary, and precarious, shelter. There had already been how many slides since that first one following the sonic boom? And each one had triggered more rock sliding, and sooner or later, the entire honeycombed structure was going to collapse. Jaime had foreseen that before they even left Santo Cristo—was it only this morning, in the early dawn?

Take your pick, he thought; be crushed to death inside the cave when the collapse comes, or be caught in the open without shelter to freeze to death.

With the clothing they had, Sue Ann, Lila, Patty and Billy would last in the open how long? An hour? Maybe.

He and Ben would last a little longer, but not much. Think, damn it, he told himself! Where is other, safer shelter? The ski basin buildings? No go. He could make it, as Wilt and Steve had, but both Sue Ann and Ben were injured, and the others were helpless. No way.

No, the cave was the only hope. And that brought a strange new thought. Across this broad land, he found himself wondering, how many people starting out in their campers and trailers or on foot with their shiny new backpacks understood that when you left the asphalt of the cities and entered the mountains, or, as far as that went, the deserts as well, you were leaving behind all convenient props and built-in safety devices, and moving toward confrontation with elemental forces which man in all his history has never been able to tame, only to evade and sometimes feebly defend himself against? And of those who did understand, how many went prepared? With proper equipment? More important, with knowledge?

Shivering, he brushed off as much snow as he could, knelt and crawled back into the cave.

Patty had moved to sit beside her mother. They were holding hands, silent, expressionless. They seemed unaware that Bart had returned.

Billy was hunkered by the fire as he had seen both Ben and Bart do. He was frowning in concentration, and all at once he looked up. "Fifteen miles," he said. "How fast can they go on skis? Ten miles an hour? More? Less?"

Ben said, "Probably a little less most of the time on that road with the sled. In some places a little faster." He looked up at Bart. "Are they good?"

"Steve is very good, racing class. Wilt and CJ are more than competent."

Ben nodded. "Then they ought to be able to do it. With luck."

Lila said quietly, "You ski?"

"Some."

"You could have gone with them."

"Now don't try to make something out of that."

"No," Lila said slowly, "of course not."

220

Ben looked up at Bart. "We're back to the waiting and hoping, no?"

"At least they'll know where we are now." It was something, but not much.

Bart squatted by the fire and held out his hands to its warmth. I might have asked Steve to call Connie, he thought. And tell her what? No. The only things I want her told I will have to tell her myself. If I get the chance. "Is there any food left in that pack of yours? I think we could all use something, anything."

18.

IN THE METEOROLOGICAL OFFICE, Brady Shaw hung up the phone and wearing a strange, self-mocking smile turned to face his assistant. "The summons has come," he said. "Another council of war in the governor's office."

"What are you going to tell them?"

The smile spread. "What they can expect in the way of a gap of clear weather to get a chopper into the air."

"You don't have to try to do that."

The smile faded. "No," Brady said, "I don't. The governor doesn't sign my paycheck. He can't tell me what to do. And there really isn't much sense in sticking my neck out by making a prediction that may be wrong, is there?"

The assistant started to speak, thought better of it, and remained silent. Only this morning, he thought, he would not have hesitated to answer. Strange.

"But," Brady said, "there are at least four people up there alive. I've never met any of them, but, by God, I feel that I know them, and if my best judgment can give them just a little better chance to get down alive, then they're going to have it, with no whereases, ifs or buts or any of the other evasions we usually try to hide behind."

"And if our prediction turns out to be wrong?"

There was that self-mocking smile again. "Then it turns out to be wrong," Brady said, "and they may cut my buttons off at dress parade for sticking the department's neck out, and you'll have a new boss. Now let's make a few phone calls." And pray to God we come up with the right answers, he thought.

Okay, roll those dice.

The first few miles went easily enough, Steve leading as before, Wilt acting as brake and rudder for the heavily loaded sled. CJ at Wilt's suggestion skied on ahead, scouting the road.

Here in the trees the wind was not as bad as it had been, but the cold alone was agonizing. With each breath Wilt could feel the hairs in his nostrils freeze, and when he exhaled, thaw. Down well below zero, he thought, and probably still dropping. Okay, think of it as a nice day in the country; or just don't think about it at all.

They had covered Warner with pine boughs as Bart had suggested, which kept the snow from his face and undoubtedly added insulation as well to supplement the sleeping bag. The man was invisible, and whether he was still alive or already dead, there was no way of knowing without pausing to look. Do not open until Christmas, Wilt thought. The poor bastard.

You were tempted always to place blame when someone landed in this kind of predicament, but it was an exercise that accomplished nothing. Worse, if you followed logic to its conclusion, and established that the victim himself was almost always at fault, then a solid case could be made for letting him take the consequences while you stayed at home with a book in front of the fire.

And if Wilt had been forced to try to explain why

he and the others did no such thing, he doubted if he could make much sense at all.

Carry it even further: how could you explain why Bart had elected to stay behind when he could just as easily have put on the skis and boots they had brought for him and now be leading this expedition?

There was absolutely nothing Bart could do by staying at the cave. If the rock structure started to collapse, he could not hold it up. If they were all forced out into the open, he could not keep them alive. Or himself. And yet he had stayed and refused even to comment on it.

When you take command, Wilt thought, you pick up the responsibility that goes with it. It's as simple as that. And if you aren't prepared to do that, then you'd damn well better stay uninvolved in the first place, because partial commitment is worse than none. The guy who had tangled with the bear understood that just as well as Bart did. Wilt had seen Ben nod almost imperceptibly when Bart had told them to take the sled and go. Wilt decided that in Bart's position Ben would have made the same decision.

As a matter of fact, if Wilt understood it correctly, and he thought he did, Ben had *attacked* the bear because he thought the rest of them were in danger. Silly, quixotic, okay, no argument, he didn't have a chance; but when the chips were down it was good to know you had somebody like that on your side.

When you got right down to it, Wilt thought, there was no substitute for people you could depend on, and maybe that was part of the explanation for doing what he and the rest did in this volunteer search-and-rescue business: in the mountains, on the trails, doing what they had done all day and were doing now, you quickly separated the men from the boys, and the men damn well included Steve, and you found out things that were very pleasant to know about a rather special kind of people.

He saw CJ coming back up the road toward them, and he snowplowed to a stop. CJ's breath emerged from his hood in a cloud of steam, and his voice was breathless. "There's a tree down across the road. I couldn't move it. Maybe together we can."

Wilt was already undoing the rope that bound him to the sled. "You stay with our passenger, Steve." He skied around the sled and together he and CJ poled off down the road.

"I thought maybe we could get around it," CJ said, "but it would be tough enough alone through the trees at best, and with him on that sled it would be impossible. What in God's name do you think he weighs, anyway?"

There was the tree. Not, thank heaven, one of the big ones, but big enough. "Let's try this end," Wilt said. "We only have to move it a couple of feet." He bent down to unlatch his skis and promptly sank up to his knees in the snow. "Okay. I'll go beyond it and pull. You push from here."

It took ten bone-chilling, muscle-straining minutes, and they both were panting steam when at last it was done.

"Stay here," Wilt said. "I'll go back and give Steve a hand." First obstacle met and overcome, he told himself. Maybe it was a good omen.

Sue Ann and Patty still sat together, hands lightly touching. "Your father—" Sue Ann began.

"Is he going to be all right?" The words came out suddenly and of their own volition, releasing the question that had weighed on Patty's mind, and, yes, on her conscience as well. Because if he was not going to be all right, if he was going to die before they ever saw him again, then a sense of guilt would remain with her forever, Patty was sure, that she had not been nicer to him, more appreciative of him, when he was alive. And why couldn't I have understood that before? It was a silent wail in her mind. "Is he?"

Sue Ann made herself smile. She hoped it was convincing. "He is," she said.

"How can you know?"

"I know."

"You can't know. You—" Patty stopped and shook

224

her head, suddenly, desperately ashamed. "You're hurt, and I'm not, and you're trying to prop me up. I guess you always have."

"That's what families are for, dear."

Patty closed her eyes. That defense of families was what you were always taught, she thought; they bombarded you with that claim from all sides. But somehow it had never seemed real, just propaganda, almost brainwashing, the kind of thing grown-ups were always doing, sometimes well, sometimes transparently, but always without shame or even embarrassment no matter how dumb it might sound.

But now in this context she had to admit there was probably something to it after all, because here she was leaning on her mother, asking for her support—and getting it, too, wasn't she? What was it she had heard once, that home was the place where when you went there they never turned you away? Well, maybe that was what family was all about too. But why did it have to take something like this—nightmare to prove it to her? Like what she felt about Daddy, why couldn't she have seen it before? She could have wept.

The big man, Bart, crossed the cave and squatted beside them. To Sue Ann: "How's the pain?"

"It's all right."

Her mother was lying, Patty thought, and the big man knew it, but she watched him nod anyway, not in agreement or even acceptance, but simply in clear approval. This kind of evasion of painful truth was more of the grown-up pattern, and it was suddenly no longer false or deceitful in Patty's eyes; it was wholly admirable.

"They'll get down," Bart said. "They know where we are. They'll send help."

And the masquerade continued. "Of course," Sue Ann said.

"They'll go first to the hospital. It's a good hospital. Their coronary care unit is first-rate, and there are some very good heart men in Santo Cristo."

"Thank you."

"I think," Bart said, "that we almost have it whipped." He wished it were true.

If a vehicle could have been sent up the road, it would have been by now, therefore they could expect no help in that direction.

Men on skis or snowshoes? He had thought of that too, and rejected it. Fifteen miles uphill with the temperature down where it was and still dropping? No way.

From a practical point of view that left what?

Until the snow stopped, nothing.

And then?

There was only one possibility he could see, and he did not like it at all: a chopper. We're already getting slides just from the weight of the snow, he thought. Add to that the blast from a chopper's blades, and the weight of the chopper itself above us if it does land, and how long will this cave roof stand? He didn't even like the question, let alone the answer.

Patty said suddenly, "Why do you do it? I mean, I know why we're here. And Ben and Lila. But why are you here?"

A man named Carter could explain that, Bart thought, and there would be those who would ask him to, who would demand it. "A mix-up," he said. "The jeep we came up in went down to town by mistake."

Patty shook her head. "That wasn't what I meant. Why did you come up in the first place? To find us? To find the plane Lila was in? But why?"

Sue Ann said, "There are men, and women, who do that, dear. I never really understood it before. I'm not sure I understand it now." She smiled at Bart. There was more than gratitude in the smile. "But I thank God, and you, for it."

Bart stood up. Bent, his head just clearing the cave roof, he looked down at them. "Hang on," he said, his breath plain in the cold air. "The cavalry is on the way." Liar.

Again CJ appeared coming back to them, and again Wilt snowplowed to a stop. "Oh, Jesus!" CJ said, "that's really torn it!" His teeth were chattering uncontrollably, and it was hard to enunciate clearly. "Somebody's got a truck stuck crosswise blocking the road! And this one we aren't going to be able to move!"

The governor presided as before, sitting behind his desk in shirtsleeves, a pad of yellow paper before him. To Brady Shaw he said, "You've got something for us?"

Technically of course the governor had no authority over him, Brady reminded himself; his was a federal position. And so he would not even have a valid claim that he had been ordered or even pressured into making a prediction that could turn out to be fatally wrong. Ah, well, he told himself, it's been a nice quiet life so far; it's probably time I ventured out of my cocoon anyway into the world of risky reality. "I'll give you my best educated guess," he said.

The governor nodded. "Good enough."

"There is no money-back guarantee."

"Get on with it."

Brady nodded. He looked down at the papers and charts he had brought for support, and found them even faintly ridiculous here in this office. He knew perfectly well what they seemed to show, and the others didn't care. He looked up and spoke to the governor. "The snow should begin to slacken in maybe an hour, maybe a little longer. There is another storm system to the south, and if it holds off—" He stopped. Damn it, he told himself, you're not here to talk about *ifs*. He went on in a loud, clear voice. "My judgment is that it will hold off, and we'll have a little time of clear, cold weather, maybe a couple of hours. Does that help?"

The governor looked at Pete Benjamin, who sat beside Captain Lopez and Carl. "How about it?"

"Plenty of time to get up there," Pete said. "The only thing is, we don't know where anybody is, do we?"

"One thing at a time," the governor said. He looked at the state engineer. "He"—he nodded toward Carl—

227

"has been up there and thinks that putting a chopper down on that rim which seems to be the only landing place just could start another slide. What do you think?"

"I'd almost bet on it," the state engineer said. "I've looked at the geology and at some studies made when they were talking about a dam for a new reservoir." He shook his head. "One of the reasons we rejected the dam was that shaky rock structure, and now with unstable snow already causing rock slides—" He spread his hands.

Brady Shaw stood up. "Do you need me any more?"

"I've got a question," Pete Benjamin said. "That storm system to the south that you think is going to hold off. If it decides not to, and does move in while I'm in the air or up there already sitting on the ground, how much warning will I have?"

"We'll be watching it," Brady said, "and we'll get to you just as fast as we can when we think we see something. That's the best I can do."

"Then," Benjamin said, "I guess that has to be good enough." He looked again at the governor. "Now how do we go about finding the people we're going after when we get our weather break?"

There were days, Wilt thought, when you just couldn't win for losing, and this was one of them. The truck was there as CJ had said, and how in hell anyone managed to get it wedged in across the road between the tree and that big rock, somebody else was going to have to figure out because Wilt couldn't, not that it made a damn bit of difference.

CJ, short, stocky and now belligerent, said, "Okay, now what?"

Working down in the canyon with Bart and then moving that tree had taken a lot out of CJ, Wilt thought, and this agonizing cold had not helped. He would have to keep a careful eye on CJ because obviously he was not standing up to punishment as well as he might. Fatigue did that to you, shortening your temper, lowering your resistance, leaving you open to all kinds of troubles including mistakes you would not otherwise make.

Steve said, "Can we get through the trees above the road?" Her voice sounded doubtful.

"No way," CJ said. "There's no room for the sled."

"Relax," Wilt said. "I don't know yet what we're going to do, and neither do you."

He poled to the edge of the road and studied the slope below for a few moments in silence. "Steve." And when she stood beside him, "What do you think?"

By himself Jaime, Steve thought looking down, would take off without hesitation and probably not even bother to slow his speed until the snow was almost smoking beneath him. And she would probably follow. She put Jaime from her mind and concentrated on the here and now, because the problem was the sled.

The slope below the road was open, treeless, probably scoured clean by some long-ago snow slide and then covered with hundreds of tons of dumped dirt and rocks from the building of the road itself. The open slope was perhaps three hundred yards long, not quite vertical, but not far from it either. At the bottom, beyond the road which swung back in a great loop, the slope was less steep and trees began again, a dense stand of second- and third-growth aspens and evergreens at which Steve stared briefly and shivered. Hitting those trees at any speed at all, she thought, would be plain suicide.

"You try to traverse that slope with the sled to maintain some kind of control," CJ said, "and you might as well turn it upside down right now and roll the poor bastard out because it'll capsize sure as hell the moment it goes at all sideways." He paused for a deep breath. "And if you take it straight down which is what you'd have to do, you'll have a runaway freight train on your hands and no way to keep it from slamming into those trees—and you with it." He glared at Wilt. "So?"

"An interesting problem," Wilt said in that light, male tone which Steve thought she now was beginning to understand.

He has made up his mind, she told herself, and what he is doing now is psyching himself, and me, for the effort. But can we—?

"All we have to do," Wilt said, as if he were explaining to a novice class, "is take the sled straight down, *and* hold it under control so it doesn't slam into the trees and take us with it. Right?"

CJ said, "You've lost your frigging mind. You might make it alone, but—"

"You're going alone," Wilt said flatly. "Steve and I will take the sled down."

CJ's breath came out in a great angry cloud of steam. "I'm not going down there, and you're by God not either. You can't—"

"And just what else do you suggest?" Wilt's voice now was cold with scorn. "You said it yourself, we can't get the sled through the trees above the road and we can't get past the truck. The only way is down that slope. So what do we do, leave him here? Is that what you have in mind?"

CJ's poles were firmly planted, and he leaned on them defiantly. "How do we even know he's still alive? Answer me that. Before we bust our asses, or worse—"

Wilt nodded. "A point. Have a look, Steve."

He watched her bend over the sled, move boughs aside, look carefully and then move the boughs back into their protective position. She straightened slowly, swallowed and nodded. "He's still breathing."

"Okay," Wilt said. "You're coming with us, CJ. We stay together." He bent down suddenly and began to unlatch his skis.

CJ said, "What are you doing?"

Wilt straightened. "I changed my mind. I'm going to ride the front of the sled. I can dig my heels in and help slow it. You two on ropes at the rear."

"Jesus!" CJ's voice was explosive. "If it gets away it'll run right over you or take you straight into those trees at the bottom!"

"And so," Steve said in quiet finality, "we won't

let it get away, will we?" She moved to the rear of the sled. "Let's get on with it." Commitment made.

Wilt picked up his skis and poles and waded back through the snow. As he passed close by Steve, "Good girl," he said.

Her reaction was instantaneous. "You wouldn't say anything like that to a man!"

"No, but I'd think it. That's the only difference." Wilt was smiling now. "Like I said, it's going to be interesting."

19.

CAPTAIN LOPEZ, Carl and Pete Benjamin walked together out to the capitol parking area. The snow was still falling, but the curtain did seem less dense. The air, however, was colder than when they had gone inside; snow squeaked beneath their feet, and after even this short distance, the captain's eyes and inner ears began to ache. The city was without traffic sounds, a dead, deserted land.

"Let's talk a bit," the captain said.

He got in on the driver's side of his car, Pete Benjamin on the other side of the front seat, Carl in the rear. The captain got the engine started and turned the heater blower on full. Its initial feeble warmth was more than welcome.

"Okay," the captain said, "what do we think?" Even within the car his breath came out in steam. He tried to ignore the cold. From lack of sleep he had reached a state of lethargy which he had to force himself to overcome. Words, and thoughts, were an effort. "Pete?"

"What choice is there?" Benjamin said. "If we get

the visibility, we give it a try, and run like hell if the weather begins to close in again."

"Do you want me with you in the chopper?" This was Carl.

Benjamin's smile was wry. "I'd love to have you, to hold my hand if nothing else, but it's a matter of capacity. If I can find them, I can take out two at a time, no more. If you came—"

"I could stay, maybe help."

"*Por Dios,* no!" the captain said. "We have played this game of musical chairs enough! What we want is to take people out, not put them back in!" He stopped and smiled wearily. "Offer appreciated, but declined, amigo."

Carl said, "You could take Carter up, and leave him there for good. He might be safer."

The captain's voice changed. "I will attend to Carter in my own way." He looked again at Benjamin. "If you cause a slide when you land, what then?"

Benjamin spread his hands. "I'll play it as easy as I can, and I'll hope, that's all I can do. There's no point in putting down on the other side of the mountain where they couldn't possibly be."

The captain turned in his seat to look at Carl. "You're guessing they might have headed for one of those caves in the canyon wall?"

How do you answer that? Carl thought. He spread his hands. "They haven't any gear. They've got to have shelter. It's the way Bart and Wilt might think. And Wilt knows that area like the back of his hand." He was suddenly silent, thoughtful. "What about making a pass over the ski basin too? It isn't all that far, and they just might have headed there." His voice rose in frustrated anger. "Goddamn it, if only we had some definite idea!"

"Don't look now," Captain Lopez said, "but the snow has almost stopped."

Over the edge and down that precipitous slope, despite Steve's and CJ's best efforts on ropes behind to hold down its speed, the sled with its heavy burden

232

seemed determined to burst out of control and hurtle down the mountainside driving Wilt ahead of it as if propelled by a juggernaut.

The snow was deep. Hidden beneath it were rocks which caught at Wilt's braced heels. He tried to keep his knees flexed to lessen the shocks and succeeded only in bouncing from position to position with the sled always plunging against the backs of his thighs.

His shoulders, hands and fingers ached from his deathlike grip on the sled, and the rushing wind of their progress brought tears to his eyes, blurring his vision, forcing him to rely solely on his sense of balance to try to keep the sled's course straight lest it veer and overturn on the impossibly steep slope.

He was suddenly conscious of a high, keening sound that filled the air, and he was unaware that it came from his own throat, a wordless scream of defiance in the cold, thin air. In all the world it was the only sound.

Once his right leg, seemingly hooked by an immovable rock, doubled beneath him, and for the kind of brief moment that seemed eternity he was afraid that he could not extricate it before the sled overran him and the leg broke, but his heel disengaged itself in time and the leg snapped back into place with a bone-jarring jolt, the moment passed and the juggernaut continued its mad plunge downward.

Ahead beyond the road at the foot of the slope were the trees he had seen, and the road itself probably had a protective ditch on its uphill side. If he and the sled crashed into any of that, it was all over. A picture went through his mind like something seen in a flash of lightning, himself, Warner Harlow and the sled jammed together into a tangle of metal and fabric and flesh best shoveled into a hole and mercifully covered over.

He heard CJ's voice raised in a sudden great shout, words indistinguishable but warning plain, and although he tried to see through the blur of his tears, he could make out nothing but light and shadows, where no shadows should be, and, braking with the full strength of his body, his legs, his shoulders and his arms, he was aware that he and the sled were into the trees. What happened next was too fast for comprehension.

There was a sudden jar as he met yielding resistance. The sled crashed into the backs of his thighs, throwing him forward into suffocation, and all at once was making desperate swimming motions as he fought for air, and it passed through his mind that he was dying.

But death could not be this cold, nor as suddenly wet against his face. He was aware that hands were tugging at him, and he obeyed their summons and came out of the snowbank, untangled himself from the sled and, brushing snow from his face and tears from his eyes in bewilderment, looked around.

They had made it. That was the essential, overpowering thought. The sled was still upright, and now motionless, and the slope rose high behind them, and it mattered not a damn that his hands and his legs and his shoulders ached as they never had, or that there was a pain deep in his chest from sheer exhaustion. Unimportant against the fact of accomplishment. He looked at Steve, whose strong hands had helped him.

She leaned now on her poles, head bent, breathing in deep, shuddering gasps. But as Wilt watched, her head came up, and she nodded faintly and tried to smile, so she was okay too. *Bravo,* Wilt thought, *bravissimo!*

CJ was something else. He was squatting on his skis, his hands, still through the loops of his poles, hanging loose at his sides touching the snow. His head was bent too, and he was panting; each exhalation blew out a great cloud of steam; beneath each inhalation was a deep rasping sound.

Wilt gathered himself slowly, lurched back along the sled and took up his skis and poles, which they had lashed beside the mummy bag. As he bent and clumsily put the skis on he wondered if the body beneath the boughs was still alive after that wild ride, or if that whole desperate effort had been for nothing.

234

Never mind. He stood erect. CJ was still in his squatting position, still blowing out steam, still rasping with each breath. "CJ," Wilt said in a tone of command.

CJ looked up then. Slowly, heaving on his poles, he got himself erect. He took a deep, angry breath. "I'm all right, goddamn it, no thanks to you! Of all the wild, stupid, goddamn silly ideas—"

"But we made it," Steve said. She was smiling.

CJ nodded wearily. His voice was that of an exhausted man. "Yeah. We made it. I don't know how." He looked at Wilt. "All right, you goddamn slave driver, don't you want us going again?"

Wilt nodded. He could even smile. "You've had lots of rest. Move out." It's got to be clear sailing from here, he thought. By God, I think we've got it made!

Bart looked around the cave, assessing morale.

Mother and daughter would stand up all right, he thought. There was a toughness in them, maybe in all women, that was showing itself.

And Lila and Ben showed no signs of panic. They waited quietly, in an apparent state of resignation, accepting what was, willing to face whatever was coming.

That left Billy, and Bart hunkered down by the fire to check on the boy. "Any new ideas?"

Billy poked idly at the embers before he looked up and smiled in a self-deprecatory way. "Oh, a couple, I guess." The words emerged through stiff lips.

"Let's hear them."

"You're sure?" Billy's voice was quiet, for Bart's ears only.

"I told you."

"Okay." He took his time. "They'll probably make it down on skis, like you told Mom and Patty. And maybe Pop will come through, at that." Sudden pride entered the boy's voice. "He's pretty tough, tougher than you'd think. I've heard about him back when he played football. At Oklahoma, it was."

"I didn't know that, Billy."

"He didn't get all the headlines, but the writers who

knew, they said he was the only reason Mr. Boone, Jake Boone, made All-America mention, Pop blocking for him."

"You're proud of him."

Billy poked at the fire some more. He nodded slowly. "But he doesn't know it. I couldn't be like him if I tried, so I never tried and just pretended I didn't care." He looked up at Bart's face. "People do that, don't they? Pretend, I mean, that something doesn't matter when it really does?"

"People do, Billy." People like me, Bart thought. Never mind. "I think he'll make it too," he said.

Billy nodded solemnly. "I hope so, even if we aren't going to know about it." He was silent a few moments, shivering. Then he looked up, and his voice took on a new adult tone. "Don't snow me. I told you I've been thinking about things. We aren't going to make it, are we? There isn't going to be any help coming, so I think what you ought to do, you ought to put on those boots they brought for you and get on those skis and go down the mountain yourself while you still can." He nodded across the cave at Ben and Lila. "Him too, if he's able."—His eyes were still steady on Bart's. "Well?"

Bart kept his voice easy, almost unconcerned. "I don't think you've figured things out quite right, Billy."

"You really think somebody's coming to get us?" Billy shook his head. "No way. If they had anything that would get up here on the ground, a tractor or one of those snow things, whatever, why, it would have been here already, and we would have heard on your walkie-talkie, wouldn't we? If they were anywhere in the area, I mean?"

The boy's reasoning was identical to his own, Bart thought. Astonishing. Or was it? "Go on, Billy." His voice held nothing.

"Okay, if they can't get there on the ground, all that's left is the air, and that means a chopper. You know the funny sounds they make, staccato, they call it, that's the shock waves from the blades, I think. We got trapped in here once just because Pop shot off his gun, and the shock waves from that set it all off. What's going to happen when a chopper gets close and those big shock waves from the blades begin sending out their vibrations?"

Across the cave there was a sound of sudden movement. Bart turned. Patty was kneeling at the cave entrance, and her voice reached them clearly over her shoulder. "It's stopped snowing! It's stopped!"

Billy was first across the cave. He squeezed past Patty and scrambled outside to see for himself. It was true, the snow had stopped, and to the west blue sky was beginning to appear behind scudding dark clouds. On the distant mountains there was even sunshine. But, oh, jeebers, it was cold!

He was unaware that Bart was standing beside him until the big man's hand took his arm and gave it a gentle squeeze. They stood watching, without words.

The sunshine was coming closer, spreading across the mesaland toward them, lighting hills and swales, distant snow-covered buildings, a microwave tower, a windmill and now the beginnings of the city itself.

There it was, pretty as a picture postcard, in the high, cold, clear air seemingly close enough to touch. There were people down there, and houses with warmth, electric lights, beds, food, all of the impossible and always before so commonplace wonders of civilization. Billy stared down as at a dream.

"We better go in," Bart said. "You'll freeze, and I'm not too comfortable either." He turned the boy around toward the cave entrance.

Billy resisted, and turned for one more look. "But it's so close!" A cry in the darkness, a wail against fate. "Don't you feel it too? I mean, look!"

"I know what you mean," Bart said. His voice was expressionless. "Inside, boy. Back to your fire. Now comes the hard part. We just keep on waiting."

Carl was again in Jaime's hospital room, deep in the visitor's chair. The door to the hallway was open. "So that's where we stand," he said. "If the chopper isn't already in the air, it will be in a couple of minutes. The weather people don't give him much time because that new storm—" He stopped, stared through the open doorway and then jumped from his chair to run out into the hallway.

"Hi, boy," Wilt said. His face was haggard and he swayed with fatigue, but in his eyes there was an unmistakable glint of triumph. "CJ's downstairs. He's okay. Steve'll be along in a moment." He nodded toward Jaime's room. "How's he?"

"He's okay." Wilt, CJ and Steve, Carl thought. "But what about Bart?"

The glint of triumph disappeared like a light flickering out. He's still up there," Wilt said, "with the other five."

"Five! Jesus!" Carl's voice was low-pitched, urgent. "That makes six! Where are they? Tell me quick, goddamn it! We've got a chopper in the air!" He seized Wilt's arm. "Come on! We've got to find a phone!"

They were gone by the time Steve came wearily down the empty hallway, walking awkwardly in the rental ski boots. Her face burned from the sudden warmth of the hospital, and her hands and feet were filled with the painful tingle of returning circulation, but sudden, overwhelming warmth was the last thing she would have complained about.

She carried her mittens in one hand; the hood of her parka was thrown back. Her hands were grimy, her hair was tousled and she supposed she looked a mess, but none of that was important either.

Wilt was nowhere to be seen, but that, too, faded into insignificance as she watched the numbers steadily increase toward the number of Jaime's room.

At the information desk downstairs where she had gone after they had skied with Warner on the sled right up to the Emergency hospital entrance normally used by the ambulances, they had told her that Jaime's condition was "serious," which did not sound at all good.

But the gods could not with one hand give Wilt, CJ, herself and maybe even Warner as well the gift of life, and with the other take Jaime away. Not now after what they had all gone through. Better by far not to

238

have let any of them get this close to freedom if the eventual design was even partial disappointment.

It was the reasoning of fatigue, of course. That she knew. When you were bone-tired, despair was never far away, and it was easy to conjure up all manner of unpleasant possibilities.

Still, "serious" could mean worse than Steve was prepared to face, and as she approached the open door to Jaime's room it took all of her strength not to turn and walk away and find out from someone else first just what Jaime's condition really was.

And now that she was actually here, almost face to face with him when earlier she had despaired that she might never be again, she wondered if her presence could even begin to be as important to Jaime as his to her, and whether she was in fact simply about to inflict herself upon him when he would far rather be left alone. Devastating thought.

At the doorway she paused, took a deep breath and then marched through, clumping loudly in the rental boots, feeling large and awkward, as uncertain as an adolescent at her first date.

He was propped up in the bed, brown face and black hair against the white pillow. One shoulder wore a large cast. He saw her as she came through the doorway and then stopped, afraid to go farther. For long moments there was only silence, and time stood still.

Slowly Jaime began to smile, white teeth in dark face, brown eyes laughing as they always had—almost. "Hi, *guapa*." His voice was soft. "Where have you been? Come in. Sit down. Tell me." And then the unbelievable words spoken almost casually: "And don't ever go away again, *comprendes?*"

Steve clumped slowly into the room, no longer large, awkward, uncertain, all doubts now suddenly wiped away. She sank wearily into the chair.

Jaime watched her, silent now but smiling still.

It was going to be all right, Steve thought, it was going to be better even than she had hoped. She knew this now with deep certainty. But there was no hurry to say all of the things they would eventually want to say because there was all the time in the world and now she could finally relax, and her smile warmed herself, and Jaime, all the way through. "You wouldn't believe," she said. "Even you would have enjoyed that sled ride."

Jaime's smile spread. "With you, *guapa*," he said, "anything."

20.

It was Sue Ann who first heard the faint staccato sounds through the small orifice of the cave entrance. She cocked her head in concentration.

Patty said, "What is it, Mom?"

"There's, I think, a helicopter out there."

Bart came across the cave in a rush. He crouched motionless to listen. Slowly he shook his head.

"If Mom says so," Patty said, "then it's there." And again the old family joke, but spoken this time with evident pride: "Mom can hear the grass grow."

From across the cave, "Fact," Billy said.

Lila said, "She knew Ben was out there with the bear."

Bart was already at the cave entrance. He stopped, and turned back. Billy's idea, one of them, was good. "A mirror," he said. "Do you have one?" He watched Sue Ann nod and burrow into her small bag. He took the mirror and crawled quickly out into the open.

At first the sunlight reflected from the snow was blinding. But he could begin to make out the faint staccato sounds. There was a chopper in the air, no doubt of it.

Despite the cold, more intense than he could remember, he left his parka hood down to listen, and slowly swung his head searching for direction. Yes, there it was, the strongest sound, from the southwest, toward the airport. He shaded his eyes and squinted.

At first, nothing. Then a few meaningless dancing spots of the kind you always saw when you strained to see. But the sounds continued, louder now, and yes, there it was, even in the high clear air barely visible, moving slightly to his left as it approached, going, for God's sake, where? We're over here!

At that moment Bart felt the same frustration Billy had felt looking down at the city almost close enough to touch. He wanted to shout, to wave his arms, to try to whistle—ridiculous, and he knew it. He had completely forgotten the mirror in his hand, and now he recalled it only because of the pain it caused him as the hand involuntarily clenched from the tension he felt.

He looked down at it, feeling almost stupid, angry with himself, and he raised it, aimed it as best he could judge at a bisecting angle between sun and chopper, and began to move it slowly in small circles.

Nothing. A friend of his who had served in the British Army in India had told him once that heliography was still used there as in Kipling's day, but that the contraptions were not merely hand-held mirrors, but carefully designed clockwork mechanisms which could follow the sun and project a reflected light beam great distances with great accuracy. Well, what he held in his hand was a damn poor substitute, but it was all he had.

The chopper continued its steady course on an angle to Bart's left, and he followed it as best he could, guessing where the tiny flash from the mirror was pointing, swinging it still in small circles trying to make as large a pattern as he could in the approximate target area.

Maybe the pilot wasn't looking in his direction. Maybe the pilot wasn't thinking. Maybe the pilot—

There. The chopper seemed to hesitate, if that was the word, cease its relentless progress in a diverging direction, and then, yes? yes? *yes!* alter course all at

241

once, and there was no question that it was coming directly toward the canyon wall where Bart stood!

(Inside the chopper Pete Benjamin said into his throat mike, "Roger. I have the message. The north canyon wall. Six of them—Wait. Someone's flashing a mirror or something. I have him. I'm on target. Over.")

Bart waited a few moments, still flashing the mirror, but in a series of quick flashes lest now that he had the target he blind the pilot. There was no longer doubt that the chopper was heading straight for him. And then from the chopper's nose there was a burst of light, and another, acknowledgment signals, and all at once the chopper was hovering out over the canyon, almost on Bart's level, and he and Benjamin could see one another clearly.

Bart pointed above, to the rim, and held up six fingers.

Benjamin nodded. The chopper swung off to one side and began to rise. Bart waited for no more.

He went down on his hands and knees and crawled back into the cave. Inside, the beating of the chopper's blades sounded like small, not too distant explosions, a string of firecrackers sending echoes into and through the rock.

"You first," Bart said to Sue Ann. "Let's go. You'll have to crawl out. Then I'll carry you." He saw resistance forming in her face, and he said in a new, commanding voice, "You'll do it the way I say. All of you. She comes first. You"—he nodded at Ben—"second. I want our wounded out. Is that clear?"

The chopper's sounds were louder now. A piece of rock broke from the cave roof and fell with a dull thud to the floor. Still Bart waited, looking at them all. "That's how we'll do it," he said. "Any comment?"

Ben said slowly, "You sound like a lieutenant I had once." The best man I ever knew, he thought, and now I can't even remember his name. But I'll remember this one. "Yes, sir," he said. "We'll do it your way. Crawl out, Sue Ann. No argument."

Patty pushed gently at her mother's shoulder. "Go on, Mom. He knows best. We'll be all right. We'll be fine." She kissed Sue Ann's cheek quickly. "Give Daddy our love. Now hurry."

Sue Ann hesitated. They all watched her, and Patty's hand on her shoulder was insistent. "I love you all," Sue Ann said, and rolling over with effort began painfully to crawl through the entrance, dragging the splinted leg.

Inside the cave there was only the continuing, but now lessened sounds of the chopper's engine and whirling blades. Another piece of rock detached itself and fell clattering down the wall behind Billy. He jumped, startled, and then composed himself and poked again at the fire.

Ben smiled faintly. "Good soldier," he said. "Stick to your post." He looked at Lila, and the smile disappeared. "You're going next."

" 'Ladies first,' " Lila said, "is that it?" There was scorn in her voice. She faced him steadily. "You're real good at giving orders. You showed that when you were in charge, keeping the rest of us alive. Now aren't you man enough to take orders? Even when they make sense?"

Ben opened his mouth and closed it again carefully in silence. The flat muscles in his cheeks worked.

"The big man said it," Lila said. "He doesn't want any cripples left that we have to take care of. You're no good to the rest of us, and you're too big to carry, so go on, do what the man says and stop this nonsense." She pushed herself away from the cave wall, got slowly to her feet and crossed the cave to kneel beside Patty, her back to Ben. "Your mom will be all right," she said. "She'll be fine. She and your dad will be waiting for both you and Billy."

Bart's bulk blocked the entrance, and his voice came to them somewhat muffled. "Room for one more. Let's go."

Lila heard the slow sounds of Ben getting to his feet and walking toward the cave entrance, but she did not turn.

Ben knelt and looked around at them all. "Luck," he said. His voice was expressionless. Patty and Billy nodded. Lila's position did not change, nor did she speak. Ben bent, crawled painfully out through the entrance and was gone.

As Patty watched, two tears appeared and rolled slowly down the sides of Lila's nose. She seemed unaware.

By the fire, Billy cleared his throat. As if on cue for introductory effect, another piece of rock suddenly rattled down the cave wall, and then was still. In the quiet, "It's on take-off," Billy said, "that aircraft, like the pilots say, they pull rated horsepower from the engine. That's when we'll get the deepest vibrations. That's when—" He stopped. "Okay. I thought you ought to know, that's all."

"I sort of thought it might be like that," Lila said. She tried to keep her voice steady. She looked at Patty, and smiled through the tears. "So now we know, don't we, honey?"

Bart was partway back down to the cave when the chopper's engine began its take-off acceleration, the blades began to whirl deafeningly, and with lift-off loose snow swirled in the sunlight in a miniature blizzard. Bart stopped and closed his eyes to hope, and to listen.

Against the chopper's clamor he could not hear the rumble of the snow slide beginning, but even through the snow beneath his feet he could feel the movement of the rock as the resultant rock slide shook the mountain.

The chopper was distant, seeming to slide downhill on a long slant for the airport before the rock movement ceased, the staccato sounds faded and there was near-silence. Bart took a deep breath that froze the hairs in his nostrils and started down toward the cave entrance.

There were new rocks on the trail, and one large piece of trail itself had broken loose, leaving a shelf no more than ten inches wide for footing, but when he reached the cave, the entrance was still open, and when he knelt and crawled through, there was dust enough to make a man cough, but the cave was still there, and Billy's fire was still going, and there was that God-given warmth without which they could not survive.

He could smile at them all. Stiff with cold, his face produced no more than a grimace, but it would suffice. It had to. "So far, so good," he said. "You three go on the next load."

Patty said, "Can't you—" She left the question unfinished.

Lila had wiped away the tears and was now watching Bart. She said slowly, "I think maybe a cup of Ben's coffee. You deserve more, but it's all the treasure we have to offer."

An ambulance waited at the airport field, its red dome light flashing, its engine turning over, keeping warm. The chopper swung in, hovered and then amid a cloud of blown snow settled to the ground. Ducking beneath the whirling blades the ambulance crew rushed in with their wheeled stretcher as Pete Benjamin swung open the door.

"The woman first," he said. "Easy on that leg."

They lifted Sue Ann down, laid her on the stretcher, hurried her back to the ambulance and tucked her inside.

Ben was already out of the chopper, with his good hand holding the injured arm and shoulder as motionless as he could. He felt faint, and still filled with anger, and, Jesus!, it was cold, but he paused, crouching, long enough to say to Benjamin, "Thanks for the lift, friend."

Benjamin smiled. "No charge. It's on the house." He started to close the door.

"Get them all out," Ben said. "All of them." His voice rose suddenly. "Goddamn it, you hear me?"

"Loud and clear," Benjamin said, and slammed the door shut.

He waited only until Ben, holding himself tight and lurching through the snow, was out of range of the downblast before he poured throttle to the engine and lift to the blades and rose in a sharp, swinging turn, headed again for the mountains. In only moments the chopper was a mere speck in the distance, and the field was still.

Ben reached the ambulance, and there he could go no farther. The attendants almost lifted him inside, stretched him out beside Sue Ann and secured him with a broad strap across his middle.

One attendant got in behind the wheel. The other climbed into the rear and shut the doors. "You must have been having a ball up there," he said.

Ben nodded. "It was—hilarious."

Sue Ann's eyes were closed. She opened them now. "My husband. He—"

"I don't know anything about him, lady. I'm sorry."

Ben said, "He came down by—sled. Two men and a woman. On skis." Painful as it was, he took a deep breath. "Did they—make it?"

"Oh," the attendant said, "them. Real Peary-at-the-North-Pole stuff like I seen on TV. Yeah, they made it. And the guy, your husband, lady? I dunno. They—"

The ambulance skidded violently, leaned, straightened and slowly resumed its slippery progress toward the city.

"Fun, huh?" the attendant said. "And another storm coming. Look, lady, last I hear they took the guy—your husband—straight to CCU. That's all I know."

"Coronary Care Unit," Ben said, translating the initials. He held out his good hand and touched Sue Ann's. "We'll hope."

The coffee was little more than lukewarm, but it was better than nothing, much better. Bart held the cup in both hands and drank slowly. They all watched him.

He was comparatively warm now, although he was beginning to wonder if he would ever really be warm again. Two trips to the top, one carrying Sue Ann, one almost carrying Ben, had taken their toll, and his body no longer threw off the cold as a matter of course. But we're near the end now, he thought, and reached

246

down for reserve strength, and confidence. He finished the coffee and handed Lila the cup.

"You three," he said then, "will go up just as fast as you can. Get what you can out of Ben's pack for warmth, and put it all on now. Billy, you lead. Then Patty. Lila, I'll follow you. It will be crowded, but all three of you can fit in."

Patty said again, "Can't you come too?"

"No." And that was that. But he did offer some explanation. "I weigh almost as much as all of you together. I'll go next trip."

Lila said, "We can go up by ourselves. Billy knows the way, don't you, Billy? You gathered wood up there that first day." Dear God, was it only yesterday? "There's no need for you—"

"We'll do it as I say," Bart said. "I'll make sure you get there."

"Then, hey," Billy said, "you'll go down on skis? The ones they brought you?"

He had thought of it, and was still not sure whether to take that course or wait for another chopper trip. Weather could close in again and the chopper could be grounded and he, sitting here in this unsafe cave, just waiting, when he could be on his way down the mountain, fifteen miles downhill, tired as he was, and in this cold—it wanted thinking, and thinking at the moment was difficult. Regardless, the first thing was getting these three safely out.

"Is that a bar of chocolate?" he said as Lila emptied Ben's pack on the floor. It was. God bless Ben. Obviously he knew what he was doing when he prepared his pack. Bart chewed on the chocolate and almost imagined that he could feel the quick energy going into his bloodstream.

Lila was bundled up again in the scarf and heavy socks and oversized sweater she had worn before. She knelt beside Bart. Her voice was quiet. "We all owe you one," she said. "I'm not going to labor the point, but if I had a medal, or a million dollars—" She shook her head. "It took us how many million years to climb up out of the ooze? The human race, I mean? And you look around sometimes and wonder why we bothered, don't you?"

Bart was silent.

"And then," Lila said, "something like this happens, and people like you, and Ben, and the rest of them come along, and it all begins to look different, lots different. You've really been alone all your life, and all of a sudden you aren't alone any more, not ever again—if you see what I mean. It—rocks you right back on your heels." She was silent, waiting for his comment. There was none. "Okay," Lila said. "Maybe it strikes different people different ways. For me, all I can say is—thanks."

They heard it then, the unmistakable pulsing of the chopper, growing louder as it approached.

"Out," Bart said. He heaved himself to his feet. "Billy, then Patty, Lila, you last. I'll follow." He watched them crawl through the entrance and he knelt to follow. When he stood erect out in the open, Lila was still there.

"Split," Bart said. "No, wait." He watched her eyes lift to search his face. "You're right, you know," he said. "We aren't alone. We just go along—thinking we are. Now go on. Scoot. For your thanks, *de nada.*"

Once more up the trail, Billy floundering ahead, Patty following close, Lila in her grotesque getup making her best pace. Each step Bart took was an effort. But the chocolate would take effect; a little blood sugar would do wonders. And they were almost to the end; there was the overpowering fact. You could stand anything when the end was in sight.

The chopper swung thunderously overhead. They looked up as it disappeared beyond the rim, but they saw the great cloud of snow it scattered as it settled, and all at once its sounds were enormously diminished. They hurried on.

Billy disappeared over the rim, then Patty. Bart gave Lila's arm a lift for the last few feet, and then they were all on top, and Benjamin had the door open.

Against the sound of the engine and the whistle of the revolving blades, speech was impossible, but Bart raised his mittened hand and made three distinct pointing motions, one each at Patty, Billy and Lila. He looked at Benjamin.

Benjamin hesitated. Slowly he nodded and held the door wide, and the three piled in, a tangle of arms and bodies in insufficient space.

Benjamin got the door shut with effort, and he waved vigorously for Bart to stand well back. Then he opened his throttle until the engine roared and the whirling blades seemed to scream.

Snow flew up in vast clouds obscuring the chopper, blinding Bart. Slowly the snow clouds diminished and there was the chopper, airborne, seeming to slide over the rim and down over the canyon, on its way, and Bart watched in silence.

He turned away at last, trudged to the head of the trail and started down. There was silence all around him now, empty silence, the silence of aloneness. Well, that was what he had always sought, wasn't it? To be alone? Well?

If you kept the world outside, you couldn't be hurt. How long ago had he learned that? Or thought he had learned it? But somehow, as Lila had said, these last long hours had made things look different, and he could not have said why or how, but it was so.

First Jaime hurt. Then themselves marooned. Then finding Ben after his encounter with the bear, and Lila almost beyond help, but refusing to give up. And the Harlow family, flatlanders who might very well have been dead already and were not—quite. An entire human community in microcosm—and where did that phrase come from?—and himself no longer looking in from the outside as in these search-and-rescue operations so often he had, as in life itself he had, but actually part of it, a new experience, illuminating.

He stumbled, automatically righted himself and slowed his pace. The cold and fatigue were getting to him, that he knew. They were responsible for the strange, confusing thoughts—or were they? No matter. Back in the cave, close enough to that lovely fire to singe his whiskers, he would recuperate, and wait, and if the chopper didn't appear quickly, there were still the skis. "I'm all right, mac, take care of the other guy first." Good God, what had dredged those words up out of memory? What——?

In the silence he heard it plainly this time, the deep rumbling, gathering force, seeming to fill the clear cold air with its thunder. And then again the shuddering of the ground beneath his feet, this time with an intensity that was hard to believe.

And there were sudden crashing sounds that had not been before, and a shower or rocks from the rim itself rained down upon him, thick as hail. He dropped to his knees and covered his head with his mittened hands, and the bombardment went on.

There was a loud crashing sound, and another not far below him. For moments he was back, under accurate fire, and what he was hearing were direct hits on bunkers, supply dumps, barracks, and all that was lacking were the shouts, and the screams of the wounded.

How long the barrage went on, he did not know, but at last it ended, and only an occasional crash of falling rock marked the last rock fractures.

He got unsteadily to his feet and stared unbelieving because the trail below him was gone, and where crevices in the face of the canyon wall had been snow-filled in low relief, there was now only fresh uncovered rock where the face of the wall had moved back a matter of feet.

Great rock sections lay tumbled in the canyon, and he imagined——or perhaps it was not imagination at all ——that on one of them he could see for the first time exposed to direct sunlight petroglyphs he had last seen carved on the walls of the cave.

No cave left. No fire. No skis. Now, he thought, I am truly alone.

He turned at last and began to make his slow, weary way back to the rim. The cold was if anything worse, or maybe it was just that he was feeling it more. And then——could it be? Dear God, it was! A wind was stirring, coming from he knew not which direction, but increasing the cold by the added chill factor, and without shelter what do you think you are going to do now, big, strong, private man?

The sun still shone, a mockery because in its rays there was no warmth. And the wind, beginning in swirling flurries, had now settled down; it came from a southerly direction. Some help, if very little.

He turned his back to the wind, and knelt in the snow, tucking himself into the smallest possible mass, protecting as best he could his hands and his vital organs, conserving what warmth his body could produce.

How long? No telling. Either the chopper came, or it did not. Whoever arranged these things had cut it fine. He found himself thinking of the dead hunter they had brought in on their last search. Maybe I'll be seeing you, he thought. But for the first time in my life I really do care, and that is what makes it so ironic.

21.

BRADY SHAW SQUINTED OUT THE WINDOW, ignoring the charts and accumulated data that cluttered his worktable. "Times I've heard weathercasters make damned fools of themselves," he said aloud, "by not bothering to look outside and see that it's raining instead of the bright sunshine they're talking about." He sighed, turned away and walked to the telephone. "As any idiot can see, it's coming at us again. Fast, and hard." He dialed a number he had come to know well, and Captain Lopez's voice came on almost immediately.

"That storm system out of the Gulf has made up its mind," Brady said. "It's not dawdling any more. It's coming at us in a hurry. Better get your chopper on the ground, and tie it down good and solid."

"*Gracias*," the captain said, and added quickly, "I means thanks. I'm that mixed up." He hung up and buzzed for his secretary. "Get on the radio to Pete Benjamin. He's run out of time. Get him on the ground and keep him there."

The secretary was back in moments. "Benjamin is just landing at the airport, Captain, but he says he has to make another trip. He—"

The captain heaved himself up from his chair and walked out to the communications room. He sat down heavily and picked up the mike. "Pete. Captain Lopez here. That storm is coming. Fast. Get on the ground and stay there. Over."

The words came clearly through the speaker. "I don't read you, Captain. Over and out." The carrier wave hum ceased abruptly.

The captain stood up. He was thinking of Carter. "If it isn't damned fools," he said, "it's heroes." ¡*Dios!* he was tired. "I want a car, and a driver this time." He walked out.

Lila was the last one out of the helicopter. Standing on the ground still bundled in oversized clothing, looking, Pete Benjamin thought, like some street urchin on a cold winter day, she said, "You'll get him? You're sure?"

Pete smiled. "Close the door, and we'll give it a try."

"Don't just try," Lila said, "do it, you hear?" She closed the door firmly and trotted after Patty and Billy toward the waiting ambulance.

The music on the FM station ended abruptly. "We interrupt this program," the announcer's voice said, "to bring you this special bulletin.

"Four of the persons trapped in the mountains behind Santo Cristo have reached the city safely on skis.

"Five others have been rescued by State Police helicopter.

"It has been reported that Joseph Martin, the origi-

252

nal cause of the search, has been found dead in his crashed aircraft. His body will be removed when weather conditions permit.

"One person remains to be rescued. He is Bart Wallace, head of the Search and Rescue team—"

Connie closed her eyes and shut out the sound until the music resumed, but she could not indefinitely ignore the talk along the counter.

"New storm on the way. Why, hell, you can see it coming."

"That guy Wallace skis. My daughter says he's pretty good. Whyn't he come out with the others?"

"One of them's in the hospital. Coronary, I hear tell. Why, damn it, it happens every year, flatlanders spend fifty weeks sitting on their duffs drinking beer and then come up here after a deer or an elk and catch a coronary, usually way back to hell and gone where somebody has to go in to get them out. Better leave them, I say."

"What I don't understand is that fellow Wallace. Think if anybody got out, he would, big and strong, and he's still there, it beats me."

You fool, Connie thought, oh, you fool! That is just why he is still there, the last one out, making sure everyone else is safe first. Oh, damn, damn, damn!

"How about more coffee, Connie?"

"Sure." She made herself smile. "All you want."

The orthopedist watched the nurse help Ben on with his shirt over the bandaged arm and strapped ribs, and then pin up the empty sleeve. "A bear," the doctor said and shook his head. "Now I've heard everything. You're probably lucky, at that. He was probably just as scared as you were, and only wanted to get away."

"If he was scared," Ben said, "he didn't bother to show it." He walked out into the waiting room, and there he stopped. Lila sat small and alone on the wooden bench.

She had taken off the extra clothing and now, except for the overlarge light turtleneck, she was dressed as

Ben had seen her first hanging upside down in the plane, shirt, slacks, rubber-soled low shoes.

She indicated the discarded clothing on the seat beside her. "I borrowed these again, and I wanted to return them. This"—she touched the turtleneck—"I'll get back to you later, after I wash it. Okay?" Her voice was expressionless.

Ben nodded in silence.

Lila stood up. "You'll have to give me an address, box number, something."

"Why don't you just keep it?" He turned away then, picked up his parka from a chair and began clumsily to put it on. With only one arm it was difficult.

"I'll help you," Lila said. "Hold still." She got the parka around him and fastened the zipper. "You're going to have your problems with only one arm."

"Goddamn it—" He stopped. "What's funny?"

"That's one way to keep the world at arm's length," Lila said, "by goddamning it."

"You say what's on your mind, don't you?"

"Not always." Lila held out her hand. "Good luck."

Ben made no move to take the hand. It was going to be Nam all over again, he thought. You share an experience with someone that neither of you will ever forget, and when it's over you just walk away without even looking back, and that's an end to it?

The hell it was. Not this time. The anger he had felt with her when he left the cave was forgotten. What was important was what had gone before, as much of it as he could remember, her coming to find him down in the canyon, helping him back by the trail. "I'd still be down there," he said, "frozen stiff by now."

"We settled that," Lila said.

"Damn it, I don't even know your name."

"Does it matter?"

"Yes, it matters!" It was almost a shout. "Now who's keeping the world at arm's length?"

For as long as it might take to count slowly to ten, Lila said nothing. Her eyes did not leave his face. Then slowly she nodded. "All right," she said. "Shall we start over?"

"Not entirely. We already have quite a bit." Now where did that thought come from? But he had no intention of retracting it.

Lila watched him quietly. "What does that mean?"

"I don't know," Ben said. Simple truth. "We'll just have to see where it goes. If you're willing." In a sense, he thought, he was humbling himself. Strange, he felt no shame at all.

Lila took her time. At last she nodded again. A smile appeared. It seemed to glow. "I'm willing," she said.

The wind here on the rim had not abated, and the temperature was if anything lower than it had been. Bart's feet were already numb, and he got himself upright with effort to walk a few steps this way and return, stamping his feet, swinging his arms, trying to keep his back to the wind.

How much longer? A good question, Mr. Bones, and I do not know the answer. Like that hunter, I will continue to stagger around until I fall and cannot get up, and that will be that. But long before that final act, I will probably cease to be able to separate fantasy from reality, and so the end will not be the painful struggle it might otherwise be. Good? Or bad?

He could not resist turning into the wind for a single brief look at the world in that direction.

Down there was the city, so close, still bathed in sunlight, sharp black shadows and glistening highlights, smoke rising from chimneys, even here and there a vehicle of some kind moving like an insect on a snow-covered path between buildings.

He tried, and failed, to locate La Cantina, although he could close his eyes and see it clearly, smell its cleanliness and warmth, almost taste the coffee Connie would automatically put before him. Fantasy.

To the southwest the sky had darkened now, and the clouds that were racing in resembled nothing so much as Disney storm clouds filled with menace and horror before which Bambi alternately cowered and fled. Reality, this, only partly mixed with fantasy.

No chopper pilot in his right mind would take off

255

in the face of that front, Bart told himself, nor could he blame him.

He turned away from the agonizing cold of that wind in his face, and took a few steps, stamping his feet and feeling only a dull sensation of impact.

It would be ridiculous to have it end here, right out in the open on the top of a ride with no attempt at shelter for survival. But with the cave gone, there was no shelter worthy of the effort within the limits of what was left of his strength, and that was that. At least when they finally did come up again, they would find what was left of him, and be spared another search as pointless as the one they had conducted for Joseph Martin in his flying machine.

He stumbled, went down to his knees and was tempted to stay there, but he drove himself to stand upright again and continue his pacing and stamping and flailing of arms.

There was in it, he thought strangely, nothing heroic because there was no enemy to face, no one at whom to shout defiance, not even something as specific as the lightning, wasn't it, Jove had sent, against which Ajax had bared his breast and damned it to do its worst? More fantasy, of course.

But some tales he had heard and read of men faced with death by freezing were not fantasy. Peter Freuchen, alone, amputating his own foot after frostbite threatened gangrene; nameless men, trappers, hunters in the Arctic, who, knowing themselves doomed by freezing, had deliberately broken through ice to cover themselves with water which would freeze as protection against mutilation by animals . . .

My God, I am wandering, he thought suddenly, and with effort concentrated on walking one step at a time, hayfoot, strawfoot, swinging his arms, stumbling and recovering his balance, refusing to allow fantasy to creep in again even when he heard a pounding in his head too fast for his pulse and a roaring in his ears which meant—what?

Another stumble and he was down again, hands and knees, head hanging, that roaring sound still filling his mind, fantasy moving in once more, almost this time seeming real.

"Get up! Get up, goddamn it! I can't lift you!" Pure fantasy.

Bart even had the illusion that someone was shaking him. Funny. The sensation was almost real.

"Goddamn it, move! Help me! We've got to get out of here!"

Bart lifted his head with effort. He had seen the face before, but where? And the roaring persisted. And there —that could not be illusion too, could it?—was the chopper, its blades turning, the sound of its engine plain.

"Up, for Christ's sake!"

One part of Bart's mind said clearly, "Well, what do you know? You'd better do what the man says, hadn't you? Even if you don't believe it?"

He got one leg beneath him and heaved strongly, got partway up with the helping hand lifting his arm, got the other foot planted and managed to stand erect. He looked down at Pete Benjamin almost without comprehension, certainly without belief. They began to lurch together toward the chopper.

Still well out of range of the blades, Benjamin made them stop. "Bend down," he said. "Duck your goddamn head or you'll have it in your lap as a present. Now. Here we go. And here we are. And in you go any way you can!"

The door read: *Coronary Care Unit, Visiting hours 11-1-3-5-7-9, Ten (10) minutes only. Family only. One visitor at a time.*

Sue Ann was in a wheelchair, her foot and ankle in cast. Billy was pushing the chair and he halted when he saw the signs. Patty stopped too. "Can you go in, Mom?" Patty said. "Alone, I mean? We'll wait here."

Actually, Patty thought, it was better that way, because she was not sure how she would be able to face —whatever awaited beyond that forbidding door. It had been bad enough back in the cave, but somehow here, surrounded by warmth and safety, back in the

257

world again, she had no idea how she would react to—jarring unpleasantness.

Sue Ann's face showed nothing. She had talked briefly with the doctor, the cardiologist, and his optimism had been guarded, but had it even been real? Why was it that doctors seemed to refuse to speak plainly?

"Your husband has been through a great deal, Mrs. Harlow. That is no news to you. But the immediate resuscitation, the external cardiac compression and the mouth-to-mouth breathing undoubtedly saved his life right then. And—" Here there was a faint smile, meant to be reassuring. Or was it? Was it merely a mask? "—I can assure you that I have had patients brought in from the mountains after heart attacks in at least as serious a condition as your husband is now—and they have recovered. That is all I can tell you at the moment."

Now, with a deep breath, "Knock on the door, Billy," Sue Ann said. She watched him make two tentative taps. "Now open it." She took another deep breath and wheeled herself through. She sensed, rather than saw, the door closing behind her.

It was not a large room, but it seemed almost filled with people, and so—busy. Four beds, spaced around three walls, and each bed occupied. One, two, three nurses; and none paid her any attention. Nor did she need it. She had located Warner at once.

He was propped up against pillows, naked to the waist, his broad chest adorned with daisy-like patches to which were attached fine wires all of which led to a adhesive tape mound on his left shoulder and a heavier covered cable that disappeared behind the bed. Above him a small television screen showed moving lines peaks and valleys, that seemed to have a life of their own and represented, she dimly understood, Warner heartbeats. She stared at the moving patterns in almost hypnotic fascination.

Warner's nose and mouth were covered by a small rubber mask, from which another tube led to a connection in the wall. Oxygen, Sue Ann thought, an watched Warner's chest rise and fall oh, so shallowly, almost exactly as it had back in the cave. Even here, she thought, he cannot be helped— No, I won't believe that! I won't!

Warner's left forearm was bandaged, and there too he was tied to artificiality by a clear plastic tube leading up to a bottle suspended from a bedside stand, and as Sue Ann watched, a bubble formed in the bottle and rose to disappear, and it seemed that the tube gulped a minute amount of fluid to feed into Warner's vein.

Warner's eyes were closed, and the color of his face was pasty; it was only by the shallow movements of his chest that he appeared alive. Sue Ann wanted to weep, and would not, not here.

One of the nurses said quietly, "Mrs. Harlow?"

Sue Ann nodded wordlessly.

"He's doing fine, much better than when they brought him in." A kindly face, dark eyes, a faint, reassuring smile. "You can believe that."

But I can't! Sue Ann thought; it was a cry of protest in her mind.

"Much better," the nurse said again. "He is responding—"

Warner's diaphragm tightened suddenly. He seemed to gag, cough, swallow with painful effort.

So helpless, Sue Ann thought, even here where everything can be done for him! He—

Warner's eyes opened, blinked, seemed to strive for focus. They searched the room, rolling in his motionless head. They saw Sue Ann, and ceased their motion. The shallow, painful breathing went on, but somehow it seemed that its rhythm had changed. Above his head the monitor flowed its ceaseless lines, its peaks and shallow valleys plain.

With the oxygen mask covering nose and mouth, no expression was possible, but it did seem to Sue Ann that his eyes were—alive! And slowly, with obviously enormous effort, Warner's right hand stirred, lifted from the coverlet only a few inches and paused. Slowly the fingers formed themselves, thumb and forefinger in a circle, the other three fingers extended, a gesture of silent defiance and near-triumph.

Warner's eyes seemed to search Sue Ann's face. She nodded, and nodded again, and found no words, but the eyes above the mask seemed satisfied as they closed once more. The hand dropped to the coverlet. The shallow breathing went on and the silent monitor above the bed continued its ceaseless vigil, the peaks and valleys flowing across the screen without pause.

"You see?" the nurse said softly. There was a mixture of sadness and pride in her voice. "Some give up. He doesn't."

No, not Warner, never Warner, Sue Ann thought, as she let the nurse turn the wheelchair, open the door, wheel her out into the hall and give her shoulder a gentle touch.

"Come back in an hour, two hours," the nurse said. "You'll see." She was gone, back into the room where life and death hung in the balance.

Patty said, "Will he be okay? Will he, Mom?"

And Billy too stood motionless waiting on the answer.

Sue Ann made herself smile. Her foot and ankle were throbbing painfully, and she could not have cared less. Nothing mattered but this, herself, Patty, Billy and Warner beyond the door living up to his creed. "Of course," she said. "Of course he will."

The fresh storm up from the Gulf had blown itself out. Stars were showing in the black sky, and the temperature had begun its steady rise.

"We'll sort it all out later," Brady Shaw said, "but I think we set a few records." There was a quality of pride in his voice, as if he had been responsible. "Someday maybe we'll be able to forecast this kind of freak weather. In the meantime, all we can do is improvise, and maybe learn a little each time."

"What did we learn?" his assistant said.

"Why, I don't know," Brady said, "but maybe a lot of people learned a lot, you never can tell."

There was the house, Bart thought. He stopped his car in a plowed area, and got out to walk slowly the last hundred yards. It was late. He had spent more time than he would have thought necessary lying on a hard table, sucking on an oxygen tube, while people put stethoscopes on him and wrapped his arm for blood pressure tests and smeared his face with some kind of stuff that wouldn't prevent peeling, the doctor said, but might help the skin to recover from its exposure to that agonizing wind and cold.

Wilt, CJ, Carl and Steve had joined him in Jaime's room for a small gathering which was not celebration because Martin was still up there dead, and the job was not yet finished. But they were all back, all safe, and so were six others who might not have been, and there was satisfaction in that.

But as he walked slowly toward the house he thought that something had been left up on the mountaintop which was just as important to him as what they had managed to bring down, which was maybe a strange way to look at it, but there it was. I left a part of myself up there, he thought, a part I could have done without for a long time, an illusion, really. It was as if a constant burden had been lifted from his mind, his thoughts, and all else was unimportant.

He knocked on the door, and then wondered what at this hour he had thought to say. He was not and had never been an impulsive man, but tonight he had been impelled here as surely as a moth is impelled to a flame. Tropism, he thought, was the word, and how do you explain that?

Then the door opened and Connie looked out, and all at once the words fell into place. "I've spent the day," he said, "since before dawn this morning when I left here, learning things." He stopped and shook his head. "No, that's wrong. I've been searching for something, maybe you could call it truth, something, anyway, I ought to have found before."

"And what is that?" Her voice was gentle. He was here, he was safe, and the long wait was over.

"I'm tired of being alone," Bart said. "I think I

261

found that out last night, but I didn't realize it until—later." And it took Lila to point it out to me. No matter. The search is over now. "I wanted you to know. It's late, and—"

"I know," Connie said. "I found it out too." She was smiling. *Es tu casa.* It is thy house," she said, and held the door wide.

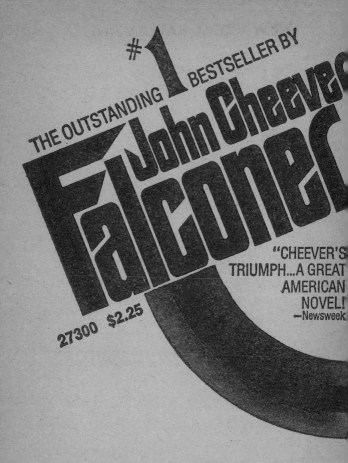

NEW FROM BALLANTINE!

FALCONER, John Cheever   27300 $2.25

The unforgettable story of a substantial, middle-class man and the passions that propel him into murder, prison, and an undreamed-of liberation. "CHEEVER'S TRIUMPH ... A GREAT AMERICAN NOVEL."—*Newsweek*

GOODBYE, W. H. Manville   27118 $2.25

What happens when a woman turns a sexual fantasy into a fatal reality? The erotic thriller of the year! "Powerful."—*Village Voice.* "Hypnotic."—*Cosmopolitan.*

**THE CAMERA NEVER BLINKS, Dan Rather
with Mickey Herskowitz**   27423 $2.25

In this candid book, the co-editor of "60 Minutes" sketches vivid portraits of numerous personalities including JFK, LBJ and Nixon, and discusses his famous colleagues.

THE DRAGONS OF EDEN, Carl Sagan 26031 $2.25

An exciting and witty exploration of mankind's intelligence from pre-recorded time to the fantasy of a future race, by America's most appealing scientific spokesman.

VALENTINA, Fern Michaels   26011 $1.95

Sold into slavery in the Third Crusade, Valentina becomes a queen, only to find herself a slave to love.

**THE BLACK DEATH, Gwyneth Cravens
and John S. Marr**   27155 $2.50

A totally plausible novel of the panic that strikes when the bubonic plague devastates New York.

**THE FLOWER OF THE STORM,
Beatrice Coogan**   27368 $2.50

Love, pride and high drama set against the turbulent background of 19th century Ireland as a beautiful young woman fights for her inheritance and the man she loves.

**THE JUDGMENT OF DEKE HUNTER,
George V. Higgins**   25862 $1.95

Tough, dirty, shrewd, telling! "The best novel Higgins has written. Deke Hunter should have as many friends as Eddie Coyle."—*Kirkus Reviews*

LG-2

The game's afoot...
and Holmes
is giving chase!